BLACK HEARTS BE DAMNED

GEORGE A. THORN

Grosvenor House
Publishing Limited

All rights reserved
Copyright © George A. Thorn, 2024

The right of George A. Thorn to be identified as the author of this
work has been asserted in accordance with Section 78
of the Copyright, Designs and Patents Act 1988

The book cover is copyright to George A. Thorn

This book is published by
Grosvenor House Publishing Ltd
Link House
140 The Broadway, Tolworth, Surrey, KT6 7HT.
www.grosvenorhousepublishing.co.uk

This book is sold subject to the conditions that it shall not, by way of
trade or otherwise, be lent, resold, hired out or otherwise circulated
without the author's or publisher's prior consent in any form of
binding or cover other than that in which it is published and
without a similar condition including this condition being
imposed on the subsequent purchaser.

This book is a work of fiction. Any resemblance to
people or events, past or present, is purely coincidental.

A CIP record for this book
is available from the British Library

Paperback ISBN 978-1-80381-752-1
Hardback ISBN 978-1-80381-753-8
eBook ISBN 978-1-80381-754-5

All rights reserved. No part of this book may be reproduced,
stored, or transmitted by any means—whether auditory,
graphic, mechanical, or electronic—without written permission
of both publisher and author, except in the case of brief excerpts used
in critical articles and reviews. Unauthorized reproduction
of any part of this work is illegal and is punishable by law.

To Brandy. My motivation. My rock.
My boo. More is to come and
I want you there every step of the way.

CONTENTS

Prologue		vii
Chapter 1:	Initiation	1
Chapter 2:	A Cordial Meeting	15
Chapter 3:	From the Desk of...	21
Chapter 4:	Family Bonding	23
Chapter 5:	A Meeting in Mexico	29
Chapter 6:	Beast of the Sea	35
Chapter 7:	Building Blocks	44
Chapter 8:	From the Desk of...II	53
Chapter 9:	Confirmation	54
Chapter 10:	Uncertainty of the Masses	56
Chapter 11:	A Word, If You Please...	63
Chapter 12:	A Year to Forget	67
Chapter 13:	A Rude Awakening	75
Chapter 14:	Shock to the System	82
Chapter 15:	A New Wave of Leadership	89
Chapter 16:	The Witch Hunt	93
Chapter 17:	The Witch Hunt Begins	104
Chapter 18:	A Biblical Announcement	110
Chapter 19:	A Pleasant Tuesday	115
Chapter 20:	Boats of Bargain	124
Chapter 21:	Reconstruction	135
Chapter 22:	Work in Progress	141
Chapter 23:	A Meeting in Mexico II	152
Chapter 24:	Sail Away	163
Chapter 25:	The Maelstrom Lives	165
Chapter 26:	Fate	178
Chapter 27:	Terror	187
Chapter 28:	Dealing with the Neighbours	200
Chapter 29:	The War Rages On	208
Chapter 30:	The Fire That Never Stops	213

PROLOGUE

Sitting across from the presidential seal was a considerable step in terms of scale the likes of which any pirate has been in, yet it wouldn't come with good consequences. Not only that, but it helped to boost the reputation of the I.I.C. (The Independent Islands of the Caribbean) as a substantial asset. Would his tone be much different from when he initially knew the address was to Lincoln and not his successor, and would the words he used be forceful? An example has to be made, and how the young leader went about it through fierce words that struck the heart of any power they would encounter. Surveying around the oval office was scarcely different from that of the young leader's own office.

While still in the height scale, the layout was much more civilised. The desk and chair was the only thing that stood out to him. So much beauty in a war-ravaged country. It put him into his family's perspective and the leaders that came before him. What carnage they must've seen in order to get where they are today. Could the I.I.C. be where it was today had one soul been cut down? He then dreaded what his great-grandfather would think if he saw the I.I.C. in the shape it was in when he took over. Would it be a look of wonder at the progress, or would it be a look of bewilderment as the traditions turned soft? A way of life turned into a parody of its once stiff-upper-lip rule-bearing tyrants. Whatever way he envisioned it, those posh snobs in Britain and France would soon have their eyes glued to everything that had been transpiring for the past several months. The weight of the Spanish died off years ago, so the I.I.C. would be seen as a scapegoat for anything, even for America. That's three sets of eyes looking across at those tiny islands.

A faint commotion could be heard outside the door, a group of three men, one of which will be the other man in the arena with the I.I.C.'s representative. The sounds were of frustration but a sudden realisation that their voices would travel far, so the closer they got to the door, the more the decibels lowered. Ultimately, it went silent for a moment, and the door opened. The President of the United States and two cabinet members by his side opened the doors for him. The silence continued as the two figureheads stared at each other from across the room. President Andrew Johnson kept his lips as thin as possible by the door, not showing any comfort in speaking to the young leader across from him. After a turbulent process with his predecessor, the weight of the loss was felt throughout the country as Johnson stepped in with his predecessor's signature top hat. He gripped it tightly like a hawk carrying its prey and walked over to his desk as the two men closed the door behind him. There is no formal introduction. There is no mutual greeting; there is already disdain for one another. Even though he hides his delight through a veil of blank expression, the young leader knows the game of chess has begun. And like the pirate he knows he is, it wouldn't be conventional.

CHAPTER 1

INITIATION

Great grandfather's jacket was a bit long in arm length but complimented the dangling mess of gold wrapped around his neck that hid his clean frilled shirt. While his beard could not match the messiness of his grandfathers (being trimmed and styled to match his striking jawline), he felt distinguished to have finally grown one which wasn't embarrassing. Too many dine-ins in the island taverns, which kept the merry tunes of old blasting to when the morning light shun, told him that what he had before wasn't working. Courting the wenches that served the island's best-tasting rum couldn't land this young lad any partnership. He has to compete with the soggy toothless regulars, whose coordination with the sea was vastly mediocre to his. The young man always winced at the idea that some of these champions of the sea would have an earring to help with their eyesight. *A load of hogwash,* he thought. However, given his love for the very thing he was born into, he had to deal with those small imperfections now. Keeping your people pleased at the highest-ranking of the islands, with a legend of the game in the back catalogue of your family tree, which started this dream, would be daunting. As his deep breaths rode his chest up and his back stood straight, the last thing to attach would be the cutlass. It laid on his desk underneath his mirror, glistening in the morning sun through his bedside window. It was something that could stand the test of time. Something that if this was to all come crashing down and sink into the deepest darkest depths of Davy Jones Locker, it would survive and let others know of the carnage it had spilt from those who wielded it. Pure silver down to the handle, engraved with the scripture of oath when Pirate captains take up the title. The text glided across the blade in tiny text reading: "A captain's word is hearsay. A pirate's blade is swift. The seas command your way. A tale of infamy, you'll bring."

As he read it, he lifted it to his eyes, familiar and bold, sweet poetry to his ears. The presentation is almost complete as the sword drops down into the pouch. One last piece, the most synonymous piece that completes the puzzle. The charred hat hung down on the corner of his mirror. A present and ever so familiar sight to anyone from the pirate nation. One local would refer to it as the crown of many captains to bring good fortune ladened with the blood of those who dare to keep it from them. The young man heard those stories, enjoyed them as a child, and went into depth as a teenager. Now, as a man, he understood the mantle. But to him, it was still the only piece his great-grandfather had bestowed upon him. The family dynasty had reclaimed power after two generations of different leaders. The Teach name he bore would be established on the pedestal of greats, but how would the young man be distinguishable from his era-defining grandfather? Even though his father would recount the tales told by his father, the name 'Blackbeard' would still not match the man they portrayed outside of the role of Captain to the I.I.C. As he reached for it, he wondered how his people would react should he not wear it.

The decorum may have changed, but the superstitious attitudes of his people would undoubtedly look on and think of the consequences should he not don the famous hat. Will the heavens open? Will the tide rise so high it will take the islands? Or will a beast rise up like the mighty Kraken and destroy the docks to a horrifying degree? Feeling the weight, he took to his pocket to draw a silver coin to decide his fate. Flicking it high into the air, he awaited to catch and see where the coin would take him, but it was not to be. A hand stretched over and snatched the falling coin. The sudden movement spooked him with a single gasp as the coin was pulled away to another pair of eyes.

"Superstition rarely gets the better of you. Something must be on your mind," the older man said. If parading around in a stolen white wig of hair used by British judges was absurd enough, the elderly man was not phased by his spotless clothing choices. Dressed in a jacket woven from two separate garments and boots, the heels were obviously used to boost his height. "Father. Where does my fate lie?" The young man asked, his voice timid with nerves.

"The unknown changing your outlook on things? That's not the Teach way, Sebastian. Your great-grandfather knew how superstitious nature clouded the workforce," the elder Teach said.

"Our people don't lose touch with the very fabric of our culture, father. There's no good tiding to those who forget the past."

"Very true. But past traditions can often lead in the wrong direction. Look where you are now. Reclaiming the very throne our family worked so hard for. You won triumphantly. You're already one-up on me. Keep playing the game, and the spoils will be yours," Sebastian's father said. Sebastian turned again to see the Captain's hat. He took it off the mirror corner and examined all its creases while his father studied the coin.

"Do you still want me to tell you the coin's fate?" Sebastian's father asked. Sebastian looked at himself in the mirror, almost anxiously awaiting his reflection to say something. That side of him that he wishes would come out more would automatically know what he wanted to do with his words and actions. But it was still hidden behind a wall of shyness. If he ever looked to break the barriers of what the I.I.C. was capable of, he would have to take away one brick at a time.

"In the hour of the Captain's course, very different eyes have steered the ship to a greater understanding of our cause. We reminisce about the golden age of our first three leaders. One of which is handing over the reins to a new yet familiar name. Sebastian Teach, son of his chosen quartermaster, Edward Teach II. Great grandson to the founding father who brought all of his here for a life away from restraint. This family knows the tricks of the trait and will control the fates of those who swear to destroy us. It is now that we say to you, Sebastian Teach, will ye serve?" The speaker asked in a loud cry that swept through to the crowd of twenty thousand pirates, all gathered around the beach stage, fashioned from a public hanging set. In the familiar territory of the pirate port, Tortuga, New Providence's land thrived from its upbeat music, shops and people. The weather was blistering hot for all in attendance but even worse for young Sebastian, who felt the sweat falling down his forehead as he donned the famous garments. Perhaps with the hat, he wouldn't have had such a hard time seeing everyone on the sandy beach of the Tortuga port. Nevertheless, he kept straight and proud and answered the time-honoured tradition of the Captain's swear.

"I will serve," he said calmly. The speaker, who wore an executioner's hood, continued the proceedings by welding a small dagger, raising it to the crowd for all to see, even the large group behind the podium, reserved for all kinds of slaves. Soon up came two wenches in rose-coloured gowns, carrying the stone slab that held a piece of parchment nailed solidly at the top. This parchment had seen better days and been through the harshest of storms. A sacred part of the Republic barely hanging on by a single nail that had rusted in its time. As they got to Sebastian, both dropped to one knee and lifted the slab high, keeping the heavy rock steady as it was presented to the new Captain. Sebastian looked at its writings and recited them in his head.

The familiarity with the I.I.C.'s constitution was burned into his memory. Its commandments were simple but effective and had stabilised the islands since its inception. The black hooded speaker brought the knife down and swiped at Sebastian's palm, gliding down his skin with blood gushing from its clean cut. It did not faze the young ruler in the slightest. He had seen much worse. He was numb to it almost. As he scrunched his hand into a fist, squeezing the blood like fresh lemon, he extended his thumb and pressed it onto the delicate paper. He was cemented now as the fourth leader of the I.I.C., forever scribbled into the history books. His bloody fingerprint now sat beside his predecessors. As he released the pressure of his thumb, he looked closely at his great-grandfathers, seeing if there was any similarity between them. Blackbeard's thumbprint was dark, but the skin pattern was visible even though a quarter of it was covered in a thick texture that looked as if it could take the paper with it if it was cleaned. First, the hat, now the blood print. In Sebastian's mind, he knew he could be different.

With enough passion as he could muster, Sebastian pounded his chest with his crimson-covered fist and brought the cutlass out from his hip guard, raising it high into the air as he screamed at the top of his lungs. The two wenches got back up to stand on two feet and turned to show the signed constitution. The crowd erupted with cheers. Swords waved, and pistols fired. The celebrations were about to commence at the famous port. The cannon fire erupted from the sailing ship behind them. The bowsprit was an old decaying ship, brought about in the famous raid victory by Blackbeard but only used for the finest occasions. Like the tropical flowers strung around the wenches beach blond hair, skulls of fallen foes were strung across its creaking stern and bow. However, Sebastian's thrill was dampened as his father came to his side, playing to the crowd before whispering in his ear: "We have to leave. We need to see him straight away."

Past the doors, the Tortuga medical house was a strong, fortified, underground dwelling dripping with moisture. Priding itself on the most straightforward and barbaric measures of practice yet lacking basic hygiene, you wouldn't feel like you were being treated for your ailments. Sebastian and his father walked through with guards on either side, brandishing cutlass swords to intimidate even the people in the hammocks. A place of aid was coated in lime green and yellow-coloured walls. Sebastian and Edward were facing one man who sat in the only wooden framed bed and didn't need any more treatment. His demise would be soon. One nurse catered to his heavy breathing and sweating by placing a cold cloth across his head as she sat by his side. The man's beard was grey, his head bald, his skin sagging, and his bones showing through his skin's thin layer. A man who once held the covenant title of Captain now laid in a bed worse for wear than he was. Sebastian thought at one stage that he and the bed would go simultaneously. He and his father looked at each other like they wanted the other to say something. It didn't dawn on Sebastian that he would be the one to speak first. Again, his newly found title still didn't make his mind sharp to the situation. He would have to change that quick. At first, Sebastian cleared his throat loudly to get the man's attention, but to no avail.

"Captain Norton?" Sebastian said. No answer. It seemed as if nothing would get his attention. Edward watched his son try to think of the solution to the problem in his head, imagining that steam would soon shoot out from his ears. In the end, Edward knew he had to be the part of his brain that thought for him outside the stone castle with lavish quarters. Taking the initiative, Edward drew out the solution; his cutlass. Sebastian looked at his father with confusion and hesitancy. "It will end quicker this way," Edward said, "Leave us." The nurse got up from the stool and walked away with the damp rag. Both men went to either side of the frail Captain Norton, soon realising how brave the nurse was to keep herself close to the decaying stench coming from the Captain for so long. As they looked down at him, all they saw was a hollow shell. "Mutiny would've been kinder," Sebastian mumbled.

"He'd pray for that more than a successor he didn't ask for," Edward said. Sebastian's father then held the sword with both hands over to his son, showing that it would be him to take his predecessor's life.

"He will be in good hands. His death will be felt, but the seas will carry his name with the wind. Live by the blade…"

"Die by the blade," Sebastian finished. An eerie sentiment, but one to have in your head constantly. As Sebastian took the blade, he and his father again had their attention on the dying Captain as the sounds of his throat distorted. Heavy and gargling, there was not much time left before the inevitable.

"The rattle. Death is playing with his new toy," Edward said. Edward was all too familiar with the Captain, he seemed relaxed, but his face showed the emotion he had for the Captain. Sebastian knew how close the two were to the pirate court. Learning about it would come with the job. He would now be the one to sever that tie. Grasping it with both hands and lifting it above his head, Sebastian waited and counted the sounds of his breathing. One. Two. Three. Four. Before the fifth gargled breath could leave the Captain's mouth, his sunken, milky eyes stared up at the young man with the blade before the eventual drop. It almost stopped Sebastian in his act of succession, but before he could faint his strike, the sword came down on the Captain's neck in a clean slice. The cutlass was now through the sheets, and Sebastian quickly drew it back to his side. The deed was done, but seeing the Captain looking up at his death would undoubtedly stay in Sebastian's dreams for a while. He tried not to let superstition get the best of him, but he knew it would haunt him.

Sebastian had only been in the Captain's quarters once. A brief visit alongside his father when he was younger. It hadn't changed since the last time. Thinly veiled curtains gave the room a shade of deep red. The mahogany wood furniture and walls would absorb the colour, while the fireplace behind the desk brought warm comfort for night time. This was to be his office daily for the remainder of the I.I.C.'s lifespan. He would be the beating heart of the operation, overseeing the quality of life for his people, the trades and the enemies. The desk was clear of anything that resembled paperwork, a guise that lured him over to the tall armchair to sit. Sebastian spread his hands along the table that was now his, he would never know what would come to his desk in the coming days, but at least today, it was his father.

"Don't get too comfortable. A pirate's life may be luxurious, but the Captain must handle everything. And it is my duty to keep you up to speed with everything," Edward said as he walked up to the desk to circle around his son.

"Now. Having relived the former Captain Norton's duties and misery, I must tell you that the Americans in Washington are not happy at the moment."

"For what purpose?" Sebastian asked.

"Since our recent blockade against the Spanish and French entering Mexico, they're a little bit twitchy at the helm. That and the north and southern states have been at war for a few years," Edward said. As he walks to Sebastian's left, he lays out a map of America and uses his finger to guide Sebastian's eyes.

"At the moment, Mexico has not said anything about the encounter on the east side of Cuba. The court feared they may be plotting a response in case we felt compelled to reach the Mexican docks."

"Are we trading with the Mexicans?"

"We almost were until Norton decided to look strong and make them beg. Now we have them and the States watching. Britain and France are just watching with their teacups in hand. I suggest an entry with level watching, but Norton rejected it."

"Can we get someone over there to explain? Perhaps if we sent a delegate to Washington, they could look the other way. They're not exactly fond of Mexico," Sebastian suggested.

"Not possible, Captain. President Lincoln is firm on his decision to lead his side to victory. His morals are questionable to ours. He'll be suspicious of any intervention whose morales side with the confederacy," Edward explained further.

"Then... We'll remain silent?" Sebastian wondered.

"It'll have to be so, Captain. Unless you say otherwise, we will remain neutral," Edward takes away the map from the desk, "Oh, I took the liberty of filling in some perfect suitors for your court. If you'd like to browse them yourself."

Edward handed his son the list and a few names he recognised insight first, and some Sebastian questioned. He first saw mayor Longstaff, Tortuga's hearty and jolly speaking head who got boozed up on all the finest occasions (finest meaning every day of the calendar year). Longstaff would be no trouble, Sebastian had met him numerous times, and everyone enjoyed his company. Scrolling through, Sebastian saw names he wasn't familiar with, such as Governor Robertson of Jamaica. Not much was known other than his slight hesitance towards taking the Captain's side in terms of providing trade stock. Most of the others Sebastian knew only from his father's circle. No sort of judgement could be made on them without inspection.

"I should meet these men immediately, father," Sebastian declared.

"Your eagerness is admirable, but the court is in disarray. Norton was becoming sceptical, and in return, his illness got worse. The only one I think he trusted, in the end, was that nurse we met."

"So you're saying I should accept them in blind faith?"

"Not blind faith, Captain. Through experience alone. And from my time besides Captain Norton, I knew these men quite well. It would show that your decision-making is fast and on track."

"Your decisions, really," Sebastian argued.

"I know it seems harsh to be walking over you already, but I'm afraid with the way the court is, we need some stability here to sort itself out. Our people will get to you soon if they disagree with it. You will have to decide if it's in their best interests by that time."

Sebastian sat back in his chair while his father walked over to the fireplace to start a new flame in the Captain's quarters. Sebastian wanted to be taken seriously at his post, but it came with a tie that could bash heads with his. This was his father he was dealing with. It crept into his head if he made the right choice regarding who will be quartermaster, but like his father said, experience came with actions. Sebastian had little to none in that regard, but it didn't hinder his decision-making.

"Did you have any doubts that these men were for themselves, father?" Edward held on to the last piece of wood in his arms as he thought.

"Difficult to say, really. With different islands come different problems. They certainly made their voices heard, but who's to say? My job was, and still is, to give the Captain both sides of the argument."

"But what if you intervened? Did you ever think that was a viable option with Norton?"

"If that would've been the case, I would have to be certain. They're honest men, Sebastian. As your father, I will try my best to not overstep my boundaries. You're my Captain and my son, and you're old enough to not take my options as gospel," Edward said, lighting a match to stoke the fireplace. He watched the flames rise through the tall stone chimney erected from the castle tower. All Sebastian could do was think it over in the night and conclude the second he woke up. But while he slept, the people of the I.I.C. would feel they were in safe hands as the colours were hoisted and the smoke rose from the castle building.

As the father and son duo walked through the town of *Norton's Steps*. The energy in the market showed why Sebastian loved this place. With no clouds in the sky, the markets were lively with stalls that bore the fruits of their labour. Spices, exotic fruit, wood and harvested animal meats. Sebastian walked down the narrow road, and the people delighted him with offerings. Small children and their mothers would be handing out fruits, which the guards had to push back. Sebastian greeted the proprietors of the stands, gracing their days before the midday mast. The bells rang in unison, louder and louder with each step closer until they engulfed every sound around you.

Coming through smoke, chatter and tarps to keep the sun out, Sebastian and his father saw the painted face of the steely-eyed depiction of Davy Jones. His beard weaved into a tapestry of battles that sunk below him and onto the large double doors. This is where the angelical side of the I.I.C. flourished. The image was burned into your eyes and would be in your brain should you decide a pirate's life was yours to uphold. As the doors opened, only one man, the pastor, stood inside at the very far end. While the outside was painted with epic encounters with the unknown, the inside of the cathedral was bare. The most striking thing you would see was the bow of the infamous Mary Rose that came through the cathedral where the pastor stood. The flags of the skull and crossbones draped along the wooden walls, which blew in the wind that fed through gaps in the boards. Though the cathedral's grandeur hooked you, the proceedings inside the creaky hall were slightly different from your standard church. As the pastor went to see his new Captain, the cathedral soon began to echo the gentle sound of children in a choir. Once the pastor made it to Sebastian to bow his head, the children stepped out. While the pastor wore an uninspired robe similar to a monk, the children were all in their everyday clothes.

"The Captain. A pleasure to see you finally," the pastor said.

"Come on, Alfred, how long have you known me?" Sebastian said with a chuckle.

"Well, it's been long enough for me to finally call you the Captain. Please, this way," Alfred said, gesturing the pair to head to the Mary Rose.

Once gathered around the Mary Rose's bow, the choir came forward to bow their heads respectfully to the Captain. Sebastian's guards walked back to the doors once the pastor waved his hand. His position at the church was in high regard, within the range of the Captain's position but not enough to influence. With a smile on his face, Alfred raised his arms and brought them down a level to his chest. Sebastian was slightly taller than Albert, and the pastor's hands almost touched his ribs.

"You swear beyond the watery mast of this, our holy ground, that you, Sebastian Teach, will swear by the blood of those before us that you will be the Captain of this ship," Albert recited.

"Aye, I swear," Sebastian said.

"You may let them in!" Albert yelled to the guards. As the doors were opened, a crowd gathered inside the church, quietly with only the sound of boots tapping on wooden floorboards. No one spoke a word, heads were bowed, and respect was given. As people flooded the church seats, the children's choir slowly raised their voices harmoniously, greeting their onlookers to the ceremony about to take place. Sebastian was feeling a lump in his throat. The joy got the better of him as the place he played around as a child would be where he was sworn by the sea gods.

"Beloved pirates of the islands. This man stands to you now a Captain. In the eyes of the many who follow our sacred oath, he was chosen as the rightful successor, and now he must be won over by the gods themselves. Captain Teach, unveil your hand." Sebastian unravelled his bandaged hand from earlier, revealing his deep cut. The blood had dried, forming a crust which fell apart as he moved his hand around.

"The blood oath is very sacred. Standing in the sands of our lands is not enough. To secure it further in the eyes of the sea gods, you must swear your blood in the oceans that they reside in," with a wave over to the choir, a small child brought out a brown bowl full of seawater, "for whom death meets shall bask in this murky water. But for you, it's a seal of destiny. As you command vessels throughout the shores of great lands, your decision leads a greater path. Now, you bear that task," Albert finished. As he did, his hand sunk into the bowl. Once he cupped a good amount of seawater, he threw it into Sebastian's face. It stung his eyes, and the taste was foul as it ran down his mouth. A familiar taste and smell but never a pleasant one. He had to endure the sting, letting it burn as he closed his eyes tight. Sebastian clenched his fists as his body fought off the initial shock. Now he would stand straight like he did before, giving off the impression to the people in the crowd that he showed no pain. After thirty seconds, Albert took a small cup of water from the alter table and tilted Sebastian's head back to dose him with clean water. The relief was splendid. The water was cooler and made him take a deep breath.

"Blessed be you, my Captain. May the peril be swift, and may the rewards drive you forward. Our Captain!" Albert cheered as he lifted Sebastian's arm to the church's applause. Reserved in their place of worship, Sebastian saw the two sides of his people: The rambunctious and the conservative. How this could be was beyond him. Pirates being reserved? It did give a perspective that showed him how they would take to his leadership. He sought to control it as much as possible, never failing them as a pirate and a worshipper of the faith. Whether or not this would break his spirit or change his rooted views would be another thing.

As the sun set along the Caribbean, the young leader and his father were back inside the castle overlooking New Providence. A busy day for what would be a lifetime soon for the new Captain. Sebastian sat in his bed, reading through the pirate code again. He had a whole collection of books to the right of him on a shelf in the middle of his wall. All stolen, of course, but the knowledge from across the seas was nothing compared to the only piece of written works he had ever known. The only one to the side of his desk by the window was the history book which was as big as a piece of driftwood. The book was thick but mostly blank pages, ready to be filled by future leaders. Only twenty-two pages had been covered so far, with the young leader's legendary grandfather starting it all. Sebastian sat in solitude. The only noise coming through was the sea from afar at the docks. He lay in bed knowing that the guards were outside his door and would never pester him unless something were to arise at any moment. Given the castle's defences, that would never happen. He sunk further into his soft pillows until his eyes became heavy, and the luxury comfort soon made him drift off into a deep sleep. From across the first floor, Edward was hard at work in the Captain's quarters, scribbling away on parchment papers to the Caribbean island's heads of state. The quartermaster spent the next two hours hard at work still after his Captain turned in for the night.

    This didn't trouble Edward at all. Compared to his temperamental predecessor, this was a step in the right direction. The former Captain Norton would profusely sweat as the hours went by, the tremble in his hands grew, and his voice rose with a simple question flung his way. Edward felt more relaxed than ever, even if his eyes wandered to the walls around him, which had the portraits of the former leaders. Norton's picture captures the very best of his chilling, empty stare. Edward's notes spoke the same, alerting the elected heads to a formal meeting with the Captain at midday tomorrow. As he sealed the last one, he slumped back in his chair, finished for the night. As he collected his thoughts and the letters, he exited through the large double doors and handed the letters over to a guard who stood by.

"Tell the mail boats to get this to the islands tonight before sunrise, immediately," Edward ordered. The guard nodded his head before leaving Edward to walk through the castle hallways, observing the majesty he had become accustomed. He wondered how his son thought of its grandeur the first time he stepped inside. With the young lad being kept under watch by his nieces and cousins down in the slum parts of Jamaica, Edward saw the glee in his eyes as he walked inside. Edward took the long route, passing his son's bedroom as he kept his hands behind his back, glazing over the stern guard who stood by and wished him a good night. Tomorrow would be very different for the young leader. Now that the celebrations were complete, the business could begin. And business was hard work for the islands.

'Tully's Catch' was where spirits were high, and the booze flowed through endlessly like a waterfall. The pungent smell of the old tavern sunk into the wooden floorboards, and the music harmonised the evening till the early morning hours. There is no closing time at Tully's. In fact, the big man Tully didn't care if you were drunk on the job as long as you could still serve and take the coins. His tavern consisted of sailor etiquette and knick-knacks. The walls had stuffed animals and fishes caught from expeditions of the Tortuga port, mainly composed of swordfish and wild boars. A warm, inviting glow radiated throughout the bar from the chandelier, probably the thing that stood out the most because it was so out of place and obviously stolen from a plantation mansion house. Three birds pitched themselves on its ring base and watched below as the merry collection of customers danced the night away to the tune of accordions and violins. Two men sat in the darkest part of the bar, just next to the looming window by the doors. One was sweating, eyes wide open, and his hands clasped together, almost like he was praying. The other had his face hidden away from his cowboy hat

and his long blond hair flowing out from the sides and back. This man was not a native by any stretch. A traveller, most likely, pulled in for the night while the night sky stopped anyone from pulling out of the I.I.C.'s docks. Curfews were tight along the islands. Arrivals would be accepted, while departures were strict and guarded in case swindlers took off without paying. Tonight, the man in the cowboy hat placed his tarot cards onto the table ever so slowly as he for told the future of the man opposite him. The last card to be set down was '*Judgement*'.

CHAPTER 2

A CORDIAL MEETING

Edward waited impatiently by the Captain's door, pacing back and forward with his hands behind his back. Mixed with anxious anticipations, coupled with his fatherly instinct to drag his son out by his hair for being late, the quartermaster continued to walk and wait. A different guard was at the Captain's door now, much skinnier than last night's guard but again held a stern expression towards Edward.

"Did you knock on his door this morning?" Edward asked.

"I did, sir, yes. I'm sure the Captain will be ready in no time," the guard answered.

"His tardiness will only get him so far," Edward mumbled. Eventually, the door unlocked and out stepped Sebastian in his Captain attire, ready for the day.

"What kept you?" His father asked.

"I have to look good, don't I?" Sebastian said with a swagger. His father was displeased by that.

"Looks will only get you so far, Sebastian. And for you today, it's looking good to some crusty old barnacles who handle most of the hard work for you. Now come on! We must not keep them waiting," Edward said, pushing his son in the right direction downstairs.

"The title of Captain will have you in high regard for any decision on the islands, Sebastian. Each and every one of them will have different issues. Now here is a list of things which I have written for you. They won't be in this order per-se, but you'll get the idea of how chaotic it has been since your swearing-in."

Sebastian scanned the paper to see an alarming number of issues from the islands, each more pressing than the last.

"What on earth did Norton do!? I can't solve all of this!"

"No, you can't, being completely honest with you there. But if anything doesn't seem right or you don't understand, just look at me, and I'll give you an answer," Edward explained.

"But then I'll look like I'm not ready! How can I impress them if I can't even figure out an answer?"

"Again, just look to me."

Reaching the main doors, Sebastian and Edward were greeted by a broad man who stood out amongst his peers as he was the most well-dressed man in all of the I.I.C. Not a wrinkle to his clothes, not a hair out of place and a smile that made anyone feel at ease. With two guards beside him, Edward extended his arms, and the two met with a hearty hug.

"Rourke! Good to see you stayed. The new Captain here will really appreciate your services to the I.I.C."

"Well, it took some convincing. Your son winning the race was a factor, I must say," Rourke said, his voice deep and smooth, adding to his charm.

"Sebastian, this is Rourke Renfold. He commanded Norton's ship in his absence. If ever you need a shipmate, there's no man better."

"Nice to meet you, sir," Sebastian said with a handshake.

"Now that I'm not accustomed to. The Captain called me sir and shook my hand, ha! I feel you will definitely turn the tide of this place, Captain," Rourke said gleefully.

"Are our arrangements all met with the mayor's, Rourke?" Edward asked.

"They are indeed. As Rourke pushed the door open and the bright morning light was let in, Sebastian and Edward looked out to the sea and saw five ships approaching. Each one was different in scale, but all flew the covenant flag of the I.I.C. high above the mast. It was always a feast for the eyes to see a sight like that every day.

"The seating arrangements are all in check. Shall it be rum or wine, Captain?" Rourke asked.

"Uh, wine, I think. Thank you, Rourke," Sebastian said.

"Look at you breaking out the French wine. I thought you hated it?" Edward said.

"Oh, I do. Just thought it would look more distinguished for the occasion."

"Then let's get you seated and ready. Remember what I said."

The table stretched out along the dining room, and the guests sat accordingly, twiddling their thumbs and sipping their glasses. The silence was awkward enough, and all that could be heard was the grandfather clock in the background. Sebastian looked across at the mayor', and he remembered what his father had said earlier. Describing his band of elected officials as "Barnacles" was just putting it nicely; these men looked decrepit. Not physically, some were more rotund than the pigs farmed in Jamaica, but in their eyes, Sebastian knew the energy was drained from them. The life sucked from their bodies and the will to carry on. Sebastian was glad Mayor Longstaff of Tortuga was here at least, but spearing new life into these other men could've been done with a simple stab of Sebastian's sword.

"Right...gentlemen. Thank you all for coming at a very troubling time. My quartermaster has informed me, uh, of the many difficulties I plunge my captaincy into. Who would like to begin?" Sebastian said as he gestured to the men to speak. Their eyes moved, looking across at one another, and their movements were that of a slug. After an uncomfortable five seconds, the man closest to Sebastian on his left sounded off. Speaking in a dry and monotone voice, like it was even an effort to speak.

"Firstly, congratulations on your victory, Captain. We'll spare you the complementarities. I can say for all of us, we're glad Norton bit the dust. The state of affairs the islands are in requires swift actions."

"That's good to know. Uh, what island are you present on, mayor...?"

"Ellis, Captain. Ellis Robertson, Mayor of Jamaica. The island is in desperate need of more slave labour. With Norton not sending any of his ships out to continue the trade down in Africa, projects have been unable to be achieved."

"Noted. I'll be onto that. Anyone else?" Sebastian asked. A hand raised further down the table. A weedy man with round glasses and a snivelling voice spoke next.

"C-Captain Teach, Mayor Williamson. A-as you know, Tortuga is r-rife with delinquents," Sebastian seemed puzzled by that statement, "This behaviour is getting too out of hand, I feel. Without the proper number of guards, it's affecting the local businesses on every island and is encouraged."

"As Mayor of Tortuga, I can honestly say that is preposterous! Captain, this is our culture! The old man clearly wouldn't know a glass of rum to a bitter serving of seawater," Mayor Longstaff rebutted.

"I can vouch for you, Mayor Longstaff, but Mayor Williamson has the floor. Carry on, sir."

"T-thank you. Will more recruitment be a priority? Since the days of rioting from Norton's time, we can't lose any more than we have. W-we're already on thin resources," Williamson continued, sounding more distressed.

"Norton pretty much put a decline on everything. I will see to it that encouragement to our brave sea guards will be sent their way," Sebastian stared out the window for a minute, "though I must ask this table of chair members: What exactly were you lot doing during this time?"

The table then perked up slightly. Like dogs, the mayor's ears pricked up, and some felt insulted. Sensing the tension, Edward rushed to his son's ear to whisper, "We're trying to solve problems, not cause them, son."

"What on earth is that supposed to mean?" The youngest mayor said.

"Gentlemen, my father has informed me of your struggles and today, I am hearing yours on the current day operations. But just then, you've shown me fear. Fear of what exactly?"

And then the room came unglued with commotion. Some of the men stood from their chairs they were so outraged. The only one to remain seated and quiet was mayor Longstaff, rubbing his face into his hand at the sight of his colleague's frustration. Sebastian didn't move a muscle in his seat, but Edward was having none of this. As he yelled from behind the Captain's chair, the men froze, and all eyes were now on Edward.

"Gentlemen! This is your Captain! There will be no more discourse like this in the briefing. You will all send in written reports before you leave. The Captain's business is needed elsewhere."

Edward wanted his son out of the dining room as quickly as possible, but Sebastian, like an immature child, merely smiled and slowly got up. Edward wanted so badly to grab him by his collar and drag him out, but he couldn't do it. Instead, the two men went outside while Rourke quietly closed the door behind them.

"Well, that was the shortest briefing of the islands I've ever heard," he joked.

"A disaster. Rourke, this is no time for jokes," Edward said, pacing around with his hands on his hips.

"Father, there's no love from them in the slightest-"

"Of course, there isn't! Do you not fully understand things right now? We don't need to be giving more reason for them to be in fear and what you did was reckless!"

"Reckless? Father, how else am I going to build back our home with a bunch of brain dead "Yes men"?" Sebastian answered back.

"That's what they are! Yes men! But on your great-grandfather's beard, please lead them in the right direction. You literally can't go wrong in your captaincy. Anything you do is going to look ten times better than what Norton did! The man cared about nothing but himself, and that is something you clearly don't do." The words resonated with Sebastian, making him reel back slightly, relaxing him.

"Now, you listen to me very carefully, young man. The I.I.C. depends on you. You're a beacon of hope to these people. The men in there may not look like the sort of people who would know how much a quarter barrel costs at your cousin Sally's distillery, but they're still people of the islands.

You want them to do their job as you pride yourself on yours. Remember that."

Sebastian finally relaxed but looked around the room to avoid eye contact with his father as his mind trailed. He listened, but he would also have to listen to his thoughts. With a simple nod, he retired up the stairs and headed back to his quarters. Rourke came to the side of Edward to watch the young captain walk.

"He'll get things done. At least he knows what he's dealing with."

"Indeed he will," Edward sighed.

"I see you didn't mention the near mass exodus?"

"If he knew about that, he would've fired them on the spot, Rourke. My boy is still impulsive, but he'll learn to control himself, with or without me. I just hope I can set him straight."

"That might be difficult," Rourke said.

"How so?"

"The seas are never a straight path."

CHAPTER 3

FROM THE DESK OF...

Across to the far west, Mexico is silent. The President, Benito Juárez, sits alone with his hands flat across his desk as he stares at the written letter. A warning has been issued, and Mexico is again a target to the French. Juárez remained vigilant but worried. Like a statue, his face remained in a frozen state of determination while his brain worked hard to devise a solution to his country's impending attack and trade struggle. It wasn't easy. Juárez just stayed inside, wasting away while the needs of his people needed an answer. That's when the door opened to his office, and in stepped a young man with a cravat tie so tight around his neck, it was a wonder he got any words out.

"It seems pretty clear what you have to do, Presidente."

"We are already cornered by the American government, they've only just recognised us, and we cannot risk the south mistaking us at this time. The Americans have battled among themselves for almost five years now. I don't want another war coming for Mexico," Juárez said.

"How does the speech look?" The assistant asked.

"Like it should: Strong, yet humble. I will address my people this afternoon in the eye of the hurricane."

"Presidente?"

"What I'm about to say might shock you, young man, but I have no choice. Sit down and listen. Tell me what you think."

Another year coming to a close, yet the brutal conflict continues in America. One man stood alone in the oval office and sat comfortably with his legs crossed by the desk. He sat in thought, pressing his hand into his cheek as his eyes wandered off to the carpet. It was a thought that crossed his mind many times, yet it never materialised.

Nevertheless, it was still prevalent at this time. The thought of a sudden attack on the White House from the confederacy didn't seem plausible, not by this time. However, the fear wouldn't go away any time soon. Not until one side conceded. Victory could be in his grasp. Rubbing his chin strap beard, he brought himself forward in his chair and looked to his desk to see it clear of paper but noticed the quill pen in the ink pot. Drawing a piece of paper from his drawer, the man begins to write a letter at a pace.

"*November 8th, 1864.*

Washington D.C.

From the Office of President Of the United States.

While the spoils of victory are far and few, today, as I write to you, I have succeeded in residing in the White House during still the horrors of the Civil War in my country. While America has recognised your efforts of recalibration during perilous times, my administration cannot help but wonder if your efforts are in aiding the opposition that is the confederacy. This is in reference to the Caribbean islands and the rule of the I.I.C., one whose core values are similar to that of the Union's opposition. I am in writing to you, President Juárez, a stark warning. While we value your input, the United States will not stand by and look the other way. My administration will take this in, and we will see fit to negotiate once the war at home has been quenched. I implore you to reason and see this as a drastic and altering deal that cannot be seen as a threat. As I resign at my desk for another four years, I guarantee my time will not be spent dealing with another foe."

CHAPTER 4

FAMILY BONDING

Edward seemed comfortable. As the afternoon came and went, the quartermaster relished in the orders requested of him to fill in the blanks of the island's governing bodies. Through written forms of declaration, he finished a lot earlier than usual, taking a moment to relish the sun coming through his office window. The island's flag (A skeleton demon piercing the heart while another prays in its might across a black background) hung behind him, and the winds coming through the window rippled through it. Nothing could interrupt him this time. Or so he thought when an apple flew in, bouncing across his desk. Disrupting and shocking the life out of him, he rushed to the window to see the commotion, Edward locked eyes with the familiar sight of his older sister, brandishing a piece of paper as she waved to him. She stood out in a half-yellow, half-brown dress as her Auburn hair bounced around.

"Can't you just knock!?" Edward called out.

"Don't be such a tight knot! Is Sebastian there? The girls were wondering if we could have you two for the tavern's anniversary?"

"For goodness sake, Abigail. He's the Captain now. We can't have him waltzing down there being rowdy with everyone. I'll be the one fishing him out from a barrel!" Edward stressed.

"Not tonight, tomorrow! We'll reserve the place for the two of you. Bring some guards and that tall fella you have under your wing," Abigail said with a playful roll of her eyes.

"Rourke is very busy, Abigail, and so are we. But...I think we can squeeze in for a meal," Edward hesitatingly said to Abigail's delight.

"Ah ha! See, I knew you couldn't resist my cooking! We shall make the place worthy of your arrival!"

23

"Wait! What time will this be exactly?" Edward asked before his sister began to turn.

"Near midnight, of course," Abigail said with a playful wink, and before Edward knew it, she was happily strolling away, knowing that the invitation would undoubtedly lead to alcohol for her brother and the young Sebastian. Edward stepped away from the window, already plotting what to say to Sebastian in his head, but unfortunately, nothing would materialise as the Captain stood inside the door, earwigging the conversation.

"I know what you're going to say, father-"

"Oh, that sister of mine! She knows fully that she can't interfere with you at the moment. I knew the second you heard such an offer, you wouldn't say no," Edward moaned.

"Father, please. We can't be isolated here. We're in need of festivities, and I haven't seen my aunties in ages," Sebastian pleaded.

"I know what it will turn into. They'll put bad thoughts into your head, Sebastian."

"No, they don't."

"Really? Well, who sat for a week under his bed, thinking that a maelstrom of all things would engulf the islands when they were younger?" Edward reminded him. Sebastian smiled; even though he wasn't at the time, the memory now was funny to relive in his head.

"Abigail may be my sister, but the family is all over the show. I don't want you going down a dark path."

"Sorry, we're pirates, father. We're already on a dark and dangerous path," Sebastian shrugged.

"Doesn't mean we can't act civilised now and again," Edward said, crossing his arms.

"Look, if it means that much to you, I won't stay for drinks. We'll just eat, and we'll go. How's that sound?"

Two hours in, and the smell of rum was overwhelming. Edward was now confined to a corner of the merry tavern while Sebastian and the family rejoiced with booze and food. The long table (just all six tables joined together) was a hodgepodge of chicken bones, shredded lettuce leaves, skins of pineapples, mushy potato, gravy-covered plates and spilt liquor. Abigail's cheeks were as red as the apple she bit into as she swayed side to side with Sebastian, whose head drooped and his hair completely ruffled. Along his left side, Sebastian was joined by his many other cousins, and to his right, the guards he invited for doing a good job recently. Rourke soon came swaggering back over to the table from the bar with another cup of rum, giggling to himself. The charm never left while intoxicated, and the infatuation still glowed in Abigail's eyes as she watched him. Sebastian clinked on his glass and called for a toast as he swung his head back up.

"Thank you all…for you-your support recently. I couldn't be more…happier to lead you all. This is the life we crave…and this…is the happy life I'll bring you! Cheers!" Glasses raised, and celebratory cheers rang out through the tavern, "and I do hope father…where ever he is, will make sure…to bore you all to sleep as he will be," Sebastian barely finished before rushing the sweet rum down his throat again. The typical noise resumed, and Edward didn't even want to finish his drink after that statement. Edward could only see it as a return to normality as he surveyed the tavern. Normality he couldn't stomach. As a youth, he remembered the days when the charismatic Jack Burchill was the leader of the I.I.C. Normality that never changed nor adapted. Edward scowled at the outrageous scenes he would see like this every night. It seemed to him that while he could never obtain the position of leader, his son basked in the reckless, drunken shenanigans that were second nature to a pirate native. Edward saw Sebastian finally get up from his chair, away from his cousins, holding on to him to stay balanced and slowly stagger his way up the stairs. Most likely heading to the restroom, Edward put his cup down and wandered off outside for some fresh air. As the door was left ajar and his back was turned, a man in a cowboy hat brushed through and surveyed the drunken tavern. From under his brim, a pair of eyes with black face paint crossed over them saw drunken dancing, passed-out bodies, and finally landing on Sebastian, stumbling along the first-floor balcony. Without any need to hide or look suspicious (even in a sober crowd, he didn't look suspicious), the man followed the young leader to the restroom. Sebastian had already shaken his trousers down to his ankles and paraded his genitals around the empty stall. Stinking of the last person who had missed his target completely. Thankfully, Sebastian didn't need to sit on the hole in the wooden box, he simply urinated with poor aim. As he felt relieved, the door creaked open, and the man in the cowboy hat walked inside and took out a piece of paper, which he had rolled up inside his duster jacket. He stood there patiently, watching the Captain like an animal, waiting to strike. As Sebastian turned after pulling his trousers up, the man in the cowboy hat simply smiled with glee like a little girl.

"The Captain! Sir, it is an honour to meet you," the cowboy said, shaking Sebastian's hand and not even attempting to cover his southern accent.

"Hey! H-how are you, sir? Oh, I love your hat!" Sebastian strung together.

"Captain, it would be an honour if I could get you to sign this for me. It's for my dear son. It'd be the birthday gift of a lifetime if he got this signed by you."

"Anything, anything, for a loyal pirate such as yourself. But I need my father. He has this thing called a-"

"Pen? Captain?" The cowboy said, brandishing it in front of Sebastian's eyes, who gave his fullest attention.

"Yeah, that! Um, it's my name you want, right?"

"Just a little signature there, please, Captain."

Without trying to tear up the paper, Sebastian managed somewhat of a signature along the dotted line, the cowboy still smiling as the initial was done.

"Thank you so much, Captain. This is going to mean the world to my son!"

"Yes, give him my best. Did I tell you you have a really nice hat? Where'd you get it from?" Sebastian got out while holding himself up against the wall. The cowboy ignored the drunken Captain and soon headed for the front door. He knew he wouldn't be remembered, but a figure would be present in Sebastian's mind the next day. A hangover could be quite the puzzle to solve. Right under his nose, the pirate captain had fallen for the ruse, but what this led to would surely hurt him.

Sebastian had difficulty keeping his head up at his desk the following day. The rain was heavy outside and the cup of water beside him was almost finished. Trying to keep his eyes open as the doors opened in front of him, Sebastian didn't see his father walk in but a guard escorting someone in.

"Miss Abigail Teach, Captain," the guard announced. Sebastian knew the dress was familiar. It was the same dress Abigail danced the last night away to, and he could see that she had not fully recovered from the shindig.

"How are you coping, love?" She asked him. Not even keeping to the code of conduct when speaking to the Captain infuriated the guard as he walked away.

"Great night, that's all I can say."

"To right it was. I just came here to see if you got here safely. Stupid question, I know, but-"

"Father had an escort carriage sent for me," Sebastian clarified.

"So he just hopped off and left, did he?"

Abigail sighed heavily as the embarrassment rushed to her.

"My brother. I could tell you loads of stories about him, but his attitude stays the same, let me tell ya," Abigail came round to stand with Sebastian as he rubbed his head as it riled in pain from his hangover. "What you working on today then?"

"Um, it's...boring treaty stuff. Something to do with food imports as well," Sebastian said, trying to sound into his work when all he wanted to do was crash back in his plump bed.

"Food imports? Go a lot on ya plate then," Abigail giggled, making Sebastian smile.

"What's it like working with the old man now? Knowing you are technically his boss?" She asked.

"I don't notice it, really. Father's been there for everything with me. You know what he's like, protective to the fullest extent. More so now." Sebastian said with a hint of dissatisfaction. Abigail could see it pestered him slightly. Last night's antics showed who Sebastian truly was to his family rather than the charade he would have to wear for the public.

"Just remember, it's not him in charge, darling. It's you. Your old man is always a boot licker and just wants things in order. He ain't right up here most of the time. Little things drone on him for too long. He wants you to be a little version of himself, really."

"You think so?"

"I know so. You weren't around when Jack Burchill was Captain, but cor' my brother did not want you turning out like him," said Abigail.

"Why's that?" Sebastian asked.

"He never was one for the pirate lifestyle. Turned his nose up to it, still does, but he won't show it to ya. Everything about it made him want to sail from these islands and never return, but he knew he couldn't. So he thought he'd show his skills in politics, and I'd be lying in saying he didn't do a little jump for joy when Burchill was killed by that filthy slave."

"I only saw little things with him when Norton was in charge. Though he tells me it wasn't a good time for anyone."

"No, it wasn't Sebastian. Everyone thought the world was coming to an end with that old bag of bones in charge."

"I get where he's coming from with his methods. He just doesn't want a repeat of what happened last time, and I get that. Just..." Sebastian wanted to say what was on his mind, but Abigail quickly said it for him.

"You want to be your own man. Remember, you're the Captain now, Sebastian. One man's moulding is never perfect," Abigail held hold of Sebastian's hands as she meant her last words, "Wield the sword strong. And I think you'll have something of this."

Suddenly the doors swung open again. Stepping in was the same guard as before with a written message in his hands.

"Captain! Urgent request that has just landed in New Providence!"

Abigail patted Sebastian's hands and went about her way, not saying a word but with a cheeky wink and grin as she strutted out past the guard.

"Yes, proceed," Sebastian said in a serious tone. The paper was placed in front of him, and the Captain read its contents. Bewilderment at first soon turned to excitement.

"All this from our delegation?" Sebastian said with a surprised smile.

"Indeed, sir. The message carrier said the President would like to see you at your earliest convenience," the guard informed Sebastian.

"Well. I guess I should arrive in style then."

CHAPTER 5

A MEETING IN MEXICO

As the rain continued to pour and the roar of the wind became intensely violent, one ship remained docked at Tortuga, which was *The Devil's Punchbowl*. A fierce navy vessel carrying twenty-five canons that could tear up a ship from any angle. Across its port and starboard, the severed skulls of the miserable souls to be caught in its path, the flag of the I.I.C. flying high and the crew members scurrying to their posts. Sebastian and Edward made their way from the coach to the wooden docks without security. The deckhands watched them stroll along to the boarding plank without uttering a word.

"Captain! The Punchbowl is ready to sail on your command!"

"Thank you, sergeant!" Sebastian inspected the fine vessel through squinted eyes as the rain hammered the crew as his father kept on.

"If you insist on doing this by yourself, then the least you can do is inform me earlier and not at the very second of your departure!"

"So if I were to tell you earlier, you would not intervene?" Edward was slightly taken aback by this response. *How dare my son get lippy with me! I'm his quartermaster, for god sake.* "Father, all I ask of you is to man the islands while my visit takes place. This could prove to be a fortune in hiding if I attend to the President's invitation-"

"We are in a circle of enemies, Sebastian. The Americans and the Mexicans will try to swindle you out of anything we have left. They know of our current climate-"

"And we know of theirs. Let this be the turning tide of this dangerous storm. Trust me on this, father. It's going to be fine. Like you said, I can't do no wrong, right?"

Edward reluctantly let his son go after the exchange. The young Captain left with a cheerful smile as he boarded The Devil's Punchbowl. The sails were brought down, the boarding platform was lifted back inside, and the beacons were lit. The force of the seas left for the west, where it was uncertain of what the Captain might encounter. Edward had all the scenarios in his head for when Sebastian would dock in Mexico. Would it be a ploy from the American government to use Mexico as a scapegoat for holding the leader of the islands hostage for bargaining? Given the past pirate Captain leader's track records with the U.S., it could be time for payback. Cursing his heritage in his head, Edward simply waved goodbye and rushed back to the castle as the rain only got heavier with each minute.

By the morning, and through a sea of rocking waves, The Devil's Punchbowl soon arrived at the Mexican docks, unshaken from its battering of the storm. A horrifying sight to the locals, who all looked on with sheer disbelief that the vessel would dare show itself again. No one moved, nor did the President, who waited patiently by his carriage with his entourage surrounding him. The cold blank expression on Juárez's face showed his supporters that he was not afraid and that progress would be made as onlookers dreaded what was to come. Soon the sergeant of the Punchbowl was to step off first, sounding off in a booming voice the oath of arrival for the Captain, a usual precursor for meetings, acquisitions or into battle. Sebastian stepped off, and the public had their first official look at the young leader since his swearing-in months ago. Juárez had the thought in his head that this had to be a joke, but as the crew still gathered around the young man, Juárez realised he would have to start walking. Which he did. The pair locked eyes as they met in the middle of the dockyard. Both parties of guards held their weapons close in case anything should break down, both unsure as to what would happen. Finally, at a foot apart from each other, Juárez formally greeted the young Captain when his stoic face changed to a pleasant smile and a shake of the hand.

"Captain Teach, on behalf of the people of Mexico, welcome," Juárez said, extending his hand, "I am most pleased you decided to visit so quickly to my letter."

"An invitation across seas will not hasten my speed, Mr President. I trust the delegation the islands sent you was put to good use?"

"Indeed it did. The sovereigns of the east are well at bay now. But that's not all I wanted to talk to you about today. Please, this way," Juárez extended his invitation into the President's carriage. Sebastian climbed inside, as did his sergeant, whisking his hands to the rest of the crew to remain stationed. The horses pulled the carriage to the President's building in the heart of Mexico City, Chapultepec Castle.

After a long journey through the Mexican heartland, the President and Captain arrived at the castle, and Sebastian was in awe of the magnificent sight. A behemoth of architecture, the striking podiums and structure of the fortified walls made Sebastian's jaw drop.

"Truly impressive," Sebastian said as he stepped off the carriage.

"Befitting, isn't it? Our people can bast in all its glory without the influence of Austrian interference. There is a reason why it sits on top here. Please, Captain, this way."

Once inside, the two men sat inside the President's main study, a royal room with red curtains, a golden tapestry and a set of plush furniture. It seemed very out of place from the renovations Sebastian walked past.

"Wonderful, isn't it? Even though we both share our disdain for a monarch, I'm sure you can appreciate its value?" Juárez asked.

"Trust me. We, pirates, know about royals and their treasures. So what do I owe the pleasure of my visit, Mr President?"

"Well, it all stems from a few years ago. Mexico was at the mercy of both kingdoms from the east. Your leader at the time pushed back these invading forces, which bought Mexico some time-"

"That was a coordinated attack through paranoia, I'm afraid," Sebastian corrected.

"Call it what you will, but what it did was a favour. We held off anything that could shake this nation, and when the delegation came from you, I saw it as an opportunity. This nation is indebted to the I.I.C, Captain Teach. Consider this invitation, as you will, an olive branch."

Sebastian took off his hat in astonishment. Things might be going the way he had envisioned them.

"You would want to trade further?"

"I would want us to become an alliance. With the events unfolding in the north and with the British and French kingdoms no longer the dominant force of the seas, it only seems necessary that a new force would come about to these lands. One for any future disturbances." Juárez then directed Sebastian's attention to the map hanging on the wall. Seeing the vast map of continents made Sebastian ponder for a moment before Juárez would fill in the desired intention.

"Kingdoms come and go, captain Teach. It would be unwise to not have someone you can rely on. The British, the French, the Spanish, the Dutch, and now the Americans. They all fight amongst themselves. We have had to fight for our survival."

"We have indeed."

"We are both in rebuilding stages. Imagine what our forces will be like together. We may be on different pages in key aspects of life, but we share a common foe: interventionists."

It made sense in Sebastian's mind. Mostly his father came to mind. Pirates have always wanted the freedom they crave with the life they chose. It would be foolish to pass up a backup in case things should go down.

"Combining forces?"

"On the common ground. The Mexican people are very patriotic to our cause. I would not turn a blind eye to their commitment, Captain."

"You understand that I will have to uphold certain…privileges, Mr president."

"And that is?" Juárez asked.

"The I.I.C's morals on contributing are very strict. If we commandeer your men, we ask that their cut be lower than our own."

"Might I enquire as to why that is?" Juárez continued.

"I value my people's work. Pirates do not like to be undermined by what they set out to achieve for the gods of the seas. And remember, we are recovering from a slew of bad decision-making. You're recovering from wars. I wouldn't bite the hand feeding you our delicious delegations."

Juárez saw the young man go stern in his bargain. He was serious. Juárez heard a hint of callousness in his voice, the mark of a true patriot of his own kind. *Very loyal.* Staring his enemies and his allies with solid intent. Juárez would have to tread carefully.

"But, to ease things through. I might propose something to this deal?" Sebastian added.

"I'm listening," Juárez said, taking a seat opposite the Captain.

"I also propose a bonding exercise. A project. One that we can both work on." "How big of a project?"

"A vessel. One where we both command it. Use it at our will. A vessel only to be used in the toughest situations. Stationed at both our lands at any time. We could make it look like something the seas' mightiest monsters have never seen before. It should strike fear to anyone looking to cross us," Sebastian went on. Juárez was leaning in more now. The idea of a ship of commendable size and artillery would prove a safe bet. Seeing the young leader's vision pan out intrigued the Mexican leader. He could see the excitement in his eyes, and Sebastian had him like a fish on a hook.

"Yes. Stationing something of immense size in the gulf would be valuable to us both. How soon would you be willing to start?"

"Immediately," Sebastian said, wasting no time, "With a joint speech effort on both patches of soil, we will rally workers to our cause faster."

"And it won't be hard to capture the purist heart for the glory of our coalition. They are already looking at us as the ones to aid their future. Captain Teach, I fully support this quest. This will be our salvation."

Juárez outstretched his hand for a shake. A great success carefully thought out by the young Captain. Capturing a nation's interest in a rebuilding phase is one thing, but bringing forth a strength in weaponry that could potentially draw in more would be another. Sebastian knew this would have to be staged accordingly. While his interests rivalled his cabinet, ultimately, they wouldn't have the final say. As his hand met the Mexican presidents, the deal was set, and the future was bright.

"We should begin preparations for when we address our people. By the way, what shall we call this vessel?" Juárez asked.

Sebastian already knew the answer to that question.

"It should be called something that would make any sailor dread the sea in general. Something that would make the faintest of hearts quiver at the sight of it. Something that would terrify a child to no end."

CHAPTER 6

BEAST OF THE SEA

"Rourke! How soon will the vessel be by the dockside?" Called Sebastian from the drawing room. "Very soon, Captain. Its crew expressed that it will be cleaned and prepared before the crowds begin to gather," Rourke assured.

"Very good. Tell them my arrival will be in ten minutes."

"Aye, aye, captain!"

Rourke signalled the crew to the dockside and then sprinted to their positions on board the Punchbowl. The ship was draped in the banners of the I.I.C.'s flag and crest badges along the starboard. Wooden box pillars were constructed on the dockside, and a crowd to the east was arriving.

As he placed his hat on his head, the guards knocked at the door and proceeded inside.

"Captain. Your shield is ready," said the guard. Sebastian walked into the door frame, and the guards stood straight. Cutlasses brandished, feet akimbo and chins pointing out. Sebastian stood in the centre of them, and they began to mould a protective shape around him, resembling a human eye.

The formation was to befit the righteous Captain in the eyes of the sea gods and his peers who would be watching. Stepping outside through the castle doors, a sea of onlookers began to cheer in unison. With great praise, they were happy to see their Captain again (a rarity in Norton's reign), but some eyes were still not as pleased as Sebastian walked down the slope towards the pier. In between his guards, he saw plain expressions wondering what to make of him, while others in small groups, dressed in blue, looked hostile. Hostility towards the Captain's seat was common, any leader is subject to ridicule, but Sebastian wanted to be different. It could only be seen as decisive in proving the right to expansion and trade with the Mexican government and the pair's shared project. At the stage, the guards dispersed, forming a line in front of the wooden pillars as Sebastian walked aboard the Punchbowl via its boarding plank. Sebastian turned around to wave his hands and show them his appreciation while at the same time keeping a watchful eye for anyone with a pistol. He may believe he has the world on his shoulders, but Sebastian knew someone would always be around to trip him up and make him lose his grip. Luckily, he was on board, and the range of faces watched and listened with hope and concern.

"Ladies and gentlemen, I come forward to you today to open your eyes to the greatest thing our islands will ever behold. Not a man or myth, not a god or demon. But from an idea. An idea where the pirate people can freely travel without isolation. Without endeavours from foreign enemies. Some of you may have caught word this week that I had taken this fine vessel to sea towards the west. It wasn't to test the durability against the seas, but for travel. Travel to Mexico, where I met with their President, President Benito Juárez," heads started to turn to their neighbours in the crowd, "There was no hostility nor any predetermined notions of us, but simply an invitation. An invitation to said idea. Effective immediately, the I.I.C. now has a new trading partner and an alliance with Mexico. While we differ on many things, we are two nations in dire need of a dream. A dream where the sea is ours to control. We are the servants of the sea's power. We know how to use it to come out on top. But lately, we could not even sail out from our own shores. Rest assured that under my command, you will sail to bring the I.I.C back as a strong, formidable nation. And with Mexico's workforce and our determined spirit, we'll make a new god of the sea!" Claps began to circulate in the crowd. Sebastian was winning his audience.

"I know, I know, sounds blasphemous. But what is a god's power to a non-believer? They may see it as a ridiculous hokum of high tides washing away their treasures or succumbing to the mighty Kraken. Yet, they laugh. They laugh at them, and in doing so, they laugh at us. The gods will see our dedication to the sea as a vessel, and you, my people, will sail it! But where is that ship, you ask? Well, that, my dear people, is what we plan to create. We will bring to life the most feared weapon of the sea this side of the Atlantic has ever seen. And in doing so, the swine of Europe and America will tremble at our feet if they ever send their ships here ever again! Together, this beast of the sea will command the strength of hundreds of cannons, immovable against any fighter ship and will be the biggest threat to any nation that dares harm our way of life. Ladies and gentlemen, we will build...the Maelstrom!"

Beneath Sebastian on the wood dock was a board placed beside him during his speech, with a tarp over it. Once the name had been spoken, the tarp was torn off, unveiling the blueprint to the Maelstrom. The front of the crowd began to marvel at the ship in question, and it was everything their Captain had envisioned for them. Fierce and dangerous, it seemed impossible, but the challenge would be commendable. As the first few audible words of excitement drew more people closer, Sebastian had to control the crowd.

"The blueprint plans will be displayed to everyone, so don't rush, please. Our guards will make sure that everyone in the island regions will get a glimpse of our dream. They will also have a sign up sheet for you to participate in the Maelstrom construction. Working on this vessel is, I feel, our nation's top priority. Any and all help will be met with tremendous gratitude and reward. And so I say to you, my pirates, go forth and be your truest self. A self that cements its legacy at sea!"

With that, the crowd erupted in cheers, but still, tiny minorities of it were hesitant to stand with anything the Captain said. Sebastian stood proud, confident in his words and love for the I.I.C.

To the west, President Juárez received the same admiration. It proved that the joint effort would bring in loyal and hard working people. The Maelstrom was a feat of engineering that needed the brightest of both countries to function. By coincidence, Sebastian and Benito were whisked away from their stages to talk with the said engineers. Sebastian sat in his chair, listening to the complicated hurdles that would encompass the making of the Maelstrom. His father was always close by his side, peering from beside the tall back chair his son sat in. As the engineers continued, Rourke stepped through unannounced, and that was all Sebastian needed to clear the room.

"I take it the speech went well from your perspective?" Edward asked.

"Not just from mine, but from everyone! Our Captain had them eating out of the palms of his hands," Rourke gestured.

"Thank you, Rourke. I suspect the Mexican President will be reaping the same results. Our speeches were the same but changed slightly."

"Oh, a joint effort speech! I see you are covering a lot of ground with the Mexican President. And all in one trip!" Rourke cheered.

"We shall have a real celebration tonight, my friend. Father, from the engineer's perspective, this needs a lot of hands-on deck. Will you be able to assemble the mayors to cover the enlisting tonight?" Sebastian asked.

Edward seemed a bit too hesitant to answer but scrambled for the words.

"Oh, now? I thought I was needed here?"

"Nonsense. Your duties stretch far beyond that tiny room of yours. Rourke, could you pass me a letter from the table behind you? I need this done as soon as possible."

Edward still continued to wrap around his son's quick thinking.

"Son-Captain, I know this is overwhelming, but I think what matters from the other islands are our main focus right now."

"But father, with this, not only will we give our people work, but the benefits they'll receive will make them work harder than ever! Leading them all further away from disruption on our own land. Look at this:" Sebastian drew out a piece of paper from his overcoat, "President Juárez drew up the list of benefits I managed to haggle for in our meeting. Not only will we have more than enough to compensate our workers, but that also covers the Mexican labour without draining us of what we already have."

"And what would they get in return from us, Captain?" Rourke asked, laying the letter and envelope in front of Sebastian.

"The use of the Maelstrom and free entry."

"What in the seven seas is this? Shouldn't we have control over this supposed weapon? It was your hair-brained scheme, after all-"

Suddenly, the doors burst open again, and Mayor Longstaff of Tortuga stepped in, slightly worried from the mixed looks he received.

"Doesn't anybody knock anymore? Guard, I'd like a word with you!" Edward shouted.

"Father, please! I invited Longstaff to be here after my announcement earlier. I think it would be best for you to complete the task I set for you."

Edward was visibly frustrated. Although he had lots to say, the thought of speaking to Longstaff was dreadful in his eyes. Never fond of the man's optimistic outlook, Edward grabbed the message and stormed out of the building, giving the guard by the door a sharp squint as he hurried off.

As he came through the door, he was not happy with the transaction. The guard at the door quickly stood to attention as the quartermaster's eyes met with his.

"Send a message to all the mayors of the districts that a meeting will be held tonight regarding the announcement of the Maelstrom," Edward seethed.

"Yes, sir. In the castle, sir?"

"No. Gavin port. See to it no one else knows of this. The Captain has said this is of strict confidentiality."

"Yes, sir."

The guard walked away, leaving Edward to his thoughts. Things felt too drastic. *Is this really what my son wants? First, he ignores me, and now he's making decisions without me?* While he felt inadequate, he could not let it steep in his mind forever. Perhaps it was just a minor hiccup, he thought. Edward let his curiosity consume him as he walked away from the door.

"I have to say, Captain, this looks impressive! Why may I ask have you invited me here when your father is gathering the mayors to your news?" Longstaff asked.

"Well, in simple terms, Longstaff. I've known you the longest and liked you the longest. You may have opinions and fondness for some of the other mayors, but I cannot see it."

"Oh, Captain! Perish the thought. Those men can work through the harshest of conditions."

"You were in that meeting, Longstaff. The slightest mention of their integrity caused them to panic, and they all squabbled like chickens. You are not like them in the slightest. You understand the people. You give them what they want."

"Well, I'm flattered you think so, Captain. But I'm merely the Mayor of Tortuga. It's hardly a big seat to fill."

"Yet you set the biggest example. Tortuga is one of our most historic ports, and you manage to draw more raw emotion from it than any other of the islands."

"Oh, that's not true, Captain. Why Mayor Beaumont in southern Cuba throws a lovely end-of-month celebration for the community-"

"It's not the same, though! It's pandering for the sake of pandering. If we want our nation to have spirit, we need to have that raw energy you possess in Tortuga. Tortuga was the pirate safe haven. Pirates have that connection to it. It's them and us there and I want that to change."

"What kind of change are we talking about, my boy?" Longstaff wondered.

The emotion left Sebastian's face as he pondered the possibilities of his plan, pouring himself a glass of brandy from the cabinet by the window.

"I shouldn't have to ask you this, Longstaff, but if we want the I.I.C. to prosper, you're going to have to do some snooping for me."

Longstaff looked horrified as he bumbled back, "Captain! Certainly not. We can't just purge ourselves in the middle of rebuilding. If we have more chaos in the boardrooms, we'll have more problems on the floor where our citizens are."

"That's what makes you perfect for it, Longstaff. It will be a learning curve for you too. It will help you sniff out the raw fish that need discarding. You are one of the few people that others can trust. The other mayors have no love for this nation. You do. But we need more proof that they don't. They're my father's men, not mine."

"Sebastian, please. Your father is your quartermaster. He's the glue that's keeping this together. You can't just discard people like they're rubbish. And I certainly hope you're not thinking of your father in that regard."

"I'm hoping it won't come to that. But, should I find something that leads me to believe that, I won't hesitate. For too long, we've had too many heads draw over the perfect vision that our nation was set for. One head or two wouldn't go a miss. I need loyalty in this government, Longstaff. Do I have yours?"

In the evening, at Gavin Port, Edward resided on a wooden log to wait for his counterparts. It was a cold dark night, and the tiki torches were the source of light and warmth. They surrounded the port like a ritual was taking place, and the sea waves gently brushed along the sandy shore. Soon, Edward caught sight of the trail of carriages, ten of them in total. One by one, the mayors of each Caribbean district stepped out, not uttering a word and staring at Edward. Edward led them inside a small dockside shack, longing for service, but was the perfect cover away from any late-night passers. It was cramped but just about fit them all in while the bales of hay towered over them, nearly reaching the roof. Once the door was shut, Edward commenced his talk.

"Thank you, gentlemen. I didn't think that we would come to this spot again, but here we are-"

"Is your b-b-boy in serious trouble, Teach?" Mayor Williamson presumed.

"No, far from it. In light of what was announced by the Captain recently, I felt the need to inform you that my son will indeed be the type to observe everyone like a hawk. He's going to push for a vessel to be made, one that is unbelievable in scope. This is merely a warning. I fear my son might be compromised like his predecessor."

A stunned silence engulfed the small shack as pairs of eyes looked at one another.

"You're not insinuating the same thing again, Edward?" Mayor Beaumont said, taking off his dusty white wig.

"It is only a precaution. He is not like Norton in any way. However, I feel our services and our way of life might be changed."

"In what way?" Beaumont said for everyone.

"I don't know. But if that should arise, then we must have a plan in place."

"You didn't fulfil that promise last time! Norton nearly crippled the I.I.C. And besides, how can we be so sure of our security when you can't even get your easy ticket under control?" Burst in Mayor Reginald, standing out from the huddled suits with a stiff upper lip.

"Reginald, please-"

"Don't you Reginald me! I have a high mind to even question if you're up to the task, Edward. If push comes to shove and we need someone to do the deed, we need it done on the day he's still walking, not on his death bed!"

"Don't you dare say that in front of me! Do not overstep the boundaries of what I can do, sir. Nor do I suggest you overstep your reach when dealing with my son," Edward warned. Reginald gave a deep guffaw.

"So much hostility, Edward. Don't think we all know what you want?"

"What's that supposed to mean?"

"Oh come, come now. Using your son as a threat. I thought we all agreed shaping him was a group effort. And I certainly would like to hear from the rest of us on how this plan should be seen, don't you?" Edward didn't move. His assertion had gotten the better of him for a second, breaking his facade. Now Edward was looking around to the collective heads of the committee, waiting anxiously for a reply. It took a few moments for the tension to leave until a smaller man, the youngest of the bunch, braved face and chimed up.

"Mr Teach, what can we do to deter us from making such an executive decision in the meantime?" Edward composed himself and stood straight, letting his pent-up anger for Reginald out with a simple exhale.

"Simply keep to your stations. If Sebastian finds anything out of place, he'll have your head. We can't risk our financial exploits being revealed. It's the only way we keep these patches of land afloat and our enemies at bay."

"What about Longstaff?" Reginald said.

"Longstaff is in Tortuga. And in Tortuga, he'll stay. Besides, he'll most likely get drunk like he is with my son. He's of little importance."

The room eased up as the answers came from the quartermaster. However, Reginald still didn't look satisfied.

"I have one final thought, Edward," Reginald said pointing to the quartermaster, "Shall we keep the original exodus plan intact, or should any steps be put into place should things go pear-shaped?"

With a long pause, Edward kept his pose with his hands behind his back and said: "I'll let you know should I get anything more that can aid us. That you'll hear from me, strictly."

Besides the carriage drivers keeping an eye along the road and paths that lead to the shack, they, unfortunately, had an unexpected listener slouched behind the barn. As he took his ear off the walls of the rickety barn, he placed his cowboy hat back on his head and drew his neckerchief over his face as he walked into the night.

CHAPTER 7

BUILDING BLOCKS

As the morning sun rose along the sea line, a new day was about to begin. Soon, the very start of a monumental shift in power would be felt along the waves. Sebastian was up as early, a far cry from when he started. A motivational push given to him by his own efforts of governing. He looked out over to the rising sun, squinting through orange haze to look down at the port, where it was quiet, but not for long. His imagination envisioned him walking along the path, overseeing the hard labour being induced into the Maelstrom's earliest construction. If it were to begin on schedule, Sebastian would have to come away from his imagination to once again see out to the sea. That was when he saw a tiny speck, a speck that was undoubtedly a ship. With a rush of excitement, Sebastian grabbed his great grandfather's hat and quickly made his way to the front door of the castle. The guard patrolling his bedroom had to quickly gain speed to be by his side.

"Captain! It's very early…hours, sir. Is everything…OK?" The guard rasped.

"Couldn't be better. I take it you heard the announcement?"

"Absolutely, sir. Is construction beginning soon, Captain?"

"That starts today. My orders were sent off via bird last night. Longstaff made good use of his penmanship yesterday."

Once outside, the sun was out over the horizon, the day couldn't have been better in Sebastian's eyes.

"Where is he!?" Edwards voice came from behind him, making that harmonious smile of Sebastian's drop to the floor in sheer agitation.

"Over here, Mr Teach!" The guard yelled back. Edward came storming to the front door.

"For goodness sake, if you are going to be up this early then kindly inform me before leaving the castle. You need security everywhere you go, Sebastian."

"Please, if anything it shows how courageous I am. A leader of the people should show solitude with his fellow workers," Sebastian said proudly.

"Yes, but if you remember half of these "workers" are going to be slaves and we cannot risk another Burchill incident. You'll need at least four guards wherever you go and that's final," Edward said firmly. Another moment of triumph for his father as Sebastian rolled his eyes in acceptance.

"Fine. Did you get my message to the mayors last night, father?"

"Indeed I did. They all know what is to be expected of them. They will contact you if anything arises." he lied.

Sebastian then focused his attention on the ship out at sea. Drawing his personal spyglass from his jacket pocket, he saw that it was indeed a ship carrying the cargo of workers that came from Mexico. A quick glance at the colours confirmed it was sent from Juárez.

"Excellent, the plan is coming together. Get a podium ready for me down there immediately. I want it all up and ready before that ship docks," Sebastian ordered the guard.

"Yes, sir!" And he turned away back inside the castle leaving the father and son alone.

"So we get the extra hands, what do they get?" Edward asked.

"Our extra hands."

"Excuse me?"

"A little something that me and Juárez agreed on. That ship will bring them to us and that ship will bring our slaves to them," An emphasis on the word slave made Edward turn in surprise,

"Free of charge labour and with the Mexican force coming here, our people will feel more at ease that our new ally is actually keeping to its word."

"Very good, my boy," Edward said, letting his professional demeanour slip for a brief moment of admiration, "Keep them within arms reach though. We don't want their influence to spread here."

"Ah, now the values of our life you agree with?"

"Sebastian, just because I disagree with one aspect doesn't mean that it encompasses all what we have. In the end, this is our home. My father, your great grandfather, paved the way for us. A life beyond those who ran the show. We are the shining star in this show. Don't let it get dirty," Edward argued.

"Far from it, father. Change must happen, but don't think I'll let it be compromised. Cause I won't. Even if it boils down to you and the mayors. Decisive nature will push us forward, not anchoring our standards with ridiculous moaning." At first, Edward doesn't take his sons word seriously, but as Sebastian finished, Edward's slight smile reverted back, and his original face of question returned.

"Right, must dash. Got the announcement to prepare for!" And Sebastian merrily strolled on down the stairs on his way to the dockside, leaving Edward alone while the morning sun hit his brow. It may have been the early days of a reform but Edward noticed a shift in his son's attitude. A sudden release of energy, catapulting his mood upward from the nervous wreck he was at the start of his reign. When his influence was not seen in his son's actions, it became clear that Edwards grip would soon begin to slip. It was something he could not let happen. He had the approval by the other governing bodies (however so slight a majority as it appeared the other night) to steer the direction in their favour, but it would take a lot more than simple people pleasing to achieve that control. Edward took himself off the stairs and followed down a pathway which would lead him into the marketplace. He had more people to appease.

Meanwhile, Sebastian watched in excitement as the crude wooden podium was being erected and the banners were flying high above him. A guard rushed to him saying: "Captain, your audience is on its way."

"Very good. Are the guards my father wanted here yet?" Sebastian begrudgingly asked.

"Uh...no sir, I haven't seen them. I'll fetch them right away-"

"No! No, we don't need to have them here. I think I've got everything under control today, soldier."

The two then suddenly turned to face the ship arriving at the dock yard as a sailor man yelled: "Lower the anchor!" The ship was packed to the gills with recruits from Mexico, all looking out to the Caribbean island of New Providence. The colours and tropical atmosphere was very different from what they had just left. They were stepping into unknown territory and the I.I.C's people were there to witness it. The crowd gathered with slight enthusiasm and walked up slowly to see the ship board and the men to step off. Sebastian turned to face the crowd of onlookers with only two guards patrolling along the outside of the dockside and composed himself.

"Ladies and gentlemen, imagine now seeing a ship like that but ten times bigger. Filled to the brim with weaponry that can withstand entire fleets of enemies. These new recruits from Mexico will work tirelessly along with us to show our share in that dream to control the seas from threats of the British and Spanish empires. I wish you all to welcome them with open arms and pour your hearts in thanks, without them, this dream would not be possible. We begin immediately!" Sebastian then took his pistol from his hilt and fired in the air. The crowd were very entertained by it, however the Mexican workforce wasn't at all thrilled. Some onlookers once again saw questionable moves that only questioned their perception of Sebastian even further until one voice crowd out: "They're not welcome to any of my goods!" Anxious rumbling weaved through the crowd, that one voice channelling in everyone's thoughts, even some of the hardened supporters of Sebastian couldn't escape it. The scepticism grew, and then, there was another: "Yeah, keep them at the docks where they belong!"

"And they will. They know of our boundaries, but do not hasten them away. Be thankful for extra hands, ladies and gentlemen. If the Maelstrom is to be completed on time and on schedule, then we must all treat each other with respect for the constitution," Sebastian reminded before drawing his gleaming cutlass out, holding it square to a Mexican workers throat, "But they must be reminded, that if anything should go arise over here, I will happily contact the president over your... unfortunate accident you had while working. Are we clear on that?"

The workers all nodded quickly in accordance to Sebastian's threat, knowing that should they run, they would be shot on the spot by anyone here.

"Now, avast everyone! Work begins now!"

A burst of cheer and gun powder from pistols lit up towards the sky as the work commenced. Supplies were lowered from the Mexican ship, carrying timber and metal. Ropes were tightly fastened in knots and the steady flow of work chatter soon rolled on in. Sebastian was beckoned over from the two guards, who appeared ready for a collision. Curious to this, Sebastian pressed: "Is everything alright?"

"We need to keep you close by us sir. A particular group have had their eyes on you for a while, I've noticed." One such group appeared to be battle scared, rancid with the odour of twenty wood barrelled aged rum and beards that could reach over their beer guts. All different in stature, race, body parts they had left that weren't replaced by smooth oak and clothing dyed in blue. As they walked up along the makeshift battle line between the four of them and the two guards, Sebastian could see their tattoos and piercings, covering them from head to toe. The tallest member, who wore only a black waistcoat with string replacing the buttons (One could only guess what made the buttons pop off) looked down at Sebastian and his guards with malice intent. They did not engage, only watching from the sidelines until a tall hooded figure approached the Captain.

"Good day, Captain Teach. I am Klaus Hamilton of the Pirate Historical Commission," the sudden switch from dread to a relaxed sense of security as the tall man addressed the Captain in a deep, booming, yet oddly calming voice broke the illusion of someone looking to cause commotion, "We recently opened with the little backing we got under the previous Captain and through donations on the street. I was wondering if we could have a little chat about things?"

Sebastian looked to his men in plated armour, the guard to his left with scraggly ginger beard raised his eyes showing Sebastian he was ready should foul play be present.

"What kind of things?" Sebastian asked.

"The commission wishes to discuss with you the importance of traditions and historical value the community has for the land we cherish. While new developments such as this is formidable, we cannot help that it goes against some time honoured traditions," Klaus explained.

"Well...that's actually what I want to champion in my time, Mr Hamilton. I don't want to just use my family name to gloss over everything. I'm much different than what my father believes in."

"Don't be so sure, Captain. Economics is one thing but the people handling the islands is what we usually voice our concern about. If you come with us I'm sure we can discuss things further," Klaus said presenting his entourage who still had their eyes locked on the young impressionable captain.

"Very well. Where will we be heading? You know the guards must accompany me anywhere."

"We're very aware. It is in the square of Bushwhack gardens where we congregate. Only a walk away, Captain," Klaus left first with his back turned and soon Sebastian followed in his shadow.

As the marketplace continued on through a snake like route, Edward felt uncomfortably out of place as he tried to weave his way past the busy street. Countless people scurried and barked out bids for their choose vendors while Edwards eyes looked for a way out. His destination was close, but the environment around him was too much for his level of comfort. With no guards to aid him at this time, he winced and moaned to himself as the dirtiness of the sand flew into his face and the mingling of bodies pushed and barged past. Suddenly, Edward saw refuge. A slither of a gap between to wooden buildings was a sanctuary as Edward darted across the oncoming traffic from both ways and he slumped away within the darkened space. For the briefest moment, he felt like everyone else on the street. Nobody seemed to care about his statuary position in the government body. It disgusted him, but relived him that he wasn't on the receiving end of an onslaught of pandering eyes that needed empty promises in return. As Edward took some slow breaths that weren't making him cough from sand particles, a meaty hand yanked him back further into the dark and before Edward knew it, a knife pressed against his neck and all he could hear was pig-like breathing, heavy and congested.

"What's a fancy fellow like you doing 'er then?" The shadowed man growled as he hocked and spat something lumpy from his throat.

"Just-just passing through, good sir! I'm nothing to you! I'm looking for someone," Edward whimpered. It only made the big man chuckle.

"Ho, ho, you'll find loads of people 'er, matey. I know you're worth more than a little splattering of silver, that's for sure," the knife pressed even more deeper into Edwards skin as the grip on his shoulder tightened, "I could shake all the gold out of you and no one will pay any mind!" The big man laughed and guffawed till he coughed hard, bringing up more phlegm which he swallowed back down.

"How-how, how about instead of doing that, you-you take me to the man I'm looking for and I'll make it worth your while!" Edward panicked.

"And how much will that be!?"

"A position at the castle guard!" The knife then eased off of Edwards neck and the big hand released his shoulder.

"How much will I earn a week?" The big man asked.

"Two gold, one silver. Good to cover you, I suspect?" A long pause made Edward feel even more uncomfortable as the knife was the only thing he could make out. While the size of the man resembled that of a cube, his features were hidden, but Edward could hear that low grumble as he scratched his stubble.

"So, who am I finding for ya?" He asked.

"Claude Boggs. He has a private boat hire. Takes people to the Dominican island to be processed whether you're travelling into the islands or your home if you're a slave. It's urgent for the higher ups at the castle, strictly confidential, especially if I'm hiring you in."

The big man broke into hysterics.

"Edward Teach! You always were one to wet your britches when under pressure!" Edward didn't understand as the big man continued to choke on his own laughter. "Claude Boggs, at your service, quartermaster!", None of the relief was gone from Edward from that revelation, "Do I still get that guard duty?" Boggs joked.

"What!? You're Claude Boggs? What was all that with the knife for?"

"There's certain things I do to understand clients, Mr Teach. Higher ups get no free pass with me. I didn't think you'd want a free ride out of here, considering how well things are going."

"Excuse me? You knew I wanted a boat before I told you?"

"I got tipped off by someone. Don't know if he works for you or not," The names and faces of who could've been the likely suspect ran in Edwards head, "So, what type of voyage are we thinking of, sir?" Boggs asked.

"Wait, wait. What did this person look like?"

"I don't know. He just came in and left a note. Sounded distressing. I honestly want to know what classes as "distressing" to you frilly collar types." Edward now had hand writing to determine, but his option for an escape was more important.

"Anyway, Boggs, I need a reservation. It is only to be used in a life or death situation. I don't think it'll be likely but it needs to be in place if something to go horribly wrong. Many aspects of the castle and the Captain are still treading delicately and they're on a tightrope right now."

"Sounds like the rumours are true then: You don't have confidence in your son." Boggs said bringing out a pipe from his jacket, the match flame highlighting the side of his face to show a grizzly man with wrinkles folding over one another.

"Those rumours are false, let's get that straight here, Mr Boggs," Edward said sternly.

"Very well. I'll put it as an insurance plan then. Either way, it makes you look like a great predictor should anything undesirable happen when it comes to the Captains castle. Now one final thing: Is this boat just for you? Or will there be others?" An impossible question, Edward had no telling what the future held for him and his colleagues. If Sebastian couldn't be turned to the way he held in his own mind, what would be the likely response from his friends? Scatter and hide? There was no way of knowing, but Edward had to be the decision maker. Even if his title of 'quartermaster' didn't resonate with him much like 'Captain' would.

Bushwhack gardens was a small area that boasted the best of the island's wildlife. Tranquillity was the best word to describe it but the pirate influence was at the heart of it. In the middle of thick green grass cut up into four square sections, was a clay stone memorial. Even though the chiselled writing was very crude and not something with remarkable penmanship, the names were easily read. Wrapping around its broad square base, the sculpture became thinner until the top carved out a magnificent head. The head of Blackbeard watching over those who gaze at him below in the gardens. Sebastian and the Commission members came through the rows of palm trees that surrounded the square and looked fondly at the first leader of the I.I.C.

"Still a presence. Even when you now hold the moniker of Captain," said Klaus. Sebastian smiled at that statement.

"I really wish he could've seen me. I could use him right now."

"Words and appraisal are one thing, Captain. But don't think that your great grandfather left you anything to communicate with from beyond. Look closely," Klaus pointed to the sculpture of Blackbeard, focusing on the necklaces.

"Is there something I should know about?"

"Indeed you should. We at the commission had a feeling about inscriptions and lost treasures to the islands that we began investigating. We now have the largest collection of history and lost treasure you have ever seen. Chests with Spanish gold, crockery befitting the King of England. And it all started, with that necklace."

"I know that symbol. Why haven't I heard of this collection?" Sebastian asked as he recognised the symbol of the earliest traces of the I.I.C's religion.

"There have been plenty of people in the castle, Captain. You never hear of the ones who were…disruptive. We four had such knowledge at our fingertips but when it came to the treasures of old, it was never discussed. Much like our routes it was always a matter of finding 'X' marks the spot," Klaus then brought his foot down on a small tile which looked out of place from the other slabs of stone. A small rumbling occurred before the circle floor surrounding the memorial slid down, grinding against the stone to reveal a staircase leading below the surface.

"You're a Captain of the future, Sebastian. But make sure that our past never stays buried. After you."

CHAPTER 8

FROM THE DESK OF...II

Juárez retreated to his bedroom, lit under a single flame. The night was young and his thoughts still clouded him. He felt tired but unable to be truly at ease unless he put his thoughts to paper. He moved over to his desk which had sheets of paper and a quill-tip pen. Seeing he had enough for his thoughts, Juárez grabbed a match stick and took some of the light over to his desk through a tall wax candle. As he took a seat, he clenched his hands tight, working back what he wanted to say before scribbling it down. What he read previously infuriated him. Made him on edge, obstructing his joy. An eye was cast onto him and his government, but that wouldn't cease the productivity, it would only fuel it. He dipped the quill into the ink and began to write.

"Dear Mr Lincoln.

While the words in your letter to me are indeed wisely timed, I must refrain from the referred offering of assistance on you behalf of your country. The Mexican leadership has been in talks with I.I.C for a long period and both parties agree that in terms of stability, trade and security, we are happy to come into an agreement that benefits both parties equally. You are the man in control of a country in turmoil, while I do value your cause for concern, I also see this as an invitation for hostile enemies in the southern territories of the American statehood. Mexico is now in a state of revival, the last thing it needs is another mindless war the depletes our resources and people. Our border is tight and so is the friendship between us and the I.I.C.

I hope you understand.

CHAPTER 9

CONFIRMATION

The state of Georgia was now in play. The Confederacy still bunkered to the southern territory of the state meant they would be back into a corner from the Unions efforts. A lone camp of raggedy tents sat along the coastline, awaiting orders. Its troops were holding onto their breath, trying to keep their heads and their morale high, but now the toll had hit them. The stench of defeat was seasoned with the sickening sight of blood from their ranks. The cold night only brought the feeling of death closer to them, while the sea brought the peaceful sounds of waves crashing to the soldiers ears. A much needed break from the sounds of canons and muskets. One lone general sat alone at his desk fashioned from crates. His head was held by his hands, propping himself up through the slump of battle, which had taken it's toll. As his eyes looked down onto the battle maps, his mind couldn't fathom what to do next. Yet in a matter of moments, the confederacy would have the break it's been looking for.

"Sir! Small boat! Coming up to the east sandbank, sir!" Shouted a short lieutenant. This made the general race up from his slump and race over with his pocket telescope to observe the scene. He could see the small boat, it only having one small sail with two ores mounted on either side. But waving out on its bow was a lone man, brandishing the Confederate flag. The general and two of his men, made their way down the sandbank and greeted the shrouded man with the cowboy hat.

"You bear the flag but no uniform. Where you from, son?" The general asked.

"Had to get your attention some how. But I have something for you, which you'll find, very important to your cause." The shrouded figure pulled a rolled op document from his jacket and the general unravelled it. What he read was brief but it was the signature at the bottom which made his tired eyes perk up.

"Is this official?" The general curiously asked.

"I watched him sign it."

"Sir, we can't take anything this guy says. Could be a bounty hunter," one of the younger men said.

"Oh I am, young man. I simply wish to give this back to the man I made the deal with in your ranks. He owes me handsomely," he explained.

"I'm not giving you anything until you give me the name," the threat made the bounty hunter bring his arms up to show he was at their mercy, "tell me or I won't hesitate to bury you out to sea."

"General Robert E. Lee."

CHAPTER 10

UNCERTAINTY OF THE MASSES

Inside the castle, looking out at the window, Sebastian could still hear the flow of workers pounding away with their hammers into the late night. Sebastian was very calm at his desk, working at a much slower pace than what he was two days ago. His father had noticed his sudden drop in ecstatic behaviour. Thinking back to Sebastian's childhood where his enthusiasm would run short after receiving any new toy from the marketplace. He watched closely as his son tended to his paperwork from the other side of the room, watching every breath his son took. Edward had his back rested against the wall, calculating what to say next to his son after an uncomfortable amount of time had past between them since coming back inside the castle. Unbeknownst to Edward, Sebastian would be doing the exact same thing. Plotting his every word out in his head, while his hand was writing something entirely different.

"Do the slaves have the exact food rationing requirements submitted yet, father?"

"Hmm? Oh, yes. The board handled it yesterday," Edward said, unenthusiastically. Silence droned from the two yet again until Edward couldn't handle anymore. "Look, it's late. Sebastian you don't need to hide your tiredness to appear dominate to me. It would do a world of good. You've been very busy these past few days."

"Is that you or the quartermaster in you saying that?" Sebastian mumbled.

"Well...both. Is something troubling you?"

Sebastian put the pen down and declined back in his chair, stretching his once arched back to feel more relaxed.

"I think I've gone about it all wrong. My approach to the public feels off. I spoke with some gentlemen two days ago, they believe something is missing. Something that could really sink the public's teeth into what we're doing is the right thing. But I just, can't convince them," Sebastian explained, rubbing his head while Edward raised his eyebrows, eager to step in with his injected politics.

"Like I said to you, we are a nation of old superstitious attitudes and some have sadly embedded those tired old tropes-"

"That's the thing, it's that! The majority know of this and we've been watering it down. I believe new change is needed to see that we all collectively follow the same thing," Sebastian exploded forward out from his chair. His father was perplexed by this, seeming startled by those words.

"Excuse me? In what way?" He asked.

"Think about it. The only time people were close to the Captain was during my ceremony and initiation into the realm of the gods at our church. It shouldn't be us and them, it should be all of us. That sense of being a pirate is lost after that. In order to boost that spirit, the spirit must be everywhere."

"Oh no. No, don't tell me you're thinking about that!" Edward gasped.

"There's no harm in it, father. Pirates have been guided by the unknown for decades. This will cement our boldness of the seas to greater heights-"

"But nationalising the church? This is how you think people are going to widen their arms to you? Sebastian what did I say at the beginning?"

"I know what you said, but it's not enough. I don't want to ride the gentle tide I want to grab the helm and steer through storms! To become legend, to see prosperity happen before my eyes! The Maelstrom is just the beginning. A visual aid to what will come. The I.I.C's might must not be won just in the seas, father. It has to be won on the sand we stand on. Don't you get where I'm coming from?" Sebastian said, pouring his heart and soul into every word. Passionate as it was, it did little for Edwards intentions.

"I understand where you are coming from and your ambitions are high, but it's only been a month. This doesn't have to be a sharp increase, it can be gradual. Don't crumble when you're already laying down bricks." Sebastian hadn't felt anger towards his father in a long time. He restrained himself, clenching his first to release any sort of maliciousness that had broiled inside of him. Edward too could see it. The years of watching his son meant he could sense whatever emotion was inside of him. If Edward wanted to encompass his son's decisions, it was definitely now while the rage had subsided.

"There is no need for overstepping your reach, son," Edward said placing his hand on his son's shoulder, "Consolidation from your piers is all that matters. The public are indeed your servants and they want you to do well, but I think in the long run, which you'll most certainly have, will be a wiser decision. Don't you agree?"

Sebastian brought his head up but his face was stern.

"I wish to see the mayors. One by one, individually. You're right father. The individual's who man this operation must have transparency. I've been too vague. Perhaps explaining myself would build the trust better," Sebastian agreed.

"Excellent," Edward said with a worrying smile, "See how things become clearer when you think it through with time? When would you like to see them?"

"Not now, the building has commenced and you've told me that they're up to date with the required materials for it. I should let them get into the moment and then explain everything thoroughly. Make it in a couple days time. I'll start with Longstaff as he's the closest."

"Very well, I'll get the letters ready to alert them all to an individual briefing for my late hours. In the meantime, rest Sebastian. Days, weeks, months, years ahead of you. All good things come to those who wait, son."

Edward patted Sebastian on the back and walked out of the fire pit lit office. Sebastian was now alone, hearing the roaring crackle of the wood behind him, the banging of hammers and sawing motions still was heard from outside of the castle. For a second, there was a cracking of a whip, followed by an exhale of pain. Sebastian came over to the window to observe out to the docks. The Maelstrom had only the foundation floor made and the working ribcage that would soon reach outwards to the desired shape were beginning. Sebastian saw a dark skinned man, bald and tall bring the whip down again on one worker who was on the ground in the fetal position. A loud crack once again emitted from below and the cry was louder than before. The others simply looked on with compliance and fear that they could be next, should they disobey orders. Sebastian watched for a long time like he was day dreaming out the window. But as he carried on watching, a smile of realisation spread. What looked like a stroke of genius to him, would look like malicious intent to anyone who saw it for themselves. He knew where he had to go, grabbing his coat and another coat to shroud him in the night, Sebastian kept through the corridors, avoiding his own guards. He weaved through the royal red carpet like it was a guide, even though he knew the ins and outs of the castle like the back of his hand. The back entrance, which lead to a steep staircase down the hillside was conveniently left ajar, made Sebastian dart across one final stretch of the ground floor. Particularly handy as Rourke was heard, about to leave the premises for the night. A sudden gust of wind nearly lifted Sebastian's disguise right off of him, as he carefully scurried down the stairs, avoiding to trip on his long coat which nearly wrapped under his boots. While the night was young, the islands were calm, much quieter than usual. The odd one or two patrons roamed the night but the slip towards the church was no task tonight for the young captain. Once again, Sebastian got chills from the sight of the painted gods as he rushed through the church doors, like his next actions were to be judged immensely. The old pastor, Alfred, was brushing the floors with his broom before his head snapped up, to see the doors burst open and the wind rush in.

"What in the- is everything OK there?" He asked, discarding the broom to walk over to the hooded individual.

"I'm fine. I just needed to be discreet," Sebastian said revealing himself.

"Oh! Captain! What seems to be the trouble?"

"I require some late night guidance, Alfred. I have an idea of how the people can feel more at ease with the new steps we are taking."

"Well that's splendid news, captain! What did you have in mind?" Alfred eagerly asked.

"I believe the church should be of a national level. Not a personal matter. I guess you could say..."

"Forced?," Alfred put it bluntly. Sebastian thinned his lips as the pastor's tone didn't match his. "Sit down with me, captain. I feel like this should be talked over more seriously."

Alfred walked to the stage with Sebastian and pulled out two stools for them to sit on. Alfred's creaked as he perched himself down, with Sebastian wondering if that was him or the stool creaking. Before Sebastian got to speak first, Alfred interrupted him.

"Have you prayed at all these past few months, Sebastian?" He asked.

"Well, I have put in a few hours, but with the timing of the deal with Mexico-"

"So not every day?" Alfred said sharply. This left Sebastian with a butterfly feeling in his stomach. While Alfred was a kind understanding man of faith, his patience couldn't be tested.

"You're unconvincing, do you know that? If you can't follow the faith of the sea, then how do you expect to lead with it? A plan of nationalising the faith dear boy would feel authoritarian. May I remind you that most people here are leavers of kingdoms, where faith is pressed onto their leaders like a badge of honour. They look up to someone like you because you let them worship the true gods who bless us with divine reason, not the false-idol worship of kings and queens. What brought you to this conclusion?"

"This conclusion, I feel, will not make me a figure of worship, Alfred. There's already people who don't have confidence in me. I see it, it drives me insane that they can't see what I see. But I let them have that freedom of expression. I simply feel like it will be a rallying cry. To bring back that spirit of adventure we as pirates have lost in recent times," Sebastian said.

"Does your father agree to this?"

"He doesn't."

"And what of the others?"

"I'll be speaking to each of them individually soon."

"And you thought coming to me would help better your stance towards them, weren't it?" Sebastian couldn't lie, the old man figured him out the moment he sat down.

"Yes," Sebastian sighed. Alfred pressed his hands onto his knees and did the same.

"My boy, I'm not a tactical tool for your political jargon. I am one to talk of the faith, study it tiresomely, but the truth is I am merely a gatekeeper. I hold no bearing over anything this faith delivers already."

"I can make you into one. Surely it must eat you up inside when those who walk these islands we call home divert from it? We have to be all in the same club, Alfred. Makes things easier."

"For you, that is. Sebastian, I can't force people. The signs are all there the second someone steps foot in the golden sand here. I simply cannot endorse this." Sebastian looked down in despair as the winds outside began to howl. The cold night air seeping into the church, bringing a slight shiver to him. There was still one more card to play however.

"I want you to see this then," Sebastian pulled from under his shirt a necklace that was hidden from sight. It had a long thin chain and it carried the thickest of golden covered pendants that was crudely melted down with bumps and dents. Sebastian handed it to Alfred, who upon studying the symbols, looked back up at Sebastian with shock and astonishment.

"How? Surely not. Where did you find this!?" Alfred said.

"I can't say, I'm afraid."

"Bu-but, Sebastian, you have no idea how precious this is! This confirms-"

"It confirms who wears it, the gods have blessed eternally. But it carries a curse, that I'm aware of," Sebastian said, taking the words of history from Alfred's mouth. Alfred studied it again, feeling the weight of the gold as his fingers glided across the wave-like symbol on the front.

"Blessed the blue sea, and all who sail it, only one commands, the goddess Oki," Alfred recited, "How is this possible?"

"This is between you and me, Alfred," Sebastian said, looking around first before he made eye contact with the pastor, "This cannot reach anyone else until I say so." Alfred's shocked curiosity now had an added element of fear. He listened closely but was afraid of the possible outcomes that would come of it.

"I met with four gentlemen a few days ago. They've held this in secrecy for years, decades even. This necklace was worn by Blackbeard. It resided in a place which I couldn't believe. But Alfred, what it holds is the truth behind my reasoning tonight. I assure it is real and you will see it, but you have to be quiet about it. Is what you're holding not enough to convince you?"

"Who were these men, Sebastian?"

"I can't say."

"What else can you tell me about them?"

"Nothing."

"And when can I see this place?"

"Give me your blessing and you can with immediate effect after I have spoken to the mayors."

Alfred reeled back, thinking of his original decision that was now skewered by this discovery. The faith that he had fawned over so vividly through ceremonies and gatherings now had more weight to it. The necklace confirmed his faith was far greater than imagined, but at what cost was Alfred about to see in the days to come. He who knows about the curse, would definitely preside over it and perhaps suffer from it.

"It will take more than my blessing to convince them, you know that?"

"Of course it will."

CHAPTER 11

A WORD, IF YOU PLEASE...

As Sebastian had hidden himself away that night, so did his father. Indubitably, he saw to alert the others as quick as possible, burying his head at his desk with the letters he composed. As it retained to his son's orders, it did so, but the wording was of Edwards design, convincing the mayors to speak against their captain. Four letters were sealed and ready to be delivered, as for one however, Edward felt it would be better to deliver in person.

Tortuga was again rampant with drunken shenanigans, however, Edward didn't have to succumb to passing by the locals with more rum in their system than food. Mayor Longstaff resided in his study off the coastline where Edward arrived through small boat, not needing to hide himself as a guard accompanied him. Longstaff was reading and drinking (and nearly drifting off to sleep) before he heard a knocking at his door. The book fell from his left hand and a small helping of drink splashed onto his lap as he got up to see who it was.

"Longstaff, I need to discuss something with you. It retains to the captain," Edward addressed formally to keep the guard distracted on the matter.

"At this hour? This is unusual but, please, come in," Longstaff said, wishing he was asleep in the chair he spent more time sleeping in than his bed. The guard closed the door behind Edward and waited outside.

"Things are certainly moving faster than expected, I can tell you that. Your boy works at quite the pace, Edward."

"Frighteningly so. Just an hour ago, he confirmed my suspicions. He's moving with a rule that will be quite drastic."

"For goodness sake, not this again," Longstaff said, grabbing his wooden cup, "Edward, I don't want to continue with this infighting. My loyalty is to the boy-"

"Just listen to me for a moment. Sebastian will be talking to every mayor at random points tomorrow, his thoughts have turned to nationalising the church faith," Edward explained.

"For what reason?"

"He believes it will make him stronger in his approach towards the masses. Personally, I think the idea will only backfire on us. I've already made my say on the matter and my letters will reach everyone, but you, you he'll listen to more in a more favourable manner."

"And who's fault is that?" Longstaff said.

"Excuse me?" Edward questioned.

"Edward. Don't you see what you're doing here? This is a coup, let's be frank. You're parading over the fact that your son won't see eye to eye with you and you take it upon yourself to sabotage it." "Yes because his ideas are asinine! We all nearly shot ourselves in the foot when Morgan was doing the same thing and we didn't object, now if you had any recollection of that, you'd know why my opinion matters!" Edward raised his voice.

"You've still not got over that have you?" Longstaff chuckled.

"Over what?"

"You're still not over the fact you couldn't win the captain's seat. I can see it in your face, Edward. The group chose your son because he was a fresh face. If the people saw you, they'd be taken back to when Morgan was in charge. It was only logical to choose Sebastian. The boy expresses confidence. He needs a welcome party with his ideas, not a group of pistols in his back!" Longstaff objected.

"You can't seriously suggest putting your backing into this!?"

"I'm not a superstitious man, Edward. If Sebastian believes this will increase productivity then by all means let him to do so. You don't think people here who aren't partial to a prayer on Sunday will bullshit their dedication? Besides, when have you really cared about people?"

Edward was stunned. He never thought Longstaff would be this honest when drinking. A playful drunk at best he thought, but tonight was different.

"I care enough because I don't shower them with unnecessary praise when it's not warranted. May I remind you, I've saved your arse numerous times for you to still be in this position! You would not believe the steps I've taken for all of us in the event of a catastrophe." The word 'Catastrophe' caught Longstaff's attention.

"And what are these steps?" Longstaff asked as he took another swig from his cup.

"I've arranged transportation in the event that we are… compromised."

"Oh for goodness sake Edward! Your boy, is the idealist captain that these islands need, he's not some deranged psychopath! How could you even think that?"

"Like I said, I don't shower praise when it's not warranted. Not even my own son," Edward said calmly, collecting himself, "I'm the quartermaster, my job is to prepare for anything that may harm the islands. And in turn, if the captain is compromised, then I'll need methods to try and solve these problems. I'll make it more easier for you, the majority of officials are going to side my way. You are the only one who will break that illusion unless you cooperate."

"Are you threatening me, Edward?" Longstaff gasped.

"I'm not. Just leaving you with something to think about. No one will be there to help you should something go wrong-"

Longstaff threw his cup down in anger.

"Your son is ten times the man you are! And these islands will be better off without you sticking your nose into things! I'm glad to see that your son hasn't picked up any of your traits. I will stand by what I believe is right and from what I've seen already, well, you cannot persuade me this time, quartermaster." Longstaff was now eye to eye with Edward. His puffy face was red and his expression made Edward recoil as he took in a few of the mayor's breath which stunk of rum. Edward could only feel pity for the man, he embodied the blind loyal pirate attitude, something that he was trying to get away from.

"Is that final?" Edward asked.

"It is!" Longstaff hissed.

No doubt the guard outside would have overheard everything inside the small office room, but Edward had tired his best. Even though he was staring at defeat, his methods would not go silent in the cold night.

"Very well. Let it be known it is one against eleven others. Just see how long you last in this landscape, Longstaff. You'll come to regret it."

"You'll regret the day you turned on your own family, Edward. The history books will show it all," Longstaff retorted.

"Depends on who's writing them," Edward made his way to the door but before leaving, as his head turned back around to see the podgy mayor, leaving the door slightly ajar, he gave him one final message, "I'll arrange that Sebastian visits you last. Given the circumstances, this will give you plenty of time to see if your opinion changes. Sobering up might help. Good night, Mr Longstaff." The door closed and Longstaff was the only one left in the room, unaware of what his fate will be come tomorrow. Having seen the total chaos of the previous Captain, nothing was to sure for anyone looking to make a difference. While Edwards motives were logical to a degree, he couldn't decipher whether Edward was being serious or not in his threats. The party of mayors were in his mind spineless, but callous villains? Longstaff could only look back as he slumped back into his seat, soaking in rum. *Where did it go wrong?*

CHAPTER 12

A YEAR TO FORGET

December 26th, 1863

As the night drew to a close, the only lights on on the island of New Providence were that of the castle. To the captain, the order of lights out after dusk were to encapsulate the beauty of the castle, bringing the beauty of it's leader at the forefront of the sea like a lighthouse. Towns were quiet and the citizens were inside as the guards roamed the streets on patrol. Some would take the liberty of injecting themselves through force into people's properties just to see if they were following the rules. Local children had used their size as advantage to escape and roam the streets at night, looking for food and aid under their noses. Some were successful, others were captured and made into slaves and others were simply killed on the spot. There was now an epidemic of people going missing and the guards were under 'hush' ruling when an execution on the streets took place. While the trade routes continued, fishermen and farmers were threatened with a 75% cut in their profits and it was no doubt that the proceeds, along with the stock, would go to the captain. In his mind, the castle was a beacon of hope, but to his people it was a symbol of oppression. Inside the walls, no politician would leave or enter without proper permission. The accessibility of the castle was under strict rules of protection from possible intruders or plotters to kill the captain. But inside the halls, the dialogue was that of the people outside. Two men on the inside were bickering on the lavish staircase that would usually greet visitors into a welcoming atmosphere. However, for years it was hostile rather than hospitable. One man was taller than the other while the other was younger, but their faces were becoming equally red with frustration.

"I've had it! If he doesn't express any interest in what we have to contend with, then the mutiny clause should be activated!" The taller, balding man expressed.

"No! This is us against him, we can't just make it this obvious. We have to coax this with the other members otherwise we'll just scare them off. We have plenty of time to set this in motion-"

"And risk being killed!? I'd rather take my chances with poison if I knew how to brew it!"

"Keep your voice down!" The smaller man whispered, "Your bombastic attitude is what will bring you down quicker than a pistol shot. Reginald has brewed something thankfully so we can keep that plan at the back for now."

All the while the two were arguing, a tall figure walked his way cordially around the staircase. As he was in the two men's field of view, their conversation quietened down till they eventually stopped. Visibly unnerved, Rourke Renfold spoke to the men as if he were talking to a slave, strict and sharp.

"Gentlemen. Why are you not upstairs with the captain? The yearly briefing is about to begin." "We were on our way Mr Renfold. We were simply restructuring-"

"Do it in silence. I've been ordered to make sure no one is outside the captain's quarters at this hour. I expect you to pick up the pace as it is nearly ten O'clock. And we know what happens to anyone who is not in there at that time," Rourke reminded with a glare that signalled violent intent. The two men didn't hesitate and scurried up the stairs, leaving Rourke to continue his patrol. The hall coming up to the large double doors of the captain's quarters had four guards stationed, each holding large cutlasses that reached above their height. The two men feared for their lives and imagined that shiny polished silver being covered in their own blood. They made it to the door and knocked twice, anxiously they waited until the tapping of shoes on stone floor was heard from the other side. Opening the door with a quick pull was Edward who beckoned them in. Inside the captain's quarters were the other members of the I.I.C mayoral figureheads, all standing around the captain's desk in a half circle formation. The captain's chair was empty as the man in question stood by the fireplace, his shadow darkening the room. Around the half circle, everyone was visibly nervous, it didn't help that they all wore the same tight fitting uniforms that were requested of them. Tight ring collars, stockings and heavy coats, even though the fireplace was the only source of heat, it didn't take away how uncomfortably stuffy it was for the men. Sadly, Longstaff was the one who suffered most, looking like he was going to pass out. Eventually, the captain brought his sword out and tapped the floor in a sequence before turning around. His long strides pressed down on the wooden floorboards with force as he heaved a coughing fit that was from the pit of his lungs. He mumbled to himself as he sat down in the chair stroking his beard before his pale eyes looked up to his servants. It made him sick looking at them, his frustration was seen in his eyes, they all were going to jump the second he opened his mouth, but he made them wait. It was a game this old crusty sea dog liked to play. Captain Norton played the long game by taking a sip from his wine glass, delicately wiping his mouth from the red that seeped slightly into his beard. Before his glass touched down on his desk, he threw it at his onlookers, all of them ducking and moving to the side. As they turned back around, the captain was grinding his teeth so loud that it gave off an irritating squeak.

"Once again, I have...tardiness. Once again, none of you come to me with anything new. Once again, I'm the one who sees the future, while you all bury your heads in the sand!" He yelled,

"It is unbelievable that you all continuously let men and women speak vile word of me. Punishment must be stricter like I said! The great gods of the sea are counting on me to deliver us to the way that we were intended to be. Not some hollow vessel that charges to nowhere!"

"We're sorry captain. But we can only do so much through our island districts accordingly. Some of the islands are disproportionally different to others-"

"You don't think I'm aware of that, quartermaster!?", Norton said, rushing over to stand toe-to-toe with Edward, "It still doesn't hide your lack of discipline! You all need to be harsher! At the end of the day, these people are my servants."

"What are you implying that we should do captain?" The eldest mayor asked in a snivelling manner.

"Clearly you all aren't accustomed to the very nature of your existence," this opening line made the mayors groan in frustration, as they knew what came next was burned into their heads since the day Norton took charge, "you all are part of a big picture, to which the gods see me as their crowning achievement. You want to know why I have lasted this long? Longer than anyone before me? Because they know. The gods speak to me on a level which no one can fathom. And being nice doesn't translate to these slobs that we manage! You must adhere to what I say because if not, our resistance sinks to the depths below." Longstaff who stood at the end of the left side of the half circle was driven to insanity hearing this yet again. In a brief moment, his own thoughts spoke louder to him than whatever Norton could. He finally listened to himself and shouted: "You're wrong!" Horrified expressions all turned to him as stood up straight with fists clenched.

"Captain, this is mistranslated to the highest order! As a believer myself, this is beyond the repair! Our people are suffering and day after day we are given construed responses that make no sense. We are all suffering from this bastardisation translation you've been relaying!" Again, silence swarmed everyone. Some were baffled, others were on edge, Edward was surprisingly sturdy in his presentation. Almost knowing that one of them would break from this torture. Norton walked over to Longstaff, oddly relaxed in his face which was very worrisome but Longstaff remained strong in defiance, even if the captain towered over him.

"Are you familiar with the scripture of Goddess Oki's final observation, Mr Longstaff?" Norton asked calmly.

"Yes. It details the goddess's wish for calmness in the heart of the sea," Longstaff answered confidently.

"Very good. Do you believe, right now, that we are in a sea of calmness!?" Norton's hand paint brushed the rotund mayor's face until he crashed onto the floor. "Words mean nothing until affirmative action has been brought. The gods were brutal in their rule, clamping down on those unworthy to serve, it is written in our constitution that anyone unable to contribute must suffer," Norton then brought his sword out from the hilt and pointed it at Longstaff who was left to struggle on the floor, "Perhaps we should begin with figureheads too!" Edward had enough and stood in front of his captain's sword, baffling him.

"What are you doing!?" He screamed.

"Captain, this is not how we should go about things. You're risking security by doing this. Mr Longstaff holds the front of a potential uprising. Tortuga is a dangerous place at the moment, the surge of scum that have originated from its port is troublesome, but I can assure you, Longstaff here has done good to calm its storm. We must also remember that it is not just simple sword play that can bring you down," Edward said. Norton brought the sword up the quartermaster's neck, the tip of the cutlass just resting on Edwards Adams apple.

"Is that an insinuation of an uprising. Mr Teach?" Edward could feel the sweat run down from inside his shirt as his life was on the line. The two men who had arrived last to the briefing both looked at each other, thinking that they should speak for the quartermaster, but held off for a moment.

"Just because you bare your grandfather's last name Edward, doesn't make you the leader for all eternity. I won fair and square and it'll take more than leeches to suck the life out of me-"

"You have to watch what you say, captain! The constitution states that we all bear the right to have you removed should a collective mutiny be approved," The shorter man blared out, scaring his tall companion into retreat. Unsurprised by this, Norton slowly turned to look at him.

"Confident, aren't we? But, no, you are right," Norton's calm yet creepy demeanour returned, "Absolutely, the constitution should be upheld should mutiny be, in your minds, the right way forward. All I say is-" Norton's sword then swung across the gap and the cutlass impaled through the eldest mayor's chest. Recoiling in fear from the captain's sudden burst of agility, the blood soon trickled down the mayor's creased white shirt, any sense of even trying to speak out to the captain was immediately silenced. The man then dropped to the floor as Norton drew his sword out and flicked the blood onto the corpse as he mumbled a verse of worship to himself all the while the tallest member of the group watched the man he talked with moments ago fall limp, holding back his shock.

Once the blade was cleaned, Edward cleared his throat to bravely continue on from where he left off.

"Very well, captain, you've made your case convincing enough. Is there anything else you'd like to leave us with?"

"There is," he said, hobbling back to the chair as he gasped for air, "Everyone's benefits of the castle is cut off until I say so." A collective mutter was just about audible for Norton to bring his sword down onto the desk as he fell back into his chair, "Anybody like to argue against that?" No one dared to try as they looked back at the corpse of one of their fellow bodies as a reminder. A wave of his hand and the captain's men left the office one by one until it was Teach and Longstaff last in line.

"You two can stay. Let's continue our little chat, shall we?" The two men stood in front of the desk, Longstaff looking at the blade, picturing it through him had it not been for Edward.

"So, Edward, what do you suggest then?" Norton asked, playing nice.

"Captain, dispensing of Mr Sanders like that will have an untold affect on the south side of Barbados. Need I remind you that is one of his closest aids is the reason we still have trade in the first place. This is unprofessional-"

"Disrespect like that must be shown not only to our people but to our enemies. You've seen what's happening up north, we must not let outsiders of any kind into the fold. Trading or not trading, we must stand firm against those who are not bred by the sea," Norton said. Confused by his superior's rejection of simple trade, Edward was not only frightened but rubbed his hand on his face in frustration. The captain had been smearing the gospel of the islands so much that he was now blind to anything logical. Longstaff only continued to lick his lips, waiting for the right time to speak again but was fearful that he might be the receiving end of a cutlass again, nevertheless he tried. "You just don't get it, do you-"

"It is you who doesn't get it, Mr Longstaff! If we're going about this in Bible terms, then I am that of Jesus! The secret that the goddess Oki laid out for us must not be ignored!"

"This involuntary slander of your workmen will be felt throughout! You can't just dispose of people left and right like some dictator!" The two went on and on until Edward could take it anymore. He watched and observed how twitchy Norton was near his sword, he could pounce over his table with the agility of a deranged cat at any moment. Now was the right time to not only be the peace keeper, but a reasonable visionary.

"Gentlemen! This debate over relics of gods is abhorrent! This will in no way direct us! Captain, if you want your directive towards your so-called "blessing" to be a reality, I suggest new leadership rules are needed."

Curious, Norton leaned in and said: "And what might that entail, quartermaster?"

Longstaff was also curious, but also anxious in thinking Edward was about to make a compromise with this mad man.

"I believe the status and privilege of a mayor's duty should be reduced. Giving you more control and say over the islands."

"Are you out of your mind!," Longstaff exclaimed, "There would be a mass exodus if that happened!" Norton was intrigued by this notion. In his mind, he could see the reigns of his fate easier to handle from this expansion of power. It gave him a slight smile underneath his unkempt white beard, which had blood splattered into it.

"And that is how you deal with pests. Very good, Mr Teach. But don't think this wins you a sympathy vote from me for that little stunt earlier with the whale over there. Make it be known that what you've just given me, is the last time a quartermaster's opinion matters. From now on you will serve me like a maid, understand?"

"I understand and thank you captain," As Edward expressed his gratitude, fake and forced as it was, it was enough to make Longstaff eject himself from the captain's quarters. Too angry for words but enough to be heard through the slam of the door behind him. Norton now had a full smile underneath his beard as he watched Edward walk to the corner of the room, observing the routes and names of a map hung above. Edward did this only to take his sight away from the geriatric sitting on the throne, whose beady eyes he could feel in the back of his head. Norton drew out a book from his left side drawer, it was leather bound and slightly dented, almost like teeth marks.

Norton caressed it in his hands as mumbled something again, much louder than before.

"What do you think makes a man do the things I do, Mr Teach?" He asked.

"I don't know, captain," Edward said, still refusing to turn around.

"I do it, out of the goodness of my heart. This book taught me early on that the balance of the food chain between god and sailor are always linked together. But, one requires more nurturing than the other. The funniest thing, it doesn't say which one it is. Why do you think that is?" Norton asked again.

"I don't know, captain," Edward said again, cautiously.

"Because, soon the sailors know who the gods are. It is a natural occurrence, like a pack, sailors know it and then that person, whoever he is, takes the mantle. But he is not boastful, nor is he with pride, why do you think that is?"

Edward this time turned around, the text would only bring forth a conclusion about his superior but the dread was like a weight on his shoulders. Edward looked at Norton's eyes and once again uttered: "I don't know, captain."

"Because being discreet is much easier than being boastful. Now do you see why I keep you here? There is no threat once the sailors know what they're doing pleases their god. I keep you protected as much as myself. I simply work towards us better understanding what we are meant to be from these scripts and I believe it is the best cause of action. You're not a caged rat, Mr Teach. You're a pampered feline. And I'm your owner. And sure enough, you'll come to bask in my glory once we understand the goddess Oki's word that will set us free from these walls."

Edward wanted so desperately to leave, but in order to do so, he had to tend to the captain's ego. Simply nodding his head and smiling at the notion that Norton was in anyway tending to Edward like a common boat cat was insulting.

"Indeed it will, sir. Is that all for tonight?" Edward asked.

"Yes, yes, that will be all for now," Edward spun on the heels of his feet towards the door as quickly as possible, "Oh! Mr Teach, do send my compliments to Reginald on this lovely wine he brewed. I believe he ran off in a haste and I never got to send my thanks."

"Certainly, captain. Enjoy the wine."

CHAPTER 13

A RUDE AWAKENING

Through a national town crier (the first of it's kind), the bell rang loud and so did a big burly man with his hair in dreads. In full view of the masses, the town crier bellowed a message of importance: "AVASTE! HERE YE! THE DECORATED CHURCH OF THE I.I.C WILL HAVE AN OPEN INVITATION TO FOLLOWERS OF THE FAITH THIS AFTERNOON! CAPTAIN TEACH BRINGS ABOUT A NEW DAWN IN THE EYES OF THOSE WHO FOLLOW THE FLAG!" With their ears now rung with the news from the captain's desk, people going about their day felt a sense of transparency that came from castle. It felt refreshing, new and reinvigorating to those who cast doubts upon the new captain. The steady increase of moral, boosted by the construction of the Maelstrom, was brought to make anyone wonder what the captain would do next. Sebastian felt the gods were with him at this point. The scepticism and worry of how the young prodigy would be once he stepped into office was questionable but Sebastian proved that he was willing to do battle inside his own government, much to the continuous dismay of his father. Around the islands, the message rang clear on the hour. Every island would soon be in the know, from Cuba to Barbados. Which now meant that the actions taken by it's mayors was now under observation at every turn. The sense of secrecy from the castle was beginning to shrivel away and people were anxious to see how the church would conduct a formal message seminar. Pastor Albert stood alone again in his church, where inside he heard nothing but the beating of his heart. It was comforting to know that he was inside his place of worship which he worked tirelessly on, but now that was about to change. The first batch of people about to venture in would be the first of many that would soon spread the word of the captain. Albert continuously combed his hair with a flat palm and adjusted his robes. In his head, he finally believed that what he had seen for many years was about to be realised. What the captain had shown him, pushed his excitement to the seas and back again. Eventually, they came. Sat perfectly in their seats with friends and family and others gathered around and outside the door, a full house. This was it, now the nerves had sunk in. Crossing his fingers and licking his lips, Pastor Albert spoke.

"Welcome, brothers and sisters. I take it you're all curious for this unexpected gathering. Especially after having your ears rang by the newest addition to our lives," A small chuckle came from the crowd, "Now, I won't keep you any further. It is my solemn duty as the head of this gorgeous house we call our temple of worship to instruct and teach all who practice the faith of the sea gods. In light of recent events, personally given to me by the captain himself, it is my understanding that the church requires change. Change that is…imperative to the world." From inside the pastor's dropping robes, Albert revealed the golden talisman that was shown to him by Sebastian. Raising it up, the crowd awed in its ancient yet familiar moulding with the stone in the centre gleaming out to the furthest onlooker.

"This is the sacred necklace given to our founder, Blackbeard, through it he had great insights and constructed this nation we live and breath on. The goddess of Oki resides inside this stone. Whimsical fortune or untold devastation is cast onto those who choose to lead. Blackbeard knew of its power and kept it hidden for decades. Only now has it resurfaced and make no mistake about it I believe our nation was hit from this devastation when we strayed further than we had ever been from the previous man in charge. Our sanctimonious rights of practice were forgotten in order to appease a devil in disguise. I speak to you all now, we must abide by our rules the gods have set for our course. And in doing so the captain has asked me of this for you…"

Sebastian was alone in his captain's quarters, circling his desk. He kept his hands behind his back as he paced, anxious for the arrival of someone. He turned his attention outside to see out to the docks and the sea, progression on the Maelstrom's skeleton frame was starting to take shape. The workers had been on a continuous loop of non-stop work since the inception. A knock at the door was heard and Sebastian allowed the person in. It was a guard, who's perfectly groomed beard covered his mouth.

"Captain, your vessel is ready."

"Thank you, await for my arrival outside, if you will." The guard closed the door behind him gently and Sebastian was once again all by himself. The decision to meet with the mayors was one that would, to him, strengthen ties from previous meetings. Sebastian, thought confident as he was, was still somewhat anxious. Plotting out every sentence in his head to say to every figurehead of the islands. It would be direct and short, however, the time now came to figuring out his tone. Sebastian rehearsed his lines, each varying in pitch, volume and tone. He seemed to be happy with what he wrote, yet he couldn't match it to how it went in his head. Was he being too much of a perfectionist? He had done this before making any of his addresses and it felt natural, but this was on a more personal level. Perhaps the hundreds of eyes didn't rock him the way a one-on-one interaction would. The attire was brash, mixing a strong red over coat with black leather hiding his white frilled shirt. It wasn't loose, the right fit for a captain, but something was missing. It was only then did he look over to the fireplace to see the hanging sword of Blackbeard. It didn't feel appropriate to carry it around, Sebastian hadn't touched the sword since his swearing in at Tortuga, but for some reason he felt it would be safe to bring it along. Never tempted to use it, but having it by his side felt better than actually using it. He was the captain and safety was top priority, even if there didn't seem to be anything around him or his nation that felt like a threat. Infatuated by it's pristine quality, made Sebastian feel more like royalty holding it. It seemed to impressive to be used for a pirate but now the times had changed. Knowing this, Sebastian brought the sword off from its mantle and hilted it. He made his way to the door and grabbed the necklace of Oki from his desk on the way out. Down the robust staircase to the main door, Rourke waited patiently to accompany the captain.

"Where's father?" Sebastian said confused.

"Forgive me, captain. Your father is unavailable for the time being. He was said to be at Antigua, he left a message saying he departed in the early hours of the night," Rourke said.

Troubled by this, as Antigua was one of the far off islands that Sebastian would be sailing to, Sebastian wondered where or what his father was up to. As he walked outside into the clear day, it would be nestled in the back of his head that his father was up to fowl play. Sebastian hoped that it wouldn't come to that.

Amongst the beach side huts, Longstaff resided to a bench overlooking the gorgeous sparkle of the sea. It was his break time and breaks mean rum. A small glass complimented his open shirt in which he basked in the hot rays of sunshine, helping him tan further into a mahogany colour. It was possibly the only bit of peace (in terms of noise) he would get in a day. A precious ten or so minutes to hear nothing but the sea brush against the sandy shores of Tortuga. While his office wasn't much to go by in terms of looks, this was definitely the bargaining chip that sold him on the office (possibly even the bar that was underneath him at all times as well). As he closed his eyes, Longstaff couldn't help but think back to last night with Edward. His persistent good nature always clashed with Edward's cynical sensibility that he often took the side of anyone going against him. It was no wonder he took Sebastian side in the debate. But now that he wasn't intoxicated like he was, he wondered if what Edward said was partially true. Does the over ambiguous nature of the current captain-ship need scaling down in order to reach the best outcome. Again, he judged his associates and thought of them as not the best candidates for the job but he had hope. Longstaff now knew he would be last in the pecking order and then it dawned on him as to why he was. A sense of realisation and self improvement washed over him as the rum trickled down, it's because he went with the grain. Last night he felt like he stood on his own two feet, able to take on a difference in opinion, to a higher ranking official no less. *Perhaps Sebastian needs to know more than he should and I should be the one to fill him with confidence,* he thought. In the corner of his ear, Longstaff heard commotion coming from behind the tavern. First it sounded like just a handful of people, then it was a small crowd. Slightly annoyed that he had to leave his spot, Longstaff winced as he got up from the bench to see what all the fuss was about. He straightened his clothes out as much as possible as he walked up the sand bank to see the crowd surrounding the taverns door. Taken back by the large numbers, Longstaff addressed them to ease the pressure off of the owner of the tavern who seemed to be unaware of his whereabouts.

"People! People! What seems to be the problem here?"

"Sir Longstaff, haven't you heard?" A young woman carrying her newborn said, "The church has found something amazing! Truly amazing!"

"It's a sign Mr Mayor. The goddess Oki has blessed the captain and us too!" Another local yelled. The name Oki made Longstaff tremble a little. He didn't know whether to recoil in terror or bravely face the so-called miracle they kept referring to. He knew he had to take action, to show himself and his peers he was capable of affirmative action and not just some low hanging fruit on the tree of elected bodies. But for a split second, he thought like he was hearing Norton again. Longstaff sucked in his gut and said: "Take me to the church."

Once there, it seemed like jubilations had begun early hours of the morning rather than being birthed from a seminar. The feeling in the air was euphoric, so many smiling faces, Longstaff hurried inside the church to see with Pastor Albert, who inside was still talking to a small group of three people. He was delighted to see the red faced mayor and opened his arms hoping for an embracing hug.

"Mr Longstaff! How good it is to see you on this glorious day!"

"What is happening here, pastor? The men and women here are happy as can be and there is no drink in sight."

"My boy, you've obviously heard about what transpired here just now. Isn't it wonderful, I've never seen their spirits at this level," Albert rejoiced.

"That's most likely because they haven't touched the spirits yet. What is this message from the captain they retain to?" Longstaff asked.

"Captain Teach has found it. This to be precise," Albert once again showed the talisman necklace, "I'm unsure where he found it, but in my eyes it's the treasure every pirate across these lands want the most: purpose."

"Purpose? Pastor, you know where this "purpose" got all of us into last time. Our previous captain-"

"I know what he did. But he never had anything to justify it and it drove him insane. Sebastian is of sound mind and resourceful. We have something to go on now."

"How do you know it's real?" Longstaff said, taking a moment to hold the necklace in his hand. Albert checked around him to see if he was being listened to and brought Longstaff closer to the wooden stage and began to whisper.

"It will soon be revealed, but the captain came to me the other night to explain things."

"Does anyone else know about this?"

"Not yet, but pretty soon the word will spread across the islands and he will look to give a big rallying cry for it. As we speak, he's meeting with the other mayors of the islands to see if their are...suspicious activities," Albert said.

"Activities?" Longstaff said as if he knew nothing about it.

"The captain is worried that our best interests are being suppressed by the governing bodies of the islands. He's looking for disturbances and wants to deal with them himself."

"Then he'll be coming to see me," Longstaff continued the illusion, "Why didn't he start here?" "Because it will give his movement more momentum. If word spreads now in the heartland, the rest of the islands will follow suit. Even if he has squabbles with the mayors the people will listen to him more. He will shift his power like no other, but it will be positive. I think you're the only one people believe are genuine, so I think you'll be alright."

"But he needs these people. What is there to purge? What secrets could there be that I don't know about?" Longstaff asked. Albert again checked around him and leaned in close.

"Something's been hidden. Hidden for a long time. If it is true and I see it before my eyes, which I will, then I know the mayors have something to do with this. From what Sebastian says, its something that has held us in jeopardy for years, decades even."

"When will you see this place?"

"The second he has returned. But for now, we must spread the word and be merry!" Albert chuckled, he raised his arms again and brushed Longstaff as he saw more people entering the church, keeping the message afloat. Longstaff stood still in wonder as to where this would lead him. Certain now that his safety was in safe hands, there seemed to be no obligation to turn against the captain like Edward suggested. That night will hold significance in the mayors mind, for it may have confirmed Pastor Albert's and Sebastian suspicions about Edward and the others. While Edward didn't explicitly say it, Longstaff had a good indication that interference was at hand. He wasn't angry in the slightest, in fact, he was quite relaxed, joyous even. It all came to him when he remembered that his glass of rum was still sitting at his favourite spot. *I think the break can be a bit longer today*, he thought.

CHAPTER 14

SHOCK TO THE SYSTEM

Sebastian stormed down the pathway as the onlookers looked in awe of their captain walking down their street. He had little time for pleasantries, the first meeting seemed to have him frustrated. Sebastian boarded his ship and the anchors began to raise up, onto the next island. It was only one out of several other neighbouring islands but Sebastian felt the slog of the tiresome mission he set out. From the time he stepped foot into his first meeting with the mayors, he noticed patterns on all of them. The way how they communicated, their demeanour, their conductivity, it all seemed staged. Yet there wasn't anything to pin down with hard concrete evidence, which he couldn't afford to stomach a blow of misjudgement at this time. Time was of the essence and sooner or later, Sebastian would soon have those who stood by his side. He thought to Longstaff, an easy choice but at this moment he couldn't be sure. The thoughts of a convincing character to steer away from the other mayors, who bared no personality whatsoever, could be a front of distraction for him. Then he thought to his father, even before his subsequent journey off from the homeland of Cuba seemed strange but Rourke put him at ease with words of encouragement. Sebastian knew his father conducted business with most of his labouring chores such as message relaying or meeting commitments, but he still had in his head that Sebastian's message wasn't the only one his father could send. He did not want to think this. The line between parent and quartermaster was blurred slightly when it came to the Teach family, but it couldn't be passed off. Rourke was the last one to hop on board after inspecting the ship before disembarking on the voyage, he joined Sebastian at the helm as they both looked out to the sea.

"Interesting, won't you say?" Rourke said.

"How so?"

"Well, Williamson didn't seem like he was compromised. He answered every question truly and trust me I watched his face like a hawk, captain."

"The only thing compromised with him is his speech impediment. Why do I get the feeling this is rehearsal for them. Anything I say and do could be under strong opposition, Renfold," feared. "Don't worry, captain. Your a competent man, there are simple ways to deal with troublemakers, if we find them that is." Sebastian had in his mind a simpler version of disciplinary action, however it would be disastrous if he even attempted it. The thought blew away with the wind as the sails were dropped down from the masts and the workers on board scrambled to their positions, reeling in rope with force and jostling supplies while Rourke steered the ship port side. As the ship, creaked in direction to sail around the islands perimeter, Sebastian caught eye of something from the west. It was like a dot to his eyes but he was curious if the shape. He took his spyglass out to use and what he saw made the captain fill with anger, anger he had festering in him since the first meeting with the mayors. Suppressed through his father's remarks and careful wording, Sebastian brought the spyglass down as his jaw was clenched tight, feeling like he could grind his teeth down to tiny stumps with the pressure.

"Renfold, take us west. Now." Sebastian said sternly.

"Captain? That takes us towards Jamaica," Rourke said.

"I know what's over there, take us there now!" With the harsh order, Rourke shouted out to the crew to brace for an new destination. The sails soon turned and the movement of the boat made everything and everybody steer sideways. Regaining balance, Sebastian then ordered: "Rourke, have the men bring down the captain's flag. I want this to be a surprise."

Robertson looked to himself in the mirror as he adjusted his frilled lace tie. A small smirk made the wrinkles in his face lift up which beat the typical expression of stern tiredness that would plague his face for years. Robertson walked slowly around his office, the third biggest in terms when it came to the captain's quarters and playful flicked his hands across ornaments in a brush like manor. Just then, the door knocked.

"Enter!" He grumbled. In stepped a oldish man, furry stuck out sideburns in a shade of grey which matches his stockings. His face was like Robertson, only more friendlier and frailer. The two reached out and shook each others hands in greeting.

"Mr Grant, pleasure to have you," Robertson said in droll voice.

"My pleasure to be here. I never saw an opportunity I couldn't meet in person" The two chuckled at the statement, "The crown is extremely excited that we could cross through at such short notice, you understand the perplexity of this deal?"

"I do indeed, by which time, when the agreements are written in writing, I and other won't have to worry about it at all for the remainder of our lives. Please, have a seat," Robertson gestured to the seating arrangements by the large window to the west of the office. Robertson's office was more simplistic; the floor was wooden, the wall was dry and they held nothing of value for the eyes to gaze upon.

"So, your government has been held up for quite some time" Grant said.

"It has, I apologise for the rather late update but the previous captain made things extremely difficult to process things," Robertson explained.

"And the new one?"

"Our quartermaster has been comfortable in engaging talks with us to subdue any doubt, but the sentiment of the group hasn't been moved by his efforts. Which is why I set this plan into action. The I.I.C, it's floundering, let's be honest."

"Well, that is why the king believes it will be a great interest to have hold of the islands again, with the delegates from you and others, we can safely assure that reasonable action can be taken. You're comfortable with the prospect of being labelled a prisoner under the captain once you return to the kingdom? It will be more convincing," Grant asked.

"Absolutely. I have no time in my life now to be worried about labels. I simply want what's best for my family and I don't want to see them carting around like workers when luxury is just a sail away," Robertson answered.

"Very well. Can you vouch for the others?"

"They'll come around. Once this venture proves successful and unhindered, they'll see the light." Grant was pleased by this and so was Robertson.

"Right. If we do this now, you can guarantee a swift intervention. The royal navy will see to it the liberation of the Caribbean is of utmost importance. Resources and labour will come under rule and slaves will be granted a right to citizenship. You and the other mayors will be taken in as prisoners of war and any assets seized will be returned to you in compensation through acts of retaliation towards your ruler. Correct?" Grant recited.

"Indefinitely," Robertson said. Grant brought the rolled up scripture from his jacket pocket, Robertson was impressed when he read the scripture, knowing that Grant committed time to memorise everything from it. Grants signature sat in the bottom left hand corner and a open space to the right for Robertson. He got up to grab the pen from his desk when all of a sudden, the doors burst open. Sebastian and Renfold stood inside the office, casting seething eyes at Robertson as he was frozen with his arm outstretched for the pen.

"Captain Teach! I-I thought I was to be second to last on your journey around the islands?" Robertson staggered.

"We decided on a detour," Sebastian said, sinisterly walking slowly towards him, "Care to explain this?"

"I-I can. Captain, this is-"

"I don't need an introduction, I need an explanation. An explanation as to why a British colonial is here, sitting in the office of an official without my understanding."

The dreaded silence could've suffocated the elderly mayor, as for Grant, he thought best to sit still in his chair, never turning to face the commotion.

"This was never my intention-"

"It was before I arrived! Who else is in league with you?" Robertson slowly backed away from the desk, holding his hands up in defence as the two walked around the desk.

"Please, Captain Teach, I can explain without this hostility."

"Oh, you haven't felt hostility until now. Rourke, grab that man in the chair," Sebastian ordered. The big burly man in the lavish suit wasted no time in gripping Grant by his arms as he cooperated by getting up from the chair, he now faced the interrogation, unsure what would happen next.

"I want names, now!" Sebastian yelled. All Robertson could do was swivel in place as the young captain prowled around him like a game of cat and mouse. Robertson backed up close to his chair, steadying himself on the arm of it as his heel hit the leg. He had no words to muster, only gilt ridden pleading was all he could produce.

"Please, captain. Just give me a chance, just give me a chance to explain!"

"You know what? I don't need to hear it. The scene here pretty much paints a picture. A very telling picture. Are you sorry for what you've done?" Sebastian asked.

"I am captain, I am very sorry." Sebastian's eyes now looked to Grant, being held in an arm hold by his assistant Rourke. Sebastian asked him: "Does this go all the way to Blighty?" Grant looked scared, his mouth was slightly open and his eyes were fixated onto Sebastian who never moved nor blinked. The young man's eyes had become demonic, fuelling the fear in Grant as to what would come next if he spoke. He reluctantly answered with a mouse-like "Yes." Sebastian saw the fear and for a brief moment, he liked it. Revelled in it, even. His suspicions had now been confirmed and all he could do now was relax.

"Mr Robertson, answer me this, before you die," Robertson grasped both arms of the chair now behind his arched back, "You all had your doubts, your motives, your tactics. There's one thing I'd like to ask you: Did my father oversee this?" Robertson could no longer hide how much he was sweating, his collar felt so tight around his neck.

"He didn't oversee me," he said. Sebastian shook his head in disappointment but it wasn't for long, the punishment was quick. Sebastian glided his silver blade up from the hilt, swiping the mayors neck in a perfect diagonal cut. The back of the chair was tall enough to hide the mayors gasps and gargling throat from both Grant and Rourke as the blood flew into the dull coloured walls and lost in the grooves of the wooden floor. Mayor Robertson was dead. In a flash, his body fell limp in the chair and his eyes rolled back as the blood continued to drench his clothes. Sebastian brought back that sinister stare as he watched the life drain right out from him but his shock was still visible. Rourke could see the captain's hand stocking out from the side of the chair, still holding the beautiful blade but it was trembling. Sebastian knew what he had done would dramatically turn everything upside down. His mind worked fast as he finally averted his gaze from the dead man and onto the sword which he brought back inside the hilt. The blood was sprinkled on his dark coat, the colours hiding the stains, except for his face where splatters of blood went up his right cheek and above his eyebrow. Sebastian calmly collected himself, brushing himself down and rummaging the corpse in front of him for it's handkerchief.

"Renfold, bring him here."

Rourke moved the elderly man like a piece of wood around the desk to face the captain, his grip tightened to where Grant could feel strain on his shoulders.

"Now you listen to me. Take a good hard look at that and let it fester in your head. These islands are not for sale and neither are we. If I see you or anyone else, you will be swiftly dealt with. The British have no business to come to these lands, understood?" Sebastian explained. Grant simply shook his head. "You will be escorted off the islands, but your crew and ship will be commandeered by us. Think of it as a tax, seeing as how you have technical crossed the treaty line, illegally."

"What are you going to do with my crew?" Grant wondered.

"They'll be put to good use. Rourke, get him out of here." Rourke yanked the defenceless Grant from the office leaving Sebastian on his own with the horrid stench of blood, now beginning to grown stronger as a puddle built up underneath the chair. The deceased Robertson stared up to the ceiling and Sebastian was left to face with what to do next. An announcement would have to be made, preparation for the replacement must be a quick and that choice of successor wouldn't be divisive. However, it made Sebastian's job that little bit easier. Confirming that corruption which he knew was nestling behind his very eyes. It was infuriating, being used like a tool for their own needs. And then came the thoughts of his father. He didn't oversee me, Robertson's final words sounded off again in his mind. If this was one thing his father didn't know about, what were the things he did know about? The undisclosed trips, the obvious defence for the mayors and the one overly cautious about everything. More had to be done but the anger soon left Sebastian as he brought out the sword again, piercing it right into Robertson's chest and through the wooden chair. As the blood gushed out, Sebastian's head was clear and the message spoke to him: Vengeance will not always be this swift.

CHAPTER 15

A NEW WAVE OF LEADERSHIP

"A witch hunt! That's what it will turn into Edward, one big witch hunt!", Yelled mayor Reginald, "I warned you, Edward, you have no choice now but to scramble them all before things go south."

"And how do you propose to that? I may have the direct line to the boats off of these islands, but we can't jump ship at the same time," Edward tried to explain.

"Easy for you to say, you couldn't organise a knees-up in a brewery! We can't just stand around and be interrogated all the time. The second one of us slips, we all slip and fall overboard," Reginald placed both his hand on his head as he sat at his desk. Both he and Edward were in a small office space that resembled that of a broken down barn. The floor had missing wooden panels, the ceiling was covered with tarp and nothing hung on the walls. It was an image of decadence, very odd for an official, Reginald's status as the mayor of Puerto Rico would assume he would have higher status. Edward stood opposite of the desk, lamenting about his steps taken to resolve the issue of discourse within his circle off officials. Reginald may have given the most criticism out of everyone but this time it was warranted.

"Look, nothing is going to happen. So far, all I've heard is complaining that I didn't do anything. I have managed to secure us an escape should something go wrong. But, if we keep up the charade that nothing is happening then we can sway Sebastian even further to an easy retirement."

"Edward, stop. We tried that and it's clearly not working," Reginald sighed in defeat, "These troglodytes are backwards people. They believe in fairy tales of the seas. You grandfather knew of this, but the luxury got to him first. We can't allow that to happen to us."

"I know, it's just…" Edward turned away as the thought nearly creped out of his voice. It tormented him and now it was suddenly starting to etch closer and closer to reality. Reginald recognised this and helped Edward finish: "You can't bare to leave your only son?" Edward held back the emotion, clenching his jaw and sealing his eyes as he knew Reginald was right.

"That and my sisters," Edward finished.

"He'll still have family beside him, Edward."

"But he won't ever forgive me. In his mind, I'll be dead to him."

"Which do you prefer though?" Reginald asked.

"Excuse me?"

"Edward, your son is captain. Ergo, he has the power to bring us all to his form of justice. There's two types of dead in your case-"

"My son would never!" Edward shouted, bringing his hands down on Reginald's desk, shaking him up from his slouched position. Reginald could see Edward seething, the quartermaster's fingers clenched harder into fists as the stayed pressed into the desk. Edward just brought his head down as the two locked eyes for a moment.

"If we can't get the reward we need, then being compensated from others willing to take us in will be substantial. We could start again, Edward. This has been in the works for a long time," Reginald stretched over to place his hand on Edwards shoulder, "We're obsolete here, Edward. A fresh start away from disaster is what we need."

Clutching at straws as to what to choose, Edward could only come to terms that Reginald indeed have the best solution. However, rounding up the mayors in rapid succession would be imperative between life or prosecution.

"Do we all still have something from the trove?" Edward asked.

"I kept mine, wherever we sail, will pay more than just a shiny penny for it," Reginald brought out a small bag from his desk drawer and placed it onto the table in front of him. Edward only needed to hear the jingling of its contents to know what was inside.

"You're certain that's all we found?"

"I'm certain, Edward. Everyone else took their fair share. Pillaging from Norton was easy once we poisoned him. He took a fair amount of time to keel over, but when it came to his little stash, he barely put up a fight." Edward grasped the bag, feeling the contents from the brown leather. It was doubloons, no question about it. Whether they were silver or gold, Edward knew they'd be financially stable in the escape. He made his choice, weighing his son to his memory like an anchor to the shore line and asked: "So, where do we start?"

The night fell over the islands but the fires burnt a warm orange glow around the Bushwhack park. Klaus, standing with his back to one of the palm trees was a clever recluse. His tall stature and dark robes made him blend in with any environment. He was all alone, waiting without his pack like a watchdog. He saw the odd couple retreating to their home after the evening light sank away beyond the horizon. Klaus then returned his attention to the tree on the opposite side of the square, a robed figure now stood by it's tree. It was one of the congregation, shorter than Klaus, stockier too. The two met in the middle where the path led to the bust of Blackbeard, both trading glances over their surroundings before they spoke.

"How goes the spread of gospel, Griswold?" Klaus asked.

"Exceedingly well. The Pastor, Sebastian told us about has been swayed in our favour. Pretty soon the islands will be in unison," Griswold told in a raspy voice.

"And the captain?"

"He departed the early hours of this morning. Travelled to Haiti first, not sure when he'll be back," Griswold said, being the eyes of the congregation.

"He'll weed them out, I know he will. That spirit in him is something this nation needs. And I know those men too well, he'll have to break them if they don't cooperate," Klaus lamented. Griswold noticed the hint of disdain in Klaus's voice as his eyes looked to the bust if Blackbeard.

"When do you think they're going to do?" Griswold asked.

"What they always do. They're like rats, when the going gets tough, the rats swim as far as they can, hoping to find better scraps. It's them I don't care about, it's the captain's father that troubles me. I want to know everything he as done since we last met," Klaus said, the hatred building behind his every word.

"What if he's not behind it? What impact will that have on the captain? It could be dangerous, Klaus."

"These islands don't know the meaning of the word dangerous. To them, it will be change. And it can't come soon enough."

CHAPTER 16

THE WITCH HUNT

Sebastian stood near the helm of the ship, still dripping in the blood of the slain mayor Robertson. Rourke had his eyes trained on docking correctly than his captain, he did not feel it was appropriate to ask the captain for anything from the journey back to Cuba. Sebastian didn't move or emote, his face remained permanently scowled as he let his body loose and his hands to blow in the wind. He seemed like a permanent ornament on the ship like a scarecrow, scaring the crew to not look, speak or approach him. A voice though, rang loud as it sounded off that the anchor would be lowered. The crew threw lines to the dock and they were tightly fastened in knots, securing the ship. As the boarding plank was set up, Sebastian finally leaned to Rourke to speak. It came in a faint broken voice but the orders were very clear, "Rourke, when the British bastard is taken back, you will own Jamaica and this ship, along with its crew." Without a word more, Sebastian descended down the stairs and to the plank leading off the ship. The crew spread away from his path as they watched in confused horror, not knowing what had happened in Haiti. All they knew was that they had prisoners on board, Rourke began to chart the course for them loudly as Sebastian sped up his walking on his way back to the castle unaided and unprotected. It wasn't long until the locals in the early morning saw their captain rise up the banks of the sandy shores like the sun, although the sight was more horrific. Men, women and children watched Sebastian in horror as their captain returned from what seemed like a horrific deal, they followed him, curious of the captain's well being as his eyes still looked vacant, never moving, fixated to the path. It didn't take long until a crowd gathered to follow their leader. Like a swarm of ants, they huddled and looked over each other to see the bloody mess.

Sebastian sensed he wouldn't be able to make it back quick enough at this rate, he finally stopped and his expressionless gaze was broken. Sebastian looked around him, his people had come to him like a sheep to their Shepard, a human wall of worried faces begging to hear something from him. That's when Sebastian reached into his jacket and grabbed the large squishy heart of Robertson that had the deep puncture from Sebastian's cutlass. He gripped it tight, squeezing the blood until it ran down his arm as the crowd backed away in shock. Horrified at this, Sebastian cried: "The heart of a traitor! He has been dealt with! You all will know, the entire I.I.C will know of this! Gather everyone you know at the castle tomorrow afternoon! My announcement will shock you, but you all will be thankful that I have exposed this corruption!" As heads turned and whispers began circulating, Sebastian dropped the heart and carried on walking through the town with people making way for their captain. Fear was now present and the gossip would soon flood Cuba come tomorrow. Sebastian couldn't waste no time, everything was now in his hands, the feeling of being the captain started to run through his body, his emotions captivated by what he had seen and done. Whatever was left of the boy that took control was now lost, but not the sincerity and love he had for his family. Sebastian took a detour before reaching the castle, arriving at his Auntie Abigail's inn. The inn was empty, devoid of life in the early hours. Sebastian needed the comforting quite atmosphere of the rural pub to keep him steady. The chairs were stacked on top of the tables and the floor looked somewhat like it had been cleaned last night before closing. Sebastian opened the doors with the key, hidden behind a decorative clam shell and walked in. He stood at the bar area as the morning sun shun brightly through the windows. The bar radiated, like it was a little slice of heaven to those who frequently came by, to Sebastian, it symbolised what he would have to put aside. He could remember the last time he was here, strung out and barely walking straight. He was captain then and he was captain now, but he looked to where he sat last and saw someone else. A past self that was easily exploited and showered with praise, even though he had accomplished nothing of note except to be inaugurated. Sebastian stretched over the counter and wrapped his arm underneath the counter to grab the first bottle his fingertips felt. It was a wide dirty bottle, carrying with it the last drop of port, fit for a small glass. The captain took the cork out and basked in its rich fragrance, taking away for a brief moment the metallic stench of blood. As Sebastian closed his eyes, thinking of the pleasurable taste, he tasted the sweet port, chugging down the last drop in seconds. Relieving his tension, Sebastian then opened his eyes and relaxed his head, all the while his Aunt Abigail watched him from the corner of the small hallway which led to her bedroom. She slowly lowered the fireplace poker she wielded as she made it out it was her nephew.

"Sebastian?" She said, making him swivel back from his trance. As Sebastian turned, the blood was visible and Abigail's jaw hung slightly.

"What have you done?"

"What I thought was right," Sebastian said, stretching his arms out. Abigail sensed that he was weirdly proud of how he presented himself.

"Who was it? Anyone I know?"

"You'll keep this in confidence?"

"Does your father know?" Abigail sternly asked. Sebastian turned away, ignoring the question.

"Something is happening right under our noses-"

"Who was it, Sebastian?" Abigail pressed.

"Mayor Robertson. I caught him red-handed, about to sell off our islands to the British. There are some officials actively sabotaging us till we have nothing left. Selling our life, reaping the benefits."

"Did he try to kill you?"

"No. But his death was the only way I could send a message to any of the others if they're out there. I'm making an announcement tomorrow." Abigail didn't know what to think. The information was horrible, yet she couldn't get over the sudden change in Sebastian's presentation of things.

"Was that the only option you could think of? Sebastian, what is your father going to think-what are the people going to think-"

"At this point, I don't give a damn what my father thinks! It's just like you said, he's a weasel who does nothing but belittle me. I'm the captain. And just before I arrived here, I held that stinking traitors heart in my hands and they felt every word I said. I know what my people want and I'm not letting them or you become lambs to the slaughter," Sebastian emphatically promised. He turned round again, facing the empty bottle on the counter, collecting his thoughts. Abigail was frightened, unsure if she should say these words, but in the end, Sebastian was family and she needed to speak up.

"You have to be calmer than this Sebastian. I said you were captain, but I didn't expect this from you. Please promise me you won't do anything like this again."

"Why shouldn't I? And what do you mean you didn't expect this from me? We're pirates Aunty, that's what we'll always be, people have lost their identity. That sense of being able to take what we want, now I've given us something that can make us strong all by myself. I don't want our identity taken away, we need our identity! I thought you'd understand that."

"Just don't...just don't hurt your father. At the very least. He's my brother at the end of the day, Sebastian. If you don't let this sense of pride ease up it's going to eat you up." Sebastian hid a delicately etched smile before he turned around to face Abigail.

"I haven't felt this good in a long time, Aunty. Trust me I've found something that makes me love myself. Our name, the Teach name. Pirate royalty. I intend for it to stay that way." Abigail looked at her nephew with grief, she knew right then that nothing she could say would change his mind. The thirst of blood is what all pirates knew, she served them after all, she knew what kind of violence a pirate could make.

"Why did you come here, Sebastian?"

"To leave the old world behind. Like the pirates before us. You'll see what I mean come tomorrow," Sebastian said.

"Will I have any say in this?" Abigail asked.

"Of course you won't, I am the-" Sebastian spun round to meet Abigail's disappointment. Caught red handed in Sebastian's shun, she pointed to the door.

"That right there is the one thing I thought you wouldn't turn out to be. I think you need to keep that in mind the next time you do things, Sebastian. Pirates have freedom of what they say and do. That's what makes us great. And when the crew out number the captain and he doesn't listen, that's when things become disruptive. Now, you may be the captain, but I'd like for you to get out of my pub."

Cold words that froze sharply in Sebastian's ears. Though the rage was still there inside, in that moment it was extinguished and Sebastian didn't feel like a captain anymore. He did what he was told and left the pub, not a word more. He stood by the door and heard it being locked behind him. In that moment, Sebastian, the young eager student of the game was left behind in that pub. Out stepped the leader who stood on his own two feet and took daring action to the dislike of his peers. Abigail have the truth about something though that Sebastian would take seriously, he would have to think things through, and he did have a day till his announcement.

As he barged back inside the manor of the castle, Sebastian headed straight for the first guard he saw to his left. Both guards on either side of the staircase stood at attention as quickly as they could once they realised it was the captain.

"I want you to deliver a message to the second ranking general. Tell him to meet me in my office immediately, it is of a high security risk. Go!" The guard rushed off as fast as his armour would allow him and Sebastian made his way up the stairs to his office. Once inside, he slammed the door shut and took the map of the island continents off the wall, laying it across his desk. He studied it, making note of the charting courses ships would have to take. The quickest course of action was necessary, if he were to impose an active measure of a military operation, one that would go underneath the public's nose, it would have to be executed swiftly. Sebastian used his finger, gliding around the paths that were largely uninhabited parts of the islands. They mayors offices would be taken from the back. The word directed at guard patrols would have to lure them away from their posts, therefore, arrests could be made without any hostility from onlookers. Now it was down to the list of suspects. Sebastian drew up a list of names, all serving positions of the islands with Jamaica being covered by a large 'X'. The islands were as followed: Haiti, Cayman, Puerto Rico, Barbados, Barbuda and Tobago. Mayors and district officials all laid there heads on the islands, except one. Almost restraining himself to write the name, Sebastian eventually did what he thought was right and placed his father's name at the bottom, listed as top priority with a circle around it. It was hard to believe, but Sebastian took no chances. He then sat and waited for the general, looking to conduct himself with precision timing instead of reckless brutality. Earlier on with Mayor Robertson was only a taste of what he could do.

Edward Teach rested alone in his bed. Dressed and ready to go for the past hour, he laid in thought, contemplating his and Reginald's plan they discussed. He was not anxious, nor did he have any feelings towards his son's persistent attitude. In a way, he was relieved that he had come this far. Thoughts came to his mind of whether or not he saw himself as a good person. The ideas and actions he partook during the reign of Norton were not seen fondly to others, but it was all that he could do. Now with the situation with his son, Edward didn't mind if he succumbed to defeat. He was at peace. No longer anchored down to the tether of countless errands and fatherly duties. It seemed comforting; knowing that he would never be seen again. He rose up from the bed, straightening his shirt and hair. Reginald was not in the office house at this point in time, he had ventured to the local tavern for breakfast while Edward slept in. Taking in a deep breath, one of Edwards thoughts seemed the most logical. His ideas had been evaluated and it was time to get to work. He grabbed his jacket and took out the small parchment paper which had the request of the boat transport out of the islands. Edward placed the request inside a jumble of papers Reginald had been working on in the night. Next came a little thing called theft. Edward acquired the bag of doubloons from the desk drawer, tucking it away as he walked out of the office. The Dominican island was only an hour away by boat, Edward had to make sure he wasn't seen, ducking and diving his way through the towns till he reached the port side. The early morning rounds of travel boats were few but the crew men were already posted and ready for the morning rush. Aside from the workers, no one was present at the docks, Edward rushed down, his feet thumping loudly as he got to the end of the pier with a balding, bearded man standing there.

"A boat to Dominican, immediately," Edward said, catching his breath.

"Certainly sir. That will be ten silver," the man said. Edward paid the exact amount with no hesitation, like he knew the price in advance. The pair climbed aboard, Edward taking a seat near the bow of the boat while the crew mate unrolled the small sail. They set off to the small island, Dominican's port of escape was getting closer and closer, the wind was on Edwards side as the journey there was calm with no hiccups. There was no turning back now, the plan was initiated. By the time Edward arrived, the sun was up, early morning rushes of people leaving for work would soon hit the streets. Thankfully, Edward's route after docking was not far. A familiar stretch down the beach side where the rocks blocked out the growing rainforest where the last few houses resided. This was an easy and formal route to Bogg's port, although not many people ventured through this way. Boggs was known as a character you wouldn't cross paths with. There was a reason why the stone paved pathways finished at the rocks. Edward finally saw the port yard, it was as desperate as the people who used it. Run down, crawling with seedy regulars and a host of burnt or washed up boats. This was either the way for a new life or a desperate death in waiting. Edward watched his step, fearing if the dead would reawaken and pull him down in the sand. The sight of drunken or malnourished regulars made him recoil as he turned his nose up at the smell of burning wood and excrement. Moans of death itching closer were all that he heard until a hearty laugh, complimented by a rasping cough indicated Boggs was near and he was. The big man rested on a sign post to the only available boat, he was sweaty as ever, bare chested and already drinking strong stolen scotch from overseas. Edward raised his hand to him and Boggs blurted his name at decibels loud enough to reach to town behind him.

"Mr Teach! What a lovely surprise! Come to see the port? It's marvellous, ain't it?"

"It's happening now. No need for formal words Claude, I'd rather you just take me now and be done with it," Edward said bluntly making the ogre of a man question him.

"Oh, so I see. And uh, what brings this about then? I was expecting more than one."

"You're getting one and done. But I'll compensate for the unlucky few," Edward pulled out the bag of rare doubloons and lobed them over to Claude. He lifted the bag up and down, checking the weight of the payment, he was very impressed.

"An extra is in there if you forget everything about this deal. No mention of it to anyone, understand? Not even if the military come through these paths...if they're brave enough," Edward mustered. Boggs laughed and untied the bag. Jingling down in his palm was pure gold, a doubloon unmarked or scratched, perfect condition. The rest inside was self explanatory, Claude Boggs had earned more than what he bargained for and chuckled more devilishly as the joy washed over him.

"Well Mr Teach, I have enough here to rebuild the whole port! Sunny! Get off ya lazy arse and get the boat ready! Mr Teach here is looking for an escape, isn't that right?" No words left Edwards mouth. Just a simple nod to confirm as he walked past Claude to the boat where the face pierced Sunny scrambled to prepare. Boggs sat himself down on the sand, chugging back his bottle with the doubloons which he proceeded to sprinkle all over him, resting on his bloated gut. Edward looked back at the sight of him as he continuously chuckled, he would finally leave the lifestyle he was born into behind at last. When he looked at Claude he didn't see character, he saw delinquency. Someone who shouldn't be the hassle of his life trying to govern. He saw it everyday he lived on these islands, it's what he was born into. The name of his father was like the accursed black spot which would plague any man it touches. No more would he be subjugated to ridiculous notions of god's and legends, he was no free as soon as his feet were in the the small boat. The skinny Sunny let go of the anchor and steered the ship away from the port with the slimy Boggs waving like a little school girl to Edward.

"Where to, sir?" Sunny asked. Edward then turned away from the islands for the last time and said: "New York."

"Naturally, we will need to disclose something to the public should any onlookers find what our men are doing, captain. A false narrative?" An elder general in part metal armour, part tuxedo explained to Sebastian who kept his head down on the map of the islands, still scrolled across his desk.

"No. No false pretences. If anyone asks you tell them the captain will address everyone tomorrow. If they want to know on the day they must travel to Cuba to hear me speak at the castle," Sebastian said.

"Uh captain, this will drive large boats to the island on such short notice. My men will have to increase presence on the island for the sake of your safety."

"My safety is of little concern right now, I've already handled one of the conspirators myself, single handedly, may I add. If the heads of the islands have been rounded up any other associates will be isolated on the islands. The military once they've secured their targets must be stationed evenly to avoid any escapes," Sebastian explained, dropping another knife of the map.

"Very well, captain. Now, where exactly shall the assailants be held?" The general asked.

"Bring them here, but not to me. There's a basement in the castle opposite the cellar. They'll be squashed in there till I say so."

"Yes sir, understood." Soon a knock was heard at the door and in walked in was Klaus, his face hidden from his hood but his beard easy to make out.

"General, that will be all. Execute the plan the second you make it out of the grounds. And general, if there is any sign of my father, deliver him straight to me." Sebastian and Klaus were the only ones in the quarters once the general closed the door.

"I trust the inquisition is full steam ahead?" Klaus said, unveiling his face.

"Indeed. They won't be much of a problem in a days time. The dominoes have started to fall on their little syndicate," Sebastian said.

"This is most pleasing, captain. The fortune now turns the tide to those who follow the carrier of Oki's message. The faith will bring the balance of piracy back into the people's lives very soon. The heinous acts of these men will bring the morale on a scale the likes of which the Americans and the British will never see coming," Klaus went on.

"The Maelstrom will then have the numbers required to have it completed in record time. The dream will finally be alive again and we, the free man, will reign over the waters," Sebastian hailed.

"I'm anxious to hear the speech tomorrow, captain. Is the priest worthy to view the confines?"

"Alfred has shown me more affection in my life more than what my father has. The word of the goddess and the pirate fate is all he knows. He knows it better than my father ever could."

"So if your father were to be captured what would be the status of the quartermaster role? And even that of the mayoral positions, how would they fare with our new approach?" An interesting question that Sebastian knew partly how to answer.

"Rourke Renfold has already been handed the governing position of Jamaica. He will return to keep the island steady after disposing of the Englishman. Others I will have to pull from a hat."

"Do you think that's wise?"

"My authority must not be questioned, Klaus. I need to look like my head is on my shoulders if I need this to go on without a hitch."

"I understand that, but what would bring the people more favourably to your reign was if you were to let them decide."

"Snap elections?"

"Indeed. Consider it a gift to them. Once you clear the air and alert the public to your knowledge that the complete compromise of the stooges who plotted to undermine the nation, not only does it make you look like a strong handler of threats it also makes them feel rewarded. A weight will be lifted, perfect matrimony for the people to feel protected by their leader." The idea was genius. Sebastian wanted the best possible relationship with his people, much like the days he had as a young boy helping in community projects. It could've been the touch of narcissism now creeping in but Sebastian could not say no.

"I second that, Klaus. It's perfect. Perhaps your efforts in practical solutions could be rewarded with a position?," Sebastian courteously suggested. Klaus scoffed at this.

"I'm flattered captain. But I believe my best work lies behind the curtain. The circle still needs me as their leader. Besides, your eventual new cabinet will have to attain to the "out there" persona that you thrive upon. Truly, it will be a government where the positivity in the freedoms we conduct on, will be protected by people of your nature," Klaus said. He turned his back to observe outside and see the Maelstrom in construction.

"But I should need to be mindful of everyone still. Who knows how many agents these islands have, scurrying around likes rats. Perhaps checks should be in order this time," Sebastian meditated the thought until his fingers snapped, "I've got it! A book of names. Collect everything from them. Names, friends, family, occupations, businesses, income, this transparency will not only put me at ease but also the public! No seediness will ever get close to the office ever again."

"Can you be certain that what they give you is true? You will obviously need officers at them at all times to be sure their actions match their words, captain."

"Way ahead of you. This book will be for me, but they will have books dedicated to weekly reports. They must chart everything of every week as the sun dials turn. That way I can be up to speed. Military operatives will be assigned to them but they can also act on any malicious activity they suspect."

"Very good, captain. And what of Mexico? Will they be informed of this?" Klaus asked, not taking his eyes away from the multitude of slaves working away on hard wood.

"What Juárez doesn't know won't hurt him. If we retain the image of a perfect ally, he will have no suspicion to doubt any of my decisions when it comes to Maelstrom. Pretty soon I will have reason to see Mr Juárez again to discuss something."

"What might that be?" Klaus said, peering over his right shoulder.

"Immigration."

CHAPTER 17

THE WITCH HUNT BEGINS

Reginald had his face pressed in on the ground by a formidable boot which kept him down. The soldier held his cutlass pointing at him, knowing that if he wanted to, he could jab it straight into the mayors eye. Two other personnel turned his office upside down, searching the premises for anything that retained to the generals orders. Find anything relating to undermining the I.I.C. As Reginald fought to turn his head slightly to speak, the officers soon began to rip up the already broken down floorboards.

"P-please! I have nothing that-"

"Mind your tongue, sir," the officer said, gentle pressing the tip of the blade into Reginald's cheek, "The captain still wants you inside under lock and key even if we don't find something." With loud cracks, the floorboards were up and tossed aside. It was only dirt, the foundation of the house. One by one they came up and nothing was underneath. This left only his desk to be searched and that's when Reginald began to squirm.

"Not the desk! Please, it's a family heirloom!"

"Like anyone on this island has an heirloom. Search it!" With the order given, the drawers came flying out and the desk ripped and snapped to pieces. One of the men lifted drawers and emptied the contents onto the floor. A few books, a pair of glasses and a coin purse fell out. This left the military with nothing to go on, but Reginald was bewildered that the small bag of doubloons, which could've been easily traced to the captain's treasury, was mysteriously missing. Reginald tried to mutter out the word "But", but he was lifted onto his feet and pushed out the door as his hands were tied behind his back. As the group brought him outside through the back door, a horse and carriage was at the ready with two other officers patrolling it. A large metal door flung open and the silver plated guards pushed the mayor in, confiding him to a damp cart ride to which he would be taken to Sebastian. As Reginald brought his hands and face to the barred square, looking back at the road he would be trailing, he frantically thought where the bag of treasure had gone. As the carriage began to rock and move away from his former home, Reginald then pieced it together. No Edward, no treasure. His trust was broken and used by his closest ally. He would have no trouble at being the first voice to be heard before the captain.

Across the islands, raids began away from the public. Offices and homes were ransacked, documents were collected and some were not as clever to hide their treasure. Some groups were alerted to the sudden military action but we're told to keep by. Offices, once searched and no other possessions could be found, were set alight. Flames would capture the people's attention more than the small carriages carting their prisoners away. These were only small groups, which were easier to control. A mass of people had already begun making preparations to sail to Cuba, to hear the captain's speech on time. Some had intentions to camp out over night as the boats were now being packed to the gills with families and single men and women. As much as the military operation was swift, only a handful of eyes saw what really happen. One small teenage boy managed to follow a carriage on the island Puerto Rico, following the carriage from afar, hearing the screeching of Mayor Williamson. The boy was in drab hand-me-downs with a straw hat and his face was covered in soot. As he kept up, his long hair smacked his face but his pace was not hindered. The coach turned in through a block of houses in which the boy went around, climbing a wooden beam on the left house to gain a height advantage. The only place the carriage could go was to the port were a ship was stationed. Crew members immediately began to hoist the colours of the captain and set the sails as soon as the carriage was insight. The young teen saw everything from the top of the house, crouching behind a chimney to keep hidden. As the carriage pulled up, he saw Mayor Williamson being dragged out by his collar. It ripped off from the force and the soldiers dragged him across the port by his arms, scraping his knees as he was thrown onto the ship. With no time to spare, the docking board was brought on and the ship quickly turned to depart. The teenage boy gulped hard as he saw this transpire, he only knew he could relay this back to his master. Knowing he would forget the details, the boy grabbed a piece of paper from underneath his hat and wrote down everything he saw with a piece of chalk. In a frantic rush, he scaled back down from the roof and ran back the way he came.

To General Lacroix, the mission went smoothly as he stood at the bow of the ship, proudly holding his hands behind his back, his tuxedo tails blew in the wind as his men held Williamson in place behind him.

"Have you got anything to tell us, Mayor Williamson?" The general asked in his thick French accent. Williamson did well not to speak, his stutter was worse when under pressure.

"Nothing," Lacroix wondered while pivoting on his heels, "You know it will only help your case if you give us names."

"I-I have n-no idea what you mean," Williamson whimpered. With a nudge of his head, Lacroix gave the order to bring a heavy fist, courtesy of the guards across his face. The punch fractured the mayors nose, bringing a mess of blood down his mouth.

"The captain would not have made this mission possible had it not been for a certain someone sticking their noses into enemy territory, wouldn't he?"

"W-what? I have no idea w-what you're t-t-talking about," Williamson spat.

"Were you aware of mayor Robertson's deal? If so, we want names and associates, if you please?" Williamson looked at everyone around him, bewildered and scared for his life as to what was happening.

"You've all g-gone insane!" With another nudge came another fist, making the mayor fall to the floor with the blood splattering over the ship. Lacroix could only take so much of the puny mayor's cries (and his stuttering). The immaculately dressed general reached down to his armoured shin guards and pulled slightly on the top half making it click. The sharp pointed tip of the curvature released and Lacroix pulled out a two speared sickle which had a folded out handle. Examining its beautiful shape, testing it's sharp tips, Lacroix brought it to the mayors neck, lifting his head up as the claw-like weapon rested under his jaw.

"Reminds me of the old days. When my father fought for my home to be free. Before he sent me away, I had only known of bloodshed. We French are very particular when it comes to people who stand for the wrong cause. Napoleon knew of this. Pirate life is all I've known, but the French in me, well, that just gives me the upper edge on things. Like this sickle, I get to reap the benefits, even from a traitor like you. Now tell me: are there any names associated with Robertson?" Lacroix asked again.

"G-general, please," the tears now began to leave Williamson's eyes, "I don't know of anyone. Whatever R-Robertson did it had nothing to do with me. I was just doing what I was told-"

"Told by whom, sir!?" Lacroix bellowed as he pressed the sickle in harder on his neck.

"Edward Teach! Mayor Reginald! They gathered us, they set up an escape plan in case the captain overstepped his boundaries!"

"I think it is you who has overstepped his boundaries. Robertson was making deals with the British in an attempt to undermine the islands wealth and resources in exchange for safety, so why would he do that if an escape plan was already in mind?" Lacroix questioned in a sinister tongue.

"I-I-I don't know! Maybe he became paranoid. He may have acted out against what Teach proposed, I-I don't know any m-more!" Williamson blubbered.

Lacroix stared intently at Williamson and withdrew the sickle away from his neck, contemplating his next like of questioning, adding a much calmer tone to his voice again.

"How long has this supposed escape plan been in place?" The general asked.

"Since the Mexican alliance was made."

"And do you have an idea of who else may be itching to leave?"

"I don't know-" Another crack of a punch came to the already bleeding Williamson from one of the guards, this time knocking him out. Lacroix gathered himself, clipping away his fashionably hidden weapon back into the metal shin guard.

"They seem to be saying the same thing to me. Put him in the holding cell, he'll find the one he's about to stay in with his conspirators much more cramped than the one below." The guards carried the small Williamson away as the ships crew continued to work in a speed which never broke.

That's what Lacroix liked, efficiency. It's what drove him to be as violent as he could, getting the answers the captain wanted would mean a sufficient reward would be in place. He looked out to the east, his ships in the force were also on the course back to Cuba, no doubt carrying yet another of the mayors in their cargo. The information Williamson gave was indeed interesting even if the general had heard it from two previous encounters from different mayors. None were aware of Robertson's act of betrayal and almost none knew where Edward Teach was. Except one. The second name Williamson spoke of.

Beneath the Cuban castle lied a a massive underground network of tunnels, burrowing through the ground below like roots on a tree, each sprouting off into a different room. With a combination of stone, sand and dirt, it was formidable but very claustrophobic to anyone venturing down just to take a bottle of wine from its many cellars. As you descended down a straight staircase, you had five options to take, two doors on the left, two on the right and one down the middle. The side doors were where food and drink were stored all in close proximity of each other yet the walls were so thick you couldn't tell. Any sound would echo in the creamy walls while hard stone made every foot step longer in your eardrums. Then there was the doorway in the middle. Steeper steps brought you down till you went left, right and then left again until you came face to face with another door, except this one was metal barred and padlocked. If you unfortunately had to be dragged into this depressing depth, you would likely be greeted to screams and yells of profanity. Cell blocks lined along, all large enough to fit at least ten prisoners in one cell, there was twenty cells in total with one facing you at the very end as your eyes looked away from the prisoners all reaching out at you through the slips of the barred walls. Williamson was escorted personally by General Lacroix, he had come to from the journey back and was pushed with one hand while his were tied. It was a delight for some prisoners to see him, the sight of another white collar individual all had a direct line of insults hurled towards him like verbal tomatoes hitting a bad stage performer. The insults were mocked his stuttering, his short frame and articulate manor. But as soon as Williamson was at the end of this hall, he was once again acquainted with the other mayors of the islands, including Mayor Reginald who sat in the corner. Williamson was shoved inside and Lacroix slammed the door behind him, locking them away all huddled together.

"Well gentlemen, you all seem to have quite the story to tell to the captain once his ceremonial speech has concluded. Perhaps it would be a valuable time now to ready your statements, if you all can agree on one that is."

"This is totally absurd, General," Reginald said, "None of us have sacrificed the integrity of these islands. The people will see through the captain's thin veil of power once he has opened his mouth." "Perhaps. Or perhaps, you don't know your people that well, Reginald. I'll return here tomorrow to escort you all upstairs, in the mean time, sit tight." Lacroix walked away from their cell to a chorus of boos and explicit claims down the hall before the metal door slammed shut. The mayors all didn't know what to do with themselves. An uncomfortable awkwardness surrounded their cell, all not even thinking of opening their mouths to explain. It was probably best suited to when they addressed Captain Teach tomorrow, who was their judge, jury and executioner. One man however, eluded Lacroix's grasp. The man all mentioned by the arrested suspects, Edward Teach. No matter how stormy the waters became, Sebastian was hell bent on presiding over his new empire and bringing down those who defied him. Only then, over night, did the islands get hit by something only the gods could conjure. Making the men in suits glad they were below.

CHAPTER 18

A BIBLICAL ANNOUNCEMENT

As I wake from thy slumber, cast a great cloud bringing reckless untold damage. My islands face the cold wrath of her holiness, Oki.

My faith is my shield and my sword is my compass, whom shall be in my way will lead me to my quest. Treachery surrounds me, prison will not suffice their sins, nor shall it quench my thirst for victory.

The I.I.C awoke the next morning and was pulverised by harsh storms. Winds swept away discarded food and waste, wooden planks were lifted away from where they lay and house roofs held on by a thread. The relentless rain poured down and the waves rose to horrifying heights that combined with the dark overlay of cloud. It was not an ideal day for an announcement to take place, but Sebastian knew he had to face danger in the eye (In this case, given from the goddess Oki) and not be afraid. He got dressed in his usual manor, even as his bedroom window refused to stay shut. Skipping the hat and instead placing the Oki necklace around his neck, Sebastian awaited patiently for his entourage to arrive. As his father remained missing, General Lacroix would be by his side at all times. Sebastian felt liberated, the first speech he would give without his father by his side. His input was no longer necessary, the young leader could no convey his strong message of inspiration without any distraction. His distractions had been rounded up and thrown below him in the castle cellar, there was no need to spoil the fun anymore. Just then the door opened after a small knock,

General Lacroix greeted the captain but seemed uncertain if he wanted to go through with this.

"Yes. It is happening, General. Even if this storm calms down or not, I'm still getting up that podium."

"As you wish, captain."

"How was the first round of interrogations?" Sebastian asked.

"Routine. But they all had a familiar story which they refused to stray away from. Your father was mentioned as a ring leader, but no-one knows where he is. Everybody believes that Robertson went against what your father ordered."

Sebastian stood solemnly. Disappointed in his father's plot of escape, yet impressed that he was the elusive one to turn his back on his governing counterparts. A sacrifice? Sebastian knew there were people who would do anything for a payment, it seemed the search would have to be more extensive.

"Let's leave that for later shall we? I have my people to address." With that, the pair walked out from his captain's bedroom and along the halls till they reached the upper floor of the castle. Atop the highest floor was a large open rooftop room that had no walls sectioning it. No windows, just a wide half circle opening up to the balcony that looked down below. As Sebastian and Lacroix walked in, the door behind them shut as they looked round to see the emptiness of the floor. It held nothing but spare chests, a few flags hung by one nail and rolls of carpets, imported or stolen from adversaries.

"Do you intend to use this floor for anything at some point?" Lacroix wondered.

"Maybe. Could be a good meeting room one day," Sebastian entertained the thought.

Surprisingly, outside had a gathering of people. Slowly but surely, people covered in makeshift tarp coats, fought off the rain and wind and more soon flocked to hear the speech in the early morning hours. Sebastian could hear the noise pick up as the more people came. His people had gathered, bound to his word even in the harshest conditions. It pleased Sebastian to no end. He took deep breaths as the General was ready to step out with him. As the last crucial breath went in, his breath out happened as he made his way to the pillared balcony. There was a moment of silence, the rain hit the captain from the side, blowing his hair to the left. Lacroix was thankful no hair was on his head but he felt the sharp little stings from the rain. Heads soon began to look up to the castle and all were hanging on to see or hear the first thing that would come out of their captain since that horrific announcement. Sebastian saw them, heads a plenty and lifted both this hands in angelic fashion. The crowd erupted, their patience had paid off and Sebastian didn't waste any time in speaking after his hands descended.

"My fellow pillagers, plunderers and pirates, there has been a great reckoning. Some of you are aware if you live in Cuba, that I returned from a recent trip with the blood and heart of someone I labelled a traitor. The traitor is speak of was non other than Mayor Callum Robertson of the island of Jamaica," a hush of silence swept through the crowd, "Unaware of my sudden intrusion, I discovered upon entering his mayoral office, he was perpetuating in the slow, saddening decline of our nation of islands. He was dealing with a British diplomat, exchanging secrets of wealth to cover his promised security when the islands fell. Having dispensed him, I took the initial action to remove all heads of the islands. In doing so, I have acted effectively to ensure that this operation will weed out the threat to our lands. Now the decision lies with you. The due process of a snap election in your islands will be under way come tomorrow. I believe that the islands need to be governed by those who inhabit it, but with recent events, I believe the good faith that Captain Burchill bestowed upon us has failed. And just recently, Captain Norton's ruthless snatching of our faith has cost us our morale. Look at what I have brought you in the past few months: a renewed faith in our churches, our lively spirit and tradition is back on our streets and a massive project of strength and unison with our new allies in the west is being constructed in record time. If we wish for the Maelstrom, a powerful weapon that will keep anyone at bay to be built, then all of you need to bring your pride and compassion to the table. And in doing so I think a manor of gratitude must be given to those who aids this project. A compensation of two ounce of cold doubloons will be rewarded," that definitely won a smile to everyone and a look of puzzlement to Lacroix, "Make no mistake this pledge will be kept, by the blood of my beating heart I will make sure nothing like this treachery ever happens again!" Cheers and fists raised into the air. "I'll make sure that the world powers that be fear the might that pirates, who are all living breathing people who sound the act of defiance against them!" Another roar of the crowd elevated Sebastian's voice to its final crescendo. "And I will make sure, that piracy, as a whole, will be far greater under the eyes of our goddess Oki, who hangs around my neck like the hangman's noose, forever reminding me, that I will never defile your rights as worshippers of the sea! If I do, I'll hear you. If I do, you and her will strike me down. And if I do, I expect pirates show no mercy!!" Sebastian raised both his fists in the air and below him, the people through fists, swords and fire lit lanterns in the air in glorious acceptance as the thunder rumbled in the sky. The momentous occasion was wrapped in a nicely lit bow as Sebastian held his fists high till the lighting struck down along the sea. He then vanished behind the castles curtain with Lacroix as the crowds noise filled the air, but all the while in the back or crevices of the streets, some were less than impressed. A small minority now had the fuel they needed in the reason of defiance. But also, a congregation, led by the hooded Klaus, watched in sheer delight but were less vocal. Klaus saw his other hooded disciples in the crowds and each of them nodded, all weaving in direction back to the quiet garden of Blackbeard's statue. Inside, Sebastian had his hands on his knees and breathing heavily while Lacroix tended to him.

"That was fantastic, captain! They were eating out of the palm of your hands!" Lacroix said in delight. Sebastian wheezed but gave a quick thumbs up as he continued to get his breath back.

"I must ask though, we have only managed suitable trade agreements with the islands original customers and I'm aware that Mexico is part of that now but what is the promise of this gold? This surely must be a promise that cannot be fulfilled?" The general wondered.

"Not...at all," Sebastian brought himself back up, "There was always a backlog that I had no idea about. Lacroix, you have done well, very well intact. The quickness of your efficiency brought weight to my speech. You have gained my trust and therefore you must be rewarded." Lacroix had a massive smile on his face and shook the captain's hand with his.

"I look forward to this, whatever it is, captain."

"Indeed. You want to celebrate? I have guests arriving in just a moment, so there's no use leaving some good wine I've come into possession of lately," Sebastian suggested.

"Excellent! Now you are speaking my language!"

To the north, boats and large gatherings of men in grey uniforms rounded their supplies up in bulky crates. Ammunition, rifles, knives and food stored away in no particular order. This was a rush operation. An operation of retreat with no surrender in mind. The wounded were treated while they waited and a concerned officer looked out to sea. If this was the work of the higher ups, he understood the implications this would have on the war, but he also saw the brilliance of it. It may have been strategic but it could also backfire if not correctly discussed. Who knew what awaited the confederacy, all the officer knew was that once the storm blew over the Caribbean islands, the boats would be on their way down south of Florida.

CHAPTER 19

A PLEASANT TUESDAY

Two days after the ferocious storm faded, the speech from Captain Sebastian Teach never did. In it's wake, the people were more joyous than ever and as the sun rose on a pleasant Tuesday morning, an influx of people were signing their name on the dotted line of recruitment sheets. Giving hours of their time in exchange for a liveable future with no dread, promise of good fortune certainly got the ball rolling. The Maelstrom, once worked on by slave forces was now the people's project. The slaves were now taken aside away from where the people worked, focusing more of the inside of the wooden and steel beast while the public worked on the gorgeous outer shell. The Maelstrom now had cannon hatches fitted, three floors stretching a mile long and an interior strong enough to withstand the toughest offence (should anyone be brave enough). Sebastian watched from his window as the work was paying off, inside his quarters while he basked in the warm sun, were workers in shirts and ties, crafting the foundation of black books that would keep in check the next generation of mayoral bodies that would occupy the vacated office spaces. Lacroix waited patiently by the door as the men scribbled at consistent rate at the captains desk. Sebastian finally turned to face his general and walked with him out of the office.

"General, I trust you're ready to see the reward for your hard work?"

"I am, captain. Is the reward here? You honestly could pay me in a bottle of that wonderful wine we shared," Lacroix chuckled.

"Much better than wine, my friend. We will have to wait for two other individuals as well, Mayor Longstaff and Pastor Albert will be accompanying us. They two have been rewarded by me also."

"How exactly did Mayor Longstaff avoid the culling, captain? He was in dangerously close proximity to you,"

"He was willing to expose some secrets to me that were highly important. It goes towards my suspicions about the other mayors

Now some others, which you will meet, will know what to do with them. I knew I could trust him and he proved that. Pastor Albert put in a good word of the fortune to him."

"I see. These men you speak of, anyone I should know about? Are they part of the castle briefing?" Lacroix asked.

"You met one not long ago but introductions will come today. They have a great deal of knowledge that has helped the I.I.C tremendously."

As the two came downstairs, Klaus stood by the doorway, the sun shining through the windows, making his shadow loom onto the steps which the captain and general stepped through.

"Ah yes, now I remember you," Lacroix said as he made out Klaus's tall frame.

"A pleasure once again, General Lacroix. The captain said you fulfilled in your mission to round up the double crossers."

"Absolutely," The general and Klaus exchange a quick handshake, "And I've been hearing things in the woodwork about you. You have been a spearhead in this resurrection."

"Not me my new acquainted friend, the spearhead was in hiding, waiting you be thrown." Upon finishing his sentence, Mayor Longstaff and Pastor Albert arrived. Longstaff arrived in lighter colours of pastel and cream, while Albert was wearing his usual brown gown but with a decorative scarf around his neck.

"And thus, the group is complete!" Sebastian rejoiced.

"Gentlemen, a great welcome. Your honour among the cause of Oki has been plentiful," Klaus beamed. Longstaff knew the name of the tall hooded man was familiar, but he couldn't quite put his finger on it.

"Amen to you sir. Captain, we are more than ready for this," Albert said.

"Excellent, let's not waste time then. Klaus, lead the way, it's a glorious day gentlemen. You will not be disappointed." The group walked with guards on either side, conjoining the group of four as they walked down the stone staircase and into the heart of Cuba. A divergent path that kept a far from the public was needed. Even though the responses from below the five men were of respect and admiration, the guards did not let down their swords. Three of the men waved while one remained neutral, Klaus crossing his arms inside the droopy sleeves of his robes and his hood over his balding head. He had been like this in public before, blissfully unaware passers by would see yet not mind, but now in full view with the highest command of the islands, it was more noticeable than ever. His speed gathered as they all turned away from the main town and came through to the gardens, the slope was steep but the invisibility the four of them had at the bust if Blackbeard was crucial. Two guards blocked off the pathway, while others took to the separate junctions that lead to the park square. Longstaff patted his head with a handkerchief as the heat was getting to him, he never walked this far out. Usually when in Tortuga, the extremity of his travels out of his office would be to the local tavern. As the men came to observe the statues of Blackbeard, marvelling in the likeness of the statue, Sebastian and Klaus stood together to initiate the pastor, mayor and general.

"Gentlemen, the time has come. This congregation has concluded that peace within the islands will be restored. Captain Teach here has already seen the treasures lying beneath our feet and now through the completion of a new government, we will all reap of wealth more than just gold." Sebastian unhooked the necklace from his neck and proceeded to unlock the mystery behind the statue of his grandfather. The pendant slotted inside the hole effortlessly as the a crack was from below the ground, soon the staircase would became visible, bringing down the stone plates of the floor to show a dark path with fire illuminating it. The three men not privy to this were in shock with Albert muttering a silent prayer before any of them could step forth with the captain's permission. Sebastian waved his hand to indicate that it was safe while Klaus's intimidating stare made the men rush in uncoordinated. General Lacroix, braced to be the next man forward while Klaus led the way, the men unsure how his tall stature managed to fit inside the confined tunnel. Longstaff was slightly fearful of his trek down the hidden staircase and asked onto Sebastian: "There won't be any ungodly things down there, will there?"

Sebastian warningly said, "You have nothing to fear. This is the place the goddess Oki blessed the most." Swallowing back his fear, Longstaff made his way down as Sebastian followed suit. The staircase began to twist in a spiral as the door closed. The flames of the lanterns came very close to brushing everyone's hair off, Lacroix feared that the most as he tucked in his neck as much as he could behind his fashionably stiff white collar like a tortoise in its shell. The darkness was almost overwhelming as the men reached flat flooring, it was stone, large stone. Ancient almost in design, the path forward curved in an arch with scriptures of a forgotten language covered it. No one could understand it, not even Lacroix who prayed to see if it was partially a part of his mothers tongue, but it wasn't. The symbols looked other worldly, the ink or blood (which was hard to tell by now) had been there for years and the damp mold was starting to take over. Klaus darkened the path with his size, nearly covering the light beaming back to the captain and his closest confidants until they reached the end of the straight path. The door was stone, two long rectangular stones much like the ground underneath them stood, formidably strong yet a seal was placed in the middle. The seal was that of the pendant, Sebastian had to come past through his fellow patrons and once again insert it. There was no cracking of old rusty metal, Klaus simply pushed the stone doors open with both hands and the glow of the fire raging from inside soon shun on the group. Sebastian smiled with glee as he once again stepped foot inside while the other four men were in awe at the holy room beneath the Blackbeard bust. A fire raged inside a large bowl made out of clay and stone rocks surrounded the walls all piled on top of each other. The three other men of Klaus's congregation stood behind the fire, all three looking on as the band of men came inside the dungeon of mystery. "What is this place?" Albert said with enthusiastic curiosity.

"Gentlemen, welcome to the tomb of the goddess Oki. The scriptures you see around these walls were here long before we were," The writings continued on through onto the stones, painting a collage of symbols that worked around the bumps and crevices,

"Until now, we had no idea what they meant. But this gave us a good hint." The congregation members walked up to Sebastian's group, carrying opened treasure chests that had contents of gold, silver and jewels spilling out at the seems. Behind them, the eyes of the four newest members to the dungeon saw piles of chests ranging in different sizes from small compact to large two men carriers.

"What is all this?" Lacroix asked.

"The spoils of foes. And this, lead us back to our rewards," Sebastian displayed the pendant in front of Lacroix and Longstaff who marvelled at it, while Albert smiled with resounding peace, knowing that his faith had led to divine treasure, "It was lost after the fall of Burchill. Norton never acquired it and it drove him mad."

"Which you will be quite aware of, Mr Longstaff, correct?" Klaus said. Longstaff was amazed it was real. The realisation that what Norton had tormented him and his acquaintances in the governing sphere was actually true.

"Unbelievable. He put us through hell, and all this time-"

"Norton was delusional anyway," Klaus resumed, "His sheer lust for power caused these islands to suffer. Their was loss for everyone, including me," Klaus unveiled himself again, giving a better view of his face in the fluorescent light to Longstaff who suddenly realised who he was talking to.

"Wait! Klaus!? Oh my word, how did I not piece the two together? Klaus Hamilton. I thought you were dead the night after-"

"After my colleague was killed in front of me? Amazing what a year in hiding will do to you," Klaus said brushing his beard.

"But I was certain Norton had you cornered off the second that meeting was adjourned," Longstaff continued in his recollection.

"These fine men behind me were the reason for me disappearing. They knew my knowledge of the castle and of the power of the captain's chair. In return, they gave me the knowledge of the tomb. These are the treasures that has kept us afloat for so many years. In truth, Norton could have never bankrupted the I.I.C, but he was close."

"I'm not one to pass gratefulness to a passing, but it is good he was removed in the end," Albert said.

"Wait, Captain, is that the reason the top of the castle is completely empty?" Lacroix wondered. "Indeed so," Sebastian answered, "Seemed more appropriate to hide such riches far beneath than up above. The congregation takes pride in our heritage. Klaus implemented a scheme to steal every last bit of it and keep it away from Norton."

"It helps if one forgets to take back the keys he was granted," Klaus jingled a single key from its metal ring that he pulled from his robe.

"So, what is this grand scheme, captain? How are we involved in the... goddess's plan?" Lacroix asked.

"We will begin that by welcoming the traitor's first."

The door behind them flew open and the guards shoved in the heard of black blazer mayors and governors to the hard floor. They panicked, as they saw who and what were in front of them. Flabbergasted, Reginald yelled: "This is downright outrageous! What do you want from us!?"

Sebastian walked over intimidatingly yet with a cocky grin as he bent down to squeeze Reginald's cheeks as the others watched in horror.

"What's outrageous, is that one of you knows something the others don't. I won't sugar coat this you lot, but you're all going to die down here," Sebastian said as Albert and Longstaff were taken back from the sudden declaration. The men were all begging for their lives, pleading with their captain for anything that they thought could be used as a bargaining trip, but nothing worked. Sebastian didn't hear in the little skirmish what he wanted to hear, so he took his sword out and they fell silent as the distinct sound of metal brushing against the scabbard rang through the dungeon.

"Reginald, you're up first," Sebastian said, enticing the bruised mayor to stand up as he brought the blade nearer his chest. He walked him closer to the fire that seemed to burn forever, the flames continuously raging so high they brushed the stone ceiling, leaving a black patch.

"The trial of judgement is now in session! Speak your final words, only if they are truth to the word of Oki, you will have a less severe punishment. For we are the deciders, and Oki's plan will not be faltered," Klaus proclaimed. He brought his head down, along with the other three men in drab robes and began to sing hymn. The hymn itself was of a dialect no one could make out. Albert could make out some words from his teaching through scripture reading he practised at the church, but this was highly difficult to master. The hymn bounced off of every wall as Reginald faced the sword.

"You'd best come clean. You were always a troublemaker to my father, but I have reason to believe that he is the instigator of this plot. Care to elaborate while you're on borrowed time, Reginald?" Sebastian warned.

"Please, your father was a swine. And I don't care if that's the last time I ever talk about your father, or you for that matter. He couldn't do anything without being the middle man. In the end, he took the easy way out, Sebastian. He took his ball and ran, leaving you in the inevitable pit you've dug yourself into."

"Is that so? You're about to miss seeing something far greater than anyone before me. With this in place, pirates will be the dominant force of the sea. Are you willing to throw all that pleasure and riches overboard like this?"

"I am, Sebastian. This dream is going to sink harder than any vessel pirates have come across. You're playing make-believe with real world consequences. You're no saviour, you're just another Norton. Encapsulated by his own rhetoric." As the two went on, Longstaff was uncomfortable. It was never his position to say anything usually but now that he was in a position higher than he ever believed he could achieve drove him mad. Sebastian was becoming something like Edward had envisioned. However, the threat of death in sacred ground was frightening. Longstaff wanted to be proven right by his own instinct that Sebastian wouldn't go down a mad path but what came next was the deciding factor.

"I'll give you one last chance, Reginald. Where is my father and are there anymore of you on the islands?" Sebastian asked, pushing the blade slightly more into Reginald's chest making him squint. The fear subsided and Reginald seemed completely at ease, relaxing his body until he spoke again. "Do you know what the difference is between you and Norton? You're going to die much worse than what I put him through," Sebastian's anger was almost about to boil over, "Drink up me harties, yo-"

Just as Sebastian was about to swing the blade with a mighty force, Longstaff's voice cried out.

"No!" Sebastian and Reginald turned, their faces remaining still in their emotions.

"You are better than this, Sebastian!"

"Do you have anything to add to his testimony, Longstaff?" Sebastian asked. That calm yet sinister tone chilled the plump mayor to his core but it was either make or break time. Longstaff couldn't live with himself if he didn't let anything of note under the goddess's watchful eye be heard now.

The truth will set you free, he thought.

"Edward came to me about the plan, Sebastian. It wasn't of malicious intent it was a safety precaution. I told him that any slip up will trigger something like this. Robertson acted on his own and that's just one. You can't pin blame to everyone when things go wrong."

"You knew?" Sebastian asked.

"I knew but I refused to take part."

"Did my father say anything that would trigger such a fast escape?"

"No, captain."

"Very well. Thank you for sharing. It's good to hear. Like you said, there's always one bad apple. But you've just proven Longstaff, that sometimes, there's only one good apple." Sebastian drove his cutlass into Reginald's gut, the squelching noise rang into the ears of everyone inside the tomb. Klaus and the congregation rose their voices louder as the blade was pierced in and Albert turned away to avoid the sight of blood, pulling a handful of his robes across his mouth. Reginald gripped Sebastian tight as his body went further across the blade. The noises Reginald made were small seeping sounds, he hid the pain of death in front of his executor as they shared one more look with each other.

"You...worst...mistake we ever made," Reginald said with gritted teeth, "Davy Jones has a special...place...for you."

Sebastian grinned again as his fiery eyes watched the life slip away from Reginald. But before the soul left his body and the limbs went limp, Sebastian swung the mayor around and the body slid out from the blade and into large fire bowl. Reginald was engulfed in flame to which there was no escape, his final sound was two small shrieks before the life was fizzled from existence and the smell of burning flesh rose to the top, sweeping down onto the inhabitants below. Klaus and his congregation finished the hymn as the place fell silent once more.

"The first son of deception has been cast out. The goddess Oki, bounds him to eternal damnation beneath the sea. His ashes will scatter and so will his soul, leaving him separated from her mighty life. A life, that I now champion. If you wish to continue down his path, you too will meet the same fate, understand?" Sebastian recited towards the group of captives. They all nodded, some willing to accept that death by sword and flame was not the way to go out, "If you wish to live and succeed on these islands, you will work as slaves until your punishment I feel has been served. Until then, you will remain in here, to see the power of our lord." Sebastian then stared straight into Longstaff's eyes, casting doubt at the mayor from across the dungeon as he walked over, putting away his cutlass.

"I think that's the first time I've seen you step up your game, Longstaff," The mayor was surprised at this sudden shift in tone, "Good work. I knew the role of quartermaster could be filled. I'll see you back at the castle." Longstaff couldn't believe what had just happened. He had just obtained the second highest command of the islands. Lacroix and Albert congratulated him but his focus was all over the place. He felt defeated, honoured and lost all at the same time. No words. Longstaff simply followed his men up through the staircase. The mayors and governors were all left inside, terrified and hot from the enormous flame that sat in the middle of the dungeon. Scared as they just sat there, hopeless, watching the body of Reginald, who's skin was burning away and who's bones would forever be trapped in the goddess Oki's eternal flame of damnation.

CHAPTER 20

BOATS OF BARGAIN

President Lincoln read the letter in droning silence in the oval office. Unable to fathom as to why or how this could be possible. The tide had definitely turned in his favour, yet he was still weary of the trajectory of sudden change. The new year rang true and his second term would soon be written in writing, but the shadow of war was far from over. A far cry from what his projectionists and generals had believed. The union had outflanked the confederacy at every possible angle, reducing their numbers and strongholds, but a strategic retreat was not something on the cards. The president double checked it, reading from it again but the initial reaction to it was to remain. Signed by Confederate general, Robert E.Lee, the general details that the confederacy was now in the hands of the I.I.C. Men, weapons and resources were to be sailed across to the mainland of Cuba, where they were to be embraced through similar ideology. *A bold statement, considering they're pirates*, Lincoln thought, but one thing the general included was the conditions of his formal surrender. A valuable asset indeed, one that could reduce the president's headache, but how valid could this information be given that the retreat seems premeditated? Lincoln could not waste time and had to get to the bottom of this. It would be his first official duty of his second term, with the war still following him, his first address would be shaped by what is to come.

As Sebastian and his group walked their way back to the castle, a very unnerving tension was felt by two of his men. Death lingered, the smell of the dungeon clung on to the garbs of the men. Everyone now knew why Klaus had such a distinct smell in his robes. Lacroix was no stranger to the barbarity of killing, Klaus had seen it first hand in the very office that he could once again walk in without any troubles, for Albert and Mayor Longstaff, it was difficult. Although Albert faired better, as he knew the importance of sacrifice was in his religious scripts, contrived and up to debate as they were, he saw it as a last result measure. Longstaff was still in a state of shock he couldn't shake. Far be it from him to criticize the captain, but now he was in earshot from Sebastian. As quartermaster, he could do just that, even if he was for most occasions, when it came to verbal conflict, a recluse. How much his word will matter in Sebastian's handling of the islands were yet to be heard. As the group returned up the sandy stone coloured stairs to the castles front door, a messenger was seen sprinting towards the group, with a spyglass in hand.

"Captain! You better come with me quick!" The spring-heeled teen cried as he made it to the group.

"What is it, messenger?" Sebastian asked.

"Boats, sir. Loads of them, coming from the north."

"English?"

"No, sir. It appears to be American, judging by the flag they're flying. I've alerted the patrol near the Maelstrom to reach the north banks," the messenger said.

"Very good. I'll need you now to divert any citizens away from the north bank. We don't want this to become tomorrow's headline."

"Yes sir!" The messenger ran down the steps to complete his task while Sebastian gave orders to his entourage.

"General, you're with me. Klaus, you and Longstaff take residence in my quarters until I return and Albert, return to the church, we need to keep the hearts and minds happy as the situation unfolds in front of us."

"Understood, captain. Her gracefulness, Oki, shines upon us. Pray they bring good fortune," Albert said as he hurried away down back down the stairs. Longstaff wondered what he would be doing with Klaus for the time being, but he dare not speak and walked in the shadow of the tall Klaus. Sebastian and Lacroix ran to the north side of the castle, where they would see out to the sea amongst the tall hillside where it presided over. Lacroix drew his small spyglass and observed the sea, there was no large arsenal, only passenger boats, dozens of them, filled with crates of what looked to be filled with supplies and weaponry. The starred blue 'X' of the confederacy all flew from their sterns and Lacroix wondered what this large convoy could be.

"They carry rifles, but are shy to brandish them. And they don't look confident," he observed.

"What could that mean? Who are they? Do you know?" Sebastian asked.

"One side of the war up in north, captain. They fight for the south, it could be a retreat. Although, I've heard from sources as to what the southerners represent in the conflict. They're patriots, beliefs similar to ours. It might be worth bringing them to the negotiation table, perhaps?"

Sebastian pondered this thought. An integration to bolster the military force that would soon preside over the Maelstrom seemed almost like a perfect hand out to him. Indeed, it was one idea to take.

As the two arrived with arms surrounding the northern banks of the island, all drawing their out dated rifles and pistols at the arriving boats, the Confederate soldiers soon began to disembark their vessels. Sebastian and Lacroix stood feared and ready in case of disruption or a sudden attack, but the sliders arriving all carried looks of comfort as they reached unfamiliar shores. A general, brandishing a ten gallon hat with a sword of arms presented himself forward to Sebastian. Standing at attention and giving a friendly salute, the general brought forward a message in which Lacroix took to read first. Surprised and with his eyebrows raised, he handed the message over to Sebastian to read.

> *To the esteemed leader of the Caribbean islands.*
>
> *Our cause for our country is under considerable turmoil. Our prospects for a greater confederacy of states has been scrutinized heavily by the sitting president and northern union states. We are currently outflanked and our losses have been many. That is why we have made the honourable decision of laying are arms to the cause of the islands and betterment of our soldiers service to you. At which time this letter makes it to you, I have surrendered myself onto the union forces to take the brunt of*

punishment that is surely in my favour. The war will conclude with my surrender. Use what we have. Enrich your islands with my men's service which is undeniable of question.

Signed,

General Robert E. Lee of the confederate states of America.

Sebastian looked the general up and down, curious as to the validity of this written testimony. They seemed wounded, beaten enough to be asking for help. General Lacroix's thought seemed to be proven right, only one thing was left to ask.

"Are you General Robert E.Lee?"

"No, sir. Colonel Saxton, I have presided over the retreat of the confederate forces behind me. In doing so, which ever the outcome of our status should be on these islands, I know my mission was a success. We all will relinquish our titles effective immediately."

"Is that so? Perhaps we can discuss this over some rum? Maybe we could use some more military genius here," Sebastian proposed, leaving Lacroix somewhat intimidated by the prospect of bringing outsiders to the table.

Back inside the captain's quarters of the castle, Longstaff sat by the wall, gazing at the captain's desk, knowing that he would stood by that chair at all times from now on. Every detail of every matter at hand would have to be observed by him to the highest degree so there was not to be any slip ups. The pressure was mounting and so was the sweat dripping from Longstaff's brow which he patted away with his handkerchief. In a similar way, Klaus was observing Longstaff, understanding the weight of the role, knowing what the job may bring.

"Nervous?" Klaus said, breaking the uneasy tension.

"You have no idea. I don't understand why it had to be me. I'm not prepared for this in any way," Longstaff said, holding in his nervous gasping for air.

"If it helps, from my perspective, the role of quartermaster now will only be for conciliation, not by a second in command should the captain not be around."

"What do you mean?" Longstaff asked.

"Captain Teach wishes to do away with traitors, correct? Well, think how easy it would be on us and the people if the roles of governors and mayor's would be sorted in a way that is hassle free?" Longstaff looked at him with confusion yet striking a shocked look as he came to the realisation.

"What? He's not seriously suggesting installing puppets to his cause is he?"

"Rourke Renfold is intended to be the governor of Jamaica once he returns from England. We will hold elections, yes, but he'll have the final say," Klaus cleared up.

"B-but that undermines everything we've built. Do we really want to go back to the days where we were fighting for our lives like stray dogs with scurvy!?"

"The tradition is there Mr Longstaff, we're just eliminating any unnecessary obstacles. We were loosing our faith and now we will reclaim it."

"I will have serious words about this-"

"I wouldn't do that if I were you. You may be the quartermaster now, but that doesn't mean you'll be immune from any harsh punishment should your tongue spit something he doesn't want to here," Longstaff slumped back down against the wall, "Why do you think he chose you? Because you spoke up? Please, Longstaff. Your role is based on how much Sebastian spoke of you. He told me in meetings that he saw you as an uncle. Someone to trust, who embodied the traditions of old. These islands will be going through a remarkable change in a matter of days. Be that shoulder for him. Don't get in his way." The two ended their conversation on a harrowing note, one Longstaff could not shake as they both heard the door being opened. Sebastian, Lacroix and Saxton entered with Klaus and Longstaff beaming a look of uneasiness at Saxton.

"Do not threat, for he is of no threat...yet. Gentlemen, this Colonel Saxton of the confederate states of America. I have brought him here as he may be of some use to us," Sebastian said, introducing the man who donned a neatly trimmed beard and a cream coloured uniform.

"Eh, I don't think I can be too much of a service, Captain Teach. I'm only following through on orders from my former superior," Saxton reiterated.

"But you hold plenty of strategic knowledge of the north of us. Is this all that there was left?" Sebastian asked.

"Those men were the ones who got away and didn't surrender, the rest were dead on the battlefield. There used to be thousands of us. We managed to escape along the coast of Florida."

"Are the union aware of your position?" Klaus asked.

"Not to my knowledge, sir."

"And what would happen if they were to find you hiding in our lands?" Sebastian pressed.

"Knowing the so-called "president", he would most likely send the Pinkerton forces after us. Hold us trial, much like the same fate as my commanding officer who wrote you the letter."

"Captain, if I can make a suggestion? With the weapons they've brought to us, it wouldn't be a bad idea to let the colonel here teach a few things to our military. Overseen by me of course, we would have a new regiment under our wing, perhaps even a bold statement as crew on board the Maelstrom?" Lacroix said in a snivelling tone, threatened still by the American officer. Sebastian pictured them onboard the soon to be finished megaship, newly obtained soldiers to fight for a cause they see greatly than that of the country they abandoned. It was like printing his own money.

"Indeed, it could. How are you with slave labourers?" Sebastian asked.

"Ho ho, you're asking the right man, captain," Saxton chuckled, "My family owned a plantation. Seized of course, but I know the spoils of an obedient worker."

"We will need every worker on board that ship once it is complete. Our slaves and volunteers need to be trained as an entry fee for their rewards I promised them. Can it be done in a month's time if I were to give you that period?"

"I've trained privates while within close range to a battlefield before, I'm sure I can do it while on sandy shores, captain," Saxton answered with confidence.

"Very well, on behalf of the I.I.C and it's accompanying bodies, I welcome you Saxton and your confederate troops to our islands. They must integrate to our rules and customs which Klaus will happily explain to you."

"I'm still fuzzy on that, actually. How did pirates become civilized enough to have rules?" Saxton's questions made the tension rise a level or two, but Sebastian handled the question with poised confidence.

"My great grandfather understood that stability was needed in order for us to combat our foes. We still have that...nature if you will. We just now have P's and Q's," Sebastian laughed, making Saxton chuckle. Klaus, Lacroix and Longstaff all frowned collectively.

"Then may I say captain," Saxton extended his hand out for a handshake to which Sebastian complemented the gesture, "I won't let you down and thank you again for having us."

"It is our pleasure. Anybody who helps the I.I.C's cause is a welcome addition to our growing list of clients." The door came open as soon as the two released their grip, in walked in Renfold who continued to adjust his frilly cravat and sleeves.

"Rourke! At last you return! We have big news unfolding here," Sebastian said in delight, eager to share.

"I can see by how crowded it is in here. Captain, the return of Robertson's trader went well as you can expect."

"Kicking and screaming?"

"They didn't know what to do with him," Rourke laughed, "I'm surprised that they didn't throw him back in the water he was that scared!" As the two laughed away, Saxton stood frozen, looking at Rourke with sharp eyes and hiding his disdain. He curiously asked: "Let me guess, personal servant?"

"Far from it! Saxton this is Rourke Renfold, dutiful first man for over forty years and officially the new governor of Jamaica!"

"Very nice to meet you, Mr...?"

"Colonel William B. Saxton of the confederacy," the two shook hands but Saxton wasn't putting much effort into his grip this time, "How does a Negro attain such a status like this?" He asked calmly.

"It was the captain's family that brought me in. My family defied the great law that presided over captain Burchill, Sebastian's father took pity on me and I've been here since. Although, I wish the circumstances of Edward weren't so...doesn't matter."

"Rourke here will accompany you back to the beaches, Colonel. He'll escort you and your men to the west side of here, near the construction of the Maelstrom. We have slave huts that your men will rest in-"

"We'll do no such thing. I'd rather confide myself to the boat I turned up in, Captain. You must understand where I'm coming from," Saxton interrupted.

"Well you're hear now, Saxton and you will reside there until you've proven your word. Hard as it is, you're technically a slave here. Your contribution is duty bound to the nature of your arrival. I thought a new identity away from prosecution was what you wanted?" Saxton was taken aback but he knew he had to cooperate with his new superior. "You'll do as I say, or suffer worse from my blade, it's your choice."

Wanting the tension to be over with, Rourke put himself forward again as he surveyed everyone's faces.

"I'll take the lead now Mr Saxton. It is not far," Rourke said politely. Saxton shrugged his shoulders and adjusted his hat as the two walked out from the quarters.

"Colonel, no more," Lacroix said with slight glee.

"Our force in the slaves has increased and so has our arsenal. Those weapons better not be broken. General, I'll need your men to inspect the rifles and pistols, we don't want to risk it should they preside inside the Maelstrom."

"My pleasure, Captain," Lacroix said.

"Sebastian, may I have moment with you in private?" Longstaff asked as he and Klaus shared a brief glance at one another.

"Certainly. Leave us," Sebastian ordered and the two walked out from quarters. Sebastian brought himself over to the desk where rested in his chair again.

"Sebastian, Klaus has informed me of this new governing plan. What is this? This not what the people wanted."

"Longstaff, they do not know any better. Most people on these islands only care for me anyway. All they do is keep track of the islands for me, they're baby sitters essentially."

"If people get word of this-"

"If people get word it'll be rumour and rumour alone," Sebastian raised his voice, "I have a new system in place to make sure all the bodies of island governors are well recorded from now on to avoid another little band of renegades selling us out. No one will back stab the captain's place again and it certainly wasn't going to start with my father giving the killing blow."

"Why Edward wanted to do that I don't know, but we must not go down a path we won't be able to dig ourselves out of," Longstaff warned.

"We have plenty treasure to keep us going for a long time, Longstaff. That treasure is what turned others who knew of its existence to turn on the islands. Let me ask you something, what if we had more to control our enemies for good?" The captain pondered.

"More?"

"More! Mr Saxton may hold some information about the states above that we could leverage. Imagine the Maelstrom conquering them as they struggle to maintain their men." Longstaff words would only be background noise as Sebastian's mind drifted into the sea of planning.

"Sebastian, we couldn't possibly. We're but small islands and America is right on our doorstep unlike Britain."

"We have an entrance way. We have an army soon to be trained even better in the role of battle. We have more might than they ever could! I must see him," Sebastian quickly got pen to paper and began to write quickly. Longstaff could only frown as he stood there like a piece of the furniture.

Blending into the background, he stood solemnly as he watched the once respected young boy transform into a bloodthirsty leader. Change was coming, but it wasn't the type he expected to be by the drawing board watching it unfold before his very eyes.

In amongst one of the broken down shells of shipwrecked boats, anchored down to the beach, Claude Boggs lied in his hammock, snoring into the early hours of the night next to the several empty bottles that rolled back and forth with every wave that hit. A knock at his cabin door didn't disturb him, which only led to it being knocked harder. Even harder a third time, it did not budge the ballooned prospector until a swift kick brought the sounds of the waves and the cold winds inside, making Boggs roll out in shock. Grunting in pain and struggling to stand, Claude blurted:

"What in Blackbeard's beard is this!?" The figure could only be slightly made out by the one candle resting on a crate. The cowboy hat and jingle of the man's boots made, Claude realise who it is, it was the bounty hunter.

"Ugh! Do you have to kick me door in like that?"

"Is the captain's father on his way to D.C?" He asked in grizzled voice.

"He's paid and on his way. Your cuts over there, look," Boggs pointed to the small chair sitting in the corner. The bounty hunter took the bag and emptied it on the floor and what fell out was not gold.

"So where is it?"

"What do you mean ya daft beggar, it's right there! You're looking at it!" Boggs iterated. The bronze coins and small smattering of silver didn't impress the masked collector.

"You best cough up the gold now before things become heated, fat boy." Claude didn't take kindly to the remark about his size. With an incredible show of speed, Boggs got to his feet and hurled one of the bottles that were scattered beneath his hammock, smashing into pieces as the bounty hunter ducked. As he came up, he drew his six shooter while Boggs grabbed his cutlass. This made Boggs outstretch his arms, standing like a statue as the gun was pointed squarely at his gut.

"I wonder if you'll pop like a balloon if I pull the trigger? I'm on a tight schedule here sailor, why don't you spill your guts before I do." The bounty hunter clocked back the trigger, showing that he was serious. Claude dropped the sword and brought out the real bag of gold from inside his hammock, which was underneath him the whole time. The big man peaked inside again, seeing his fortune before tying it back up and chucking it across in the middle of the hunters feet.

"Do you have to report back now?" Claude asked in defeat.

"Yeah. Something's coming for these islands and I don't want no part of it. At least I know my clients informant is on the way."

"Ya know, I can get you up and out of here in time. You'll take as much time as Mr Teach did through my boats. For a small donation that is," Claude said, conjuring up the deal miraculously. The hunter couldn't take any more of the hulking masses grovelling, so in an act of begrudging acceptance, he took one gold coin and dropped it amongst the bronze and silver.

"Consider it paid. Get it ready now," the hunter demanded as he turned to walk out the door before Claude stopped him with another question.

"Is it fun?"

"What? The job?"

"No, killing two birds with one stone? I'll be gone before it happens, but I'd be surprised if you bring down two nations over a little thing like fools gold?" Claude wondered. The hunter turned back around to face out of the murky cabin while he lingered on that thought.

"I'd be surprised if I didn't."

CHAPTER 21

RECONSTRUCTION

President Lincoln waited with anguish for the arrival of his briefing party. The table he sat at the head at was long and narrow and the small room was dark with its gothic furniture. He braced for the interaction, hoping that this wasn't another gamble where the safety of his country was at stake. He took the letter of Robert E. Lee serious enough to throw a meeting together but that didn't stop his paranoia. Suddenly a light tap came at the door, at which Lincoln directs the traffic inward of the office. In stepped his newly appointed Vice President, Andrew Johnson. His frown questioning the reasoning for being here at such short notice and of the matter at hand.

"Sir, you cannot be serious," Johnson whispered.

"We'll take what he has to say with a grain of salt but if this is an end in sight, I will gladly take that path to it," Lincoln said, his hands clutched together as the pressed against his chin.

"What exactly did the letter read?"

"You'll know soon enough, Mr Johnson. It's validity will be tested in a matter of moments." The prospect of the war ending clung into the room like the dimly lit chandelier above the outstretched table. As the doors came open again, Lincoln's closest men came in side, all collectively dressed except for one man. Formidable in presence and stature with his dark blue uniform and cutlass bared across his left leg, he stood to attention and gave the president a hard salute.

"At ease, Grant," The president said.

"Sir. This sounded urgent but I'd be really eager to share with you some details about the south." "That won't be necessary, General. You see, that's why I've gathered you all here tonight, because I have received a message that will tip the balance of how this war will unfortunately prolong," Lincoln explained.

"What do you mean by that, sir?" Grant asked.

"Well Uslyess, if you turn around you'll understand why." General Grant turned sharply until his eyes were met with his adversary, matching his beard style but with grey colour and a cream uniform, General Robert E. Lee stood before him. No words left the two's mouth as the intensity of their stares was all that was needed to get the negotiations under way.

"Gentlemen, let us not bring the bloodshed to the negotiation table. General Grant, you will sit opposite me, Mr Lee, you will stay there. Shut the doors if you please," Lincoln ordered and the doors were closed behind the two men by the servant. Grant didn't take his eyes off of Lee even when taking his seat next to the president, vice president Johnson studies the room and saw the uncomfortable atmosphere that had now set inside.

"Now. Gentlemen, it is with great pleasure that I inform you that the war has finished. Only on our sovereign soil. Mr Lee here is here as a plaintiff for the confederacy, isn't that right Mr. Lee?" "Indeed, Mr President," Lee addressed formally, "I have done the correct thing. Through my guise of formal surrender on behalf of my cause, the rest of the army has begun a full retreat to the Caribbean islands of the I.I.C."

"They've what!?" Grant exclaimed, nearly jutting out from his seat as Johnson restrained him, "The I.I.C are nothing but pirates! They'll take up anyone who adheres to their barbaric nature! You've just handed them a ton of manpower!"

"We have won the war at home, General, but our efforts to suppress the enemy has unfortunately slipped into unknown territory. Worse still is they have a working relationship with Mexico. Meaning that, if they could, make way into the entrance of our country through the souther border," Lincoln said. The men at the table all looked taken back, the struggle for financial stability after the war was worrying.

"It may not be as gloomy as we thought though. You see, I had eyes and ears inside the islands for a while and those eyes and ears secured the US something very valuable, who ever the victor may be." Lee drew from his pocket a piece of paper that was torn slightly and unravelled it amongst the eyes of the board room. The corners of the page had to be held down as they turned up but what was written was baffling it's audience. Eventually, the paper is examined by both the vice and president, they marvelled at it, Lincoln had the right idea in mind to what it could be used for as he saw the signature on the bottom.

"This will be hard for the people to rally behind, Mr Lee. You must understand that by taking this action we could lose way more than what we put in towards it."

"At the end of the day Mr Lincoln, it's evidence of a surrender. Consider it the long game. Passionate men from both north and south will risk everything for the country at the end of the day. At least I can say that when I see it," Lee said with slight disdain.

"I have taken plenty of measurements to make sure your ideals were stamped out, Mr Lee. Do not make me do that to your proposed privileges at the cost of surrender," Lincoln said, raising his voice.

"Let me see this," Grant said, grabbing the paper. As he finished reading, Grant lowered it and studied his opponents face once more, locking eyes as the twos expressions mirrored each other. Both thinking alike, yet morally different that carried on through four years of conflict, "What did your men find there, exactly?" He asked.

"A man, you should say. Not a man of uniform, not a man of loyalty. Payment drew him to it. He's been amongst the pirates for a while now, surveying, interacting, relaying. What he's found is a shift in governing and it could pose a threat should it not be addressed. I'll be happy to disclose the measures of what he found there, if my demands are met. It'll only bring greater meaning to that letter, which he secured from the captain himself," Lee continued. The bargain was there on the table. Not in black and white, yet. However from his subjects around the table, Lincoln had the final say.

"Very well. We will pay your ransom and have it submitted in writing. Now Mr Lee, this government would like to know what your man found. And if what I hear is of merit, then this plan better be worth it," Lincoln sternly said.

"Thank you...Mr President."

Through a desolate street along the coastline of Puerto Rico, one lone tavern was lit in the late hours of the night. It attracted the attention of a man draped in a hooded cloak while his sandals scraped and flopped along the stone road. As he approached the door of the tavern he knocked twice, paused, then knocked three times, hoping that the people inside would let him in from the coded knock. His wish was granted when the locks began to click and turn but only a slither of the door came open and a man with the body density of a stick stared down at him, almost looking like he could fit through the ajar door.

"You for the meeting?" He asked.

"Yes. On behalf of the instigator," the hooded man whispered.

"You have payment?"

"Is this enough?" The hooded man flashed five pieces of silver from his opened palm and it succeeded in getting him inside as the thin man, who was now revealed to be bare chested and covered in crude outline tattoos, closed the door. The hooded man however couldn't rest on that for long as he was now in the presence of a gathering which appeared to be hostile. Threatening looks and brandishing flintlocks gave the hooded man a lump in his throat as he stood upon ten men resting up against pillars, sat on chairs and standing behind a bar. One thing was for sure though, they were all part of a group, a light blue colour was slapped on over their garments, either as crude strokes or thin lines riding along the bends and bumps of their bodies. A flag was draped across the bar stand, also blue yet the face of what was on it was hard to make out as, what appeared to be a ring leader in a sea of scroungers and drunks, leaned over it, eyes fixed on the hooded man.

"Has everything been cleared by the payer?" The ragged man said as he hocked away a lump of spit from behind the counter.

"In full."

"And what exactly did he say?"

It's in full swing. The older Teach has escaped, all the governor's have been rounded up. Something is happening in the castle like you suspected," the hooded messenger clarified. The burly man relished in his presumptions, laughing quietly to himself until his joyous attitude rang round the tavern.

"You hear that boys!? I was right!," The rest of the men brought their fists to the air as the toasted the notion, "That family has been a curse onto these islands for generations. While the Teach's sit on a throne of reputation and admiration from the blind beggars of the streets, those like Burchill and Norton are destroyed from within because they don't like what they do! And we don't like what they do! It's now time that we put action into this!" The bar lit up in cheers. The hooded messenger began to slowly back away as the group tightened in around the bar counter, unfortunately he tan right back into the pencil thin guard at the door who didn't budge from his position. As the messenger looked back the guard only shook his head as the camaraderie increased in front of him and the ideal chatter of a revolution grew.

"I say we kick the door in and take everything, just like our fathers before us!" One man with a scarred eye chimed.

"Too risky. The military is growing everyday, if anything we need to go on the inside. A little bit of sabotage won't go a miss and let's face it, who's gonna care if one poor soul is in the line of fire?" The men jeered and chuckled away as the plan slowly came together.

"What say you Graham? What will our leader choose?" Another man asked the grizzly leader.

"Oh, both sound great, yet why not do it together? May we forget chaps, that the captain has granted handouts for those who help in his ship building project. What say we stow away and check it out for ourselves? Find it's weak points and then boom! His credibility is shot down, his head hung low and we step up?", Graham proposed. Some were weary as the planning involved would take countless days but after a slow build, the rebellious group nodded.

"I think that'll settle it, aye lads? All in favour say aye?" "Aye!" The men responded.

"Then it'll be! Now, for the fun part...planning!" Graham yelled, making the rest of the men sigh and moan, clearly showing the men's lack of ambition but keeping tight to their morals on the workings of the islands.

"Oh, don't get too excited will ya lads? Bloody hell, ya sound like you stuck your downstairs dignity in a clamshell! Besides,

I already have the first step all mapped out," the men leaned in at the prospect of not thinking of something themselves, "You see, message boy here brought the payment of the instigator to us, but he didn't say anything about what happens after the payment." The thin topless guard held the messenger by his head and brandished a knife to his throat, making his hood flop down to the side of his face. He wriggled and clawed for an escape but the malnourished looking guard was surprisingly quite strong.

"Oh yes, a little cause of fear on the streets will get the people rooting for us in no time lads. Boy! Get the rope!" Graham projected his order upwards to the upstairs room, "They want to install who Teach wants? Well we're going to install something that we want. Revolution."

CHAPTER 22

WORK IN PROGRESS

Mexico city was a buzz on a fine sunny morning. Banners of the countries colours as well as the official flag of the I.I.C were flown in accordance with the news of the allied islands arrival in the coming days. The docks continued to fill ships with workers of the Maelstrom over to the coast of Cuba and immigration boats from both islands arrived and departed. President Juárez knew the meeting in question from the captain of the I.I.C was of great importance. The urgency of his letter which arrived to him in the evening, seemed dramatic in it's writing. Juárez was compelled to be on hand as an ally when it came to dire predicaments, yet this came to him while everything was going smoothly. The trade between both factions helped each other greatly, there was no discourse in the Mexican rebuild, no quarrels among officers and feeling of the Mexican heritage being undermined. Juárez stood outside in the castle grounds, embracing it's botanical gardens which lined through the pathways and pillars, he took in deep breaths as he closed his eyes and warmed his face in the sun. Relaxing himself outside was the only way to quail his inner thoughts of his presidency. The thought of his preservation and place in history was dawning on him. He was the first president the country had outside the rule of a monarch, moving the country forward with a big step wit an ally on hand. *Did that seem necessary or cowardly?*, he thought. His thoughts then turned to the model of the US up north, his early meditations on the war and infighting is what brought him closer to the table with captain Teach. He compared both letters he received, one from Teach and the other from president Lincoln. Both urgent but very different. "Help us" Vs "Stay in your lane." Juárez held his faith tight, for he knew then that the choices he made were the right ones and the completion of the Maelstrom would certainly confirm that.

Amongst the islands of the Caribbean, a major shake-up took place in the week. The islands were in a flux of speeches and voting parades. Sebastian's selected few were basking in the glory of the crowds, all spewing a Teach positive rhetoric. Because of the tight nature of the voting process (seemingly to avoid disruption and favourably towards the captain) none were able to see the easily spotted similarities from Teach's chosen leaders. The men were all good at public speaking, all plucked from thin air, donning black frilly shirts, all with their beards neatly trimmed and tied with a black ribbon. The eyes, face and hair were different but the image was that of a smartly designed reconstruction, away from the secretive nature of the previous incumbents. One of them was already in place, a chosen power play that didn't require an election process. Rourke Renfold arrived inside his new office at the Jamaican embassy building. His eyes surveyed the office walls and then to the chair, where he once saw the bloodied remains of Mayor Robertson. He would now sit upon it, the newly crowned Mayor of Jamaica, embracing the position of power with wondrous lust as he gripped the arms of his chair tighter.

The positions would be met with a rounding success, all of the black ribbons would win in a landslide. Faceless puppets to the captain surrounded the islands and their actions would still be monitored by the black books, which they kept firmly by their sides like bibles. Sebastian revelled in the victory of his message as he watched the construction of the Maelstrom from the tip of the castle balcony where he gave his speech to curious onlookers. Unmatched power and size rested along the coastline, it was a behemoth. Comprised of hundreds of cannons along it's port and starboard, a towering scale of sail masts and a formidable angel of death carved into it's bow, it was almost ready for the inevitable battle it would be trialled for. Once he was done marvelling at the impressive sight he returned back downstairs as the sun began to set over the horizon. *It seems like the type of occasion to start drinking early*, he thought. Before the thought of cracking open that fine bottle of handmade wine, it was interrupted by a sudden womanly shriek coming from the front door. The frighteningly ear piercing scream caught the attention of the guards as they scrambled quickly through the halls. Upon entry into the manor, they saw a man in a hood facing down on the ground as the maid stood by with her hands covering her mouth. They took her aside and inspected the body, turning it over, they saw the man's face beaten to a pulp. He bled profusely from his mouth, his eyes rolled back and he was bare chested, but his body read a message which had been carved in cruelly for his onlookers. As the guards wiped away the smeared blood, on the man's chest it read: Bluebeard's know Blackbeard, Bluebeard's don't know the Teach's. Bluebeard's outweigh the black ribbons, they'll soon follow you no more.

"Bluebeard's?" A guard wondered. Before the guards even had time to understand the meaning of the message, their heads turned to see the captain stand above them on the staircase, visibly haunted by the man laying dead with nothing but a warning inscribed on his chest.

"Captain, orders?" Sebastian couldn't take his eyes off of the body, the small lifeless corpse had traumatized him in the wake of his political gloating. Fearful although trying to overcome it, Sebastian said: "Wine. Two bottles. My quarters. Now!" The guards scrambled as Sebastian ran back to his office, slamming the doors behind him as caught his breath.

"Quite the commotion down there," Klaus said, making Sebastian audibly jump with surprise.

"Do you have to stand there like a piece of the damn furniture!?"

"I'm sorry, captain. Maybe one could get accustomed to me in a cage like a parrot?" "Don't act smart! There was a murder at the door."

"Really? Remarkable," Sebastian glared at Klaus again, "I would've thought you'd be prepared for something like this?"

"I don't expect people dead at my door! I will have choice words with whoever was meant to be watching the door after this."

"Captain, there will be detractors in any regime. The goddess Oki may be on your side but she is not your protector, she is your watcher. That's what I'm here for."

"Then where were you? Instead of standing here like a lamp waiting for your bright spark of conversation to happen, why didn't you alert me?" Sebastian furiously asked.

"To see this. This selfish brand of narcissism that believes they can't be touched. You have got to take that away captain because if you don't, you'll wind up like Burchill shot dead on the floor. I watched that man walk right up those stairs without a slight flicker of thought given from your guards, now what does that tell you?" Sebastian didn't answer. The touch of pride prevented him from answering which would confirm Klaus's point. Instead he went over to the drinks cabinet, a tower of skulls and melted wax which formed into cup holders stood nightmarishly in the corner by the fireplace.

"I'll tell you what it means, it means that too much of a good thing is going to ruin these islands. You have to get these people riled up and in doing so, you make the military put their foot down hard. The rule of law is what will put everyone in line, captain," Klaus explained as his voice became more sinister.

"Where's the wine!?" Sebastian called out, hoping the men would cater to his whim.

"It is no good drinking away yourself from a slight hiccup. Oki has blessed us all in these lands. The sooner we strike the sooner we mean business-"

"I already have something in mind, Klaus! Now please quit your babbling. I'm two steps ahead," Sebastian said in frustration as he planted a glass down on his desk, sinking into his chair as he tilted his head back.

"The wine you requested, sir," a servant said, coming through the double doors in a rush. Sebastian was not impressed.

"Knock first next time, boy," Sebastian snapped.

"Yes of course, captain. Apologies," Sebastian wasted no time in unscrewing the cork from the black bottle as the servant retreated back outside. Klaus watched the wine pour into the goblet glass and the captain's eyes, thirsty and craving it's pleasures.

"See, a little bit of discipline goes a long way, like you said, Klaus. What comes next in terms of our grand reclaiming of these lands is mine to set in motion."

"Ah, to what, may I ask, will it begin?"

"It will begin once the last branch of the islands will be taken over. Then I can take command of the Maelstrom, there is not much left to construct, so it'll need it's rightful captain."

"And what of Juárez? Will he see fit the role once you have explained to him?" Klaus asked.

"The meeting at the end of the week was a long time coming. I shouldn't have prolonged a meeting with him, not after everything that's happened. Especially now with who ever these "Bluebeard's" are. I'll have you to send a message to the American men if you can?"

"Certainly, captain. What will that be?"

"Once the weapons training is completed, have Saxton and his men move in at the top of castle tower. They will be the new security around here. The lot here can patrol the grounds and they're sleeping privileges are revoked," Sebastian ordered.

"Very well, sir. And what will you have General Lacroix do once you've left for Mexico?" Klaus asked.

"He will be leaving with me. Him and his first lieutenant, Lieutenant Bloom. I believe Mexico could find him useful in a certain demographic that anxiously needs remodelling."

"Presidente!," A guard came crashing through the door of the office, "Presidente?" stunned to not find the president inside, the guard rushed to find his superior. Frantically sprinting down the corridors, he found no one, his other option had to look outside in the gardens. As the sun glistened, he squinted with his hand over his eyes, trying to find Juárez Thankfully, two guards arriving through the gates pointed him in the right direction and soon he rushed over to the castles gardens. The young man hesitated before wanting to rush over, he sensed that the president was in deep thought as his basked in the sun's rays. Steadying himself, the young man walked over as quietly as his plimsolls would over the slated rock.

"Presidente?" He called over quietly. President Juárez opened his eyes and slowly turned to hear from the man.

"Another letter has arrived to you from the president of America." At first, Juárez begins to shrug it off, smirking at that statement as if it were a joke, but the more he thought about it, the quicker that smirk changed into a frown.

"Are you the young man who came to me before?" Juárez asked.

"Sì, Presidente."

"Come here," Juárez said politely. The young man was more at ease as he came to the presidents side again.

"Tell me something, what do you make of the relationship between us and the pirates?"

"Presidente, I feel it has improved a lot of things. You of course set this up."

"Do you think it has ever soured us as a nation?"

"No, Presidente Who says such things?" The young man said with slight shock, Juárez hoped that he would.

"Me. Some thoughts come to me during the day. How can I be the one who saves our country if all I did was hand ourselves over to another? They came in good faith, yes, but who's to say that faith runs out?" This puzzled the young man. "You shouldn't worry about these things, if you mind me saying, Presidente, you take charge all the time here. Captain Teach, he is…young. He'll actually grow around your leadership if you think about it."

"Such a positive outlook you have," Juárez smiled, "As much as I would like that outlook, unfortunately, I have to play to convictions and doubt it. How do we not know it's a charade? The love my people give to them is accepting, they show more love to them than they do their own country."

"Presidente, no, they do not think this. They think highly of them because they are joined in our efforts. We both will be seen as such a force that even America will have to take notice," the young man spoke up with passion.

"Do you believe that?" Juárez asked.

"Sì! Indeed I do. I believe our people have more of a passion for this than the pirates do."

"What makes you say that?"

"Presidente, I hear rumours. I walk along our docks, hearing from people that come from there and our workers. They are, brash. Some talk about a group making their voices heard against the captain."

"Do they have a name?"

"It's a...Bluebeard's! They're small but very vocal. They, uh... don't like generations leading." The young man's words of rumours made Juárez think for a moment. An opportunity came, one that could thrust Juárez further in his reach of control.

"Interesting. Let me ask you, boy: If say, the Bluebeard's, made a compelling argument for the captain to not be in charge, would you listen to reason?"

"Presidente! No! Any action against the captain would be against you. You're allies after all," the young man protested.

"And if we weren't?" The question made the young man freeze in puzzlement until he finally came to.

"I...I'm not quite sure. I guess it wouldn't be in our best interests?"

"It could be. Trading is one thing but differences in culture is another. I knew this when I laid the deal out on the table to Teach. Perhaps we could quail what ails them, shall we say? Never over stepping but just a little nudge in the right direction. Open dialogue is what will benefit all of us. Maybe this is what he has requested this meeting for," Juárez thought.

"Do you think it could be serious for us?"

"From the way our people have interpreted it, possibly."

"Why are you so persistent to keep this war going? We've won! There's no point in extending this isolation for the southern states. Let's just go with what Lee is telling us-"

"We cannot let our guard down for one second, Edwin," Lincoln protested, "With both generals by our side the proposed effort against the I.I.C, should they become a threat, will be managed accordingly."

"This is in no way what we discussed before Lee arrived here by his own will the other day. What has he said that has invoked this? I already have people in departments breathing down each others necks cause they believe them to be traitors to the union, so what makes you think this is going to help? Need I remind you who your VP is?" Edwin argued, scratching his beard as his anxious worries fell on the presidents ears.

"This is in no way a direct war, Edwin. This is simply a matter of surveillance until we see there is no threat. Now, if you would kindly leave, Mr Lee and I have a meeting to have about the said topic, so please," Lincoln said waving his hand to the door of his office. Edwin shrugged himself back as he left unfulfilled. The president took the small amount of time before the generals arrival to pat his forehead and drink from his glass filled with water. As the glass sat back down on the table, the brief break the president had was gone as the doors opened and General Lee stepped forward with the door being pulled closed again.

"I must say you have a knack for not being tardy with your meeting times," Lincoln complimented the Confederate general.

"Thank you and thank you again for the accommodation, Mr President-"

"Right, flatteries over, who is this we've been waiting for anyway? My whole cabinet is in panic over this and I'm going with my gut on yours and Grants decisions here," Lincoln hurried.

"He's just being inspected at the door downstairs. Like how I was, only less forceful."

"Did you come here to propose a solution or to cast judgement on my hospitality?"

"Not at all, Mr President. I simply am a man accepting defeat and bringing to you the spoils of vital information should something come about these...pirate people. The war was good for nobody but I stood at my post. I think you'll need to continue at yours for the foreseeable future," Lee said.

Lincoln reclined back in his chair, slightly arching his back and wondered: "Tell me something, you knew your forces were being depleted by the day and yet you held off for as long as possible without the I.I.C, who I know would of happily helped you in this situation. Why didn't you ask them for help?"

"I could never allow a bunch of drunken buffoons take charge of me. They hold their own up in high regard with no sense of what a mirror is. We on the other hand, had morals, we had a chance."
"Yet, here you are," the president said bluntly.

"Only because my intel has found something that could be quite favourable to a national rebuild."

"So you would claim the spoils from your intel?"

"It is not a popularity contest, Mr president-"

"It certainly is in the long run. Grant's been considering, why can't you?" Lincoln asked.

"Sometimes the office makes people forget who they are, you're no exception," Lee suggested. "Then please explain to me how you would understand what I'm going through? This whole war is a calamity of both parties, I'm the one trying to stitch a wound while the blood is still pouring out of it!"

"And yet you vilify and degrade half of the lives of those who have survived said wounds. I know how your games play, Mr president, and they always end up with you looking good and your enemies banished." The two locked eyes, uncomfortably sitting across from one another before the door knocked. President Lincoln was relieved to not have this conversation continue. In stepped the doorman and he announced the arrival of the informant.

"Mr President, Mr Edward Teach Jr. Quartermaster to Captain Sebastian Teach."

In stepped Edward, presentable, upright, relived. It seemed to the other two men that the security pat down didn't deter the quartermaster's proud smile as he walked through the halls of the white house. Lee and Lincoln could see his admiration for the White House as his eyes continued to inspect every aspect of the room.

"Mr President, honour to meet another head of state. Mr Lee, glad to see you in person as well," Edward said shaking Lee's hand first in front of the bearded commander.

"I'm so glad nothing happened to you on your way out. I trust the bounty hunter did everything as planned?" Lee enquired.

"Without a single person knowing. The fat lard who gave me the boat will whip him and the others to shape-" The sound of wood screeching across the floorboards was heard as Lincoln got up from his chair in disbelief.

"You have got to be kidding? This was your informant?"

"Much like how I reached out to you, Mr Teach here reached out to me," Lee said.

"We've had a few message cycles going on since the previous captain, Mr president," Edward said.

"I'm not extending my gratitude, this much I can assure the both of you."

"You will, once I've told you about the treasure, Mr president," Edward said confidentially.

"Don't tell me we're going on a story or myth? There is no room for that after this war, it'll be catastrophic if I lead a battle on a silly pirate story!" Lincoln argued.

"It is true, sir. My son has only just learnt about it. He followed the trail and it led him to it. Perhaps this may show you how real it is." Edward took out the gold that he carried with him. One gold doubloon, old Spanish gold lost for centuries.

"My son has now followed the paths of the old "stories" as you call them. I held out hope that he would see it my way, but he took it by force. I do believe the rest of my colleagues have either been captured or killed. It's very likely that he is reshuffling the cabinet as we speak," Edward continued.

"You were second in command to him. What has he done since his ascension?" Lincoln questioned.

"Well like I said, he took his own path instead of mine and he has bolstered a stronger force that will easily set them up to be looked on in fear. Thankfully the I.I.C only has one partner and they're depleting their resources just to complete this new project."

"Mexico," Lincoln said with certainty.

"Correct. Mr president, leading my forces onto these islands is enough for the people to rally behind an invasion. All it takes is one spark, one discourse, two parties to set things up," Lee carried on the case.

"What is it exactly that they've made for this project?"

"A ship. The largest battleship imaginable. And trust me, that's disservice. It's barbaric but powerful. Slave forces and willing participants have nearly completed it's construction. You have that, you can control an entire coastline. Partner that with the treasure? Then you have yourself a worthy pay off," Edward explained. President Lincoln was wary about this, he read the quartermaster's face trying to see if what he was saying or that his actions was true.

"Answer me this, Mr Teach, why come to us now? Why build this up for months and months near when this weapon is close to being finished? Don't think I don't know about the British diplomats trying their hand with your colleagues? It sounds desperate now."

"Desperate times, Mr Lincoln. So are you in those times," Edward's words rang true in the president's ear, hurting his strong image yet he smiled as he uttered his rebuttal.

"Desperation doesn't lead me to abandon my family, Mr Teach. I'm aware of your family clan. A rather deadly name in the Caribbean. Is freedom really what you desire?" Lincoln wondered. Edward didn't want to answer the president's question, but he knew that honesty would be something Abe would hold in high regard. Edward laid the doubloon on the table and slid it down the shiny surface until the president caught it.

"This is all they care about. It always has been. If you can do anything, I want you to save my son. They're going to die out eventually. I'd much rather piracy be snuffed out quick rather let it be a lingering flame. You guarantee my son's safety, even if you have to do a public scrutiny, I'll offer you my life, Mr President. That boy is worth more than gold to me." Studying the coin, Lincoln was drawn to its ancient design and value that his eyes only met back with Edward once he hid it from sight, grasping it tightly in a fist.

"Mr Lee?"

"Yes, Mr president?"

"Who ever you relay your messages to in the rebellion group, tell them this: Make Captain Teach a priority to keep him alive at all cost once the match has been lit," General Lee nodded in accordance with the message, "Your son is going to put up a fight," Lincoln continued.

"He won't fight, Mr president," hesitancy kept the horrid description from Edwards lips until he finished with his warning, "He'll butcher."

CHAPTER 23

A MEETING IN MEXICO II

President Juárez stood firm in his place by the castle doors, not moving his body not his expression of a somewhat penultimate dread. However, he would bring a welcoming smile when Captain Teach would climb up the stairs through the presidential carriage that took him from the docks. His closest confidants stood by his side in formation while guards drew a line in the stone in front of them. The sun radiated that morning with not a cloud in the sky, a fitting day for the arrival of the Captain, as the president had hoped. Far to the west, Mexico city's docks were surrounded by cheers and admiration, as they saw The Devils Punchbowl make port. Spectators waved flags for both Mexico and the I.I.C, Sebastian waved his hands to the onlookers as the anchor was lowered and the docking board was placed. General Lacroix observed everywhere like a hawk as the black carriage pulled up in front of the main road, guards had to physically hold back a few people as they tried to barge their way through just to hold hands with the captain. It seemed strange to the general, this type of admiration would be seen most to that of their own leader, not a second party from the western islands. Perhaps it was a custom but Lacroix had to be open to every possibility even as the carriage door closed behind them as he sat besides Sebastian. The Captain, on the other hand, was enjoying the respect given from the Mexican people. Sebastian saw the love they gave to him, the very same enthusiasm that his own people back home gave. Everything was coming exactly as he hoped, the Maelstrom nearing completion, the force of the military expanding and men and women of his own wave length cornering the islands from those willing to exploit it.

The thoughts of his father never crossed his mind, it was as if he never existed anymore. Although, the thoughts could be weighed by down as the captain took out a small flask which carried his now favourite wine with him, with which he took a sharp swig as the bumps in the road rocked the carriage. Lacroix noticed this also, the young man's face was becoming more rosy like the wine. His cheeks were a bright pink, faded but noticeable as it was on Sebastian's nose. Sebastian smiled as he saw the general noticing his drink.

"Thirsty?" Sebastian said.

"Non, captain. I didn't think that this was an celebration?" Lacroix answered honestly.

"Indeed it is my fine French friend," Sebastian decreed, "Mexico's leader is about to be informed of a glorious passing. One that will shoot us into the stratosphere. The goddess Oki will shine brightly on all of us today."

"Do you think the people know what is going on?" Lacroix asked, twiddling with his beard.

"Perhaps. It has been months and months of waiting. Family men sailing over to us in the hopes of creating a great weapon that will keep us safe. I think they know."

The carriages scrolled across the gorgeous terrain until the last onlooker, who frantically ran to get a glimpse of his foreign ally couldn't catch up anymore. The blistering heat made the two men and their guards sweat from their brows, the black wooden walls of the carriage didn't help their situation. Very soon though, the castle was in sight and so was Juárez The carriage slowed down and the formation line in front of the Mexican leader began to march and form two lines for where the captain and his general could walk. Sebastian walked down to Juárez with a swagger that was most likely brought on by the wine while General Lacroix still arched his back with his locked hands, still observing the perimeters.

"Benito! Ha ha, wonderful to see you again!" Sebastian called halfway through the rows of guards. Juárez awkwardly smiled and nodded his head, waiting to speak until curious ears were muffled by the castle walls. Juárez darted his eyes to the doorman to get them inside immediately as he began to shuffle back closer to the door.

"I have got so much to tell you my good friend, you won't believe what we have done!" Sebastian sounded again, clasping his hand in Juárez's for a handshake.

"Sì, pleasure to have you again captain. And this is?"

"Oh! This is General Lacroix, first hand commander in my military," Sebastian brought his head down and close to Juárez as he whispered, "He's French." The laughter from his captain only made Lacroix shake his head even more while Juárez didn't know what to make of the captain's outlandish behaviour.

"Quite. Shall we proceed?" He asked.

"Oh yes! Massive news to tell you on the Maelstrom."

"Senior, is it finished already?"

"All to be revealed," Sebastian playful catered to Juárez's intrigue and excitement as he stepped in the castle first. Lacroix waved the president in before him, but this was only to pass on a whispered message to the doorman. The doorman's shock was quickly hushed as the French general placed a delightful payment into his hands which soon turned the disgusted guard around very sharpish. He closed the doors as the general walked inside, counted his earnings and rushed down to the gateway where he met the carriage driver.

"Senior! Bring the coach around the back. Presidents orders."

Inside, Lacroix followed the distant natter of political proceedings and admired the design and luxury of the castle. It's views of impossible landscape photographs and tapestry pieces, weaving the very history of Mexico in front of him made him relax a little. The focus of the chat from his captain was overly positive, glossing over the past couple of weeks of bloodshed in order to relax the already tense president. It bothered the French general somewhat. His senses were already heightened at the start of the voyage from the east coast, Lacroix never let his guard down even in friendly territory. But even so, the demeanour of the captain's briefings were becoming shorter than usual, often skipping over days and certain events when it wasn't deemed "Too necessary". Failings of a working mind or a stressed state of coping? Lacroix knew from the moment he stepped into the chamber below Blackbeard's statue that his position would be highly valuable in this new pirate world, but that didn't mean he had to like every aspect. He crept up the stairs slowly as the chatter came from the presidential suite, the voices of both the Mexican president and his Captain getting more acquainted as liquor was poured. Like a mini celebration of sorts, Lacroix would have to indulge in the pleasantries of politics the second he came through the door.

"That is absolutely marvellous, captain Teach!" Juárez said with relief as he held a bottle of tequila, ready to pour it into his favourite glass goblet, "This has come about quicker than I expected!"

"Absolutely! We managed to pick up more workers than we expected and what do you know, we finished two months earlier. Now, I do have to come clean with you Mr Juárez, I haven't been keeping my end of the bargain," Sebastian said.

"What? How so?"

"Well I wasn't in contact with you through many ups and downs. I thought it was quite ill-fitting for our relationship across the seas," Sebastian explained as Juárez endured the smell of wine on his breath.

"Not at all, this whole operation has been one long trust campaign. We in Mexico have seen nothing ill-fitting to our bond that we signed. But, if it's regional, you don't need to hide anything from me. What has happened exactly on the islands?"

Sebastian took another quick sip of his wine flask again as he walked sombrely over the plush couch, slowing his movements down like he was about to cry.

"There has been a... dramatic change in governing positions since we last spoke, Benito," Juárez filled his glass half way as he took to the opposite couch in the middle of the room, "My father is no longer quartermaster."

"For what reason?" He asked.

"Conspiracy to bewilder the finances of the I.I.C. If it were successful, I doubt the Maelstrom could've been completed, let alone set to sail. We wouldn't have survived. But, I took action and it has been dealt with," Sebastian continued.

"Diplomatically?" Juárez said taking a small sum from his goblet.

"In a pirate sort of way, yes," Sebastian broke the illusion of grief by laughing, showing what little remorse he had for those he had killed. Juárez's eyes flicked to General Lacroix from across the room as the both shared a worrisome look at the young leaders eerie tone. It all but confirmed to the Mexican president of what levels of diplomacy it was across the east to them.

"I am in no way disparaging your methods, captain Teach, but there must be some level of some democratic-"

"No. No there won't," the captain said defiantly, "My father betrayed me for money. To sell us off to that fat bitch back in Britain. Behind my back, just because I wasn't going the way he wanted me to. I hope you're not doing that."

"No, captain. We both agreed that we would both express ourselves freely within our dialogues. I share my sympathy with your situation but you must hold strong. Your people might become hostile." The words Juárez spoke were not reassuring to the young captain. He bit down and flexed the muscles in his jaw as he etched out another smile.

"Can you prove to me that you support this cause, Benito?" The Mexican raised his eyebrow.

"Prove? I thought our collation was more than enough. I traded workers, resources to get that ship built. Need I remind you of our own rebuilding here."

"I mean really prove it. Answer me this and you must be truthful: Have you had any contact from the Americans?" Sebastian asked.

"I have. The president has been sending me warnings about this collaboration. It's no doubt that they look at us as a threat as the war has ravaged them from the inside-" Juárez noticed how intent Sebastian's eyes were as they looked at him across the low coffee table. Waiting on every breath he said in hopes of catching him out, "No, no, no captain, I have never considered anything with President Lincoln. Mexico has a past with them," he scrambled.

"Yet you yourself have said you're still under reconstruction. It wouldn't be daft to presume your getting some imported goods over without me knowing," Sebastian speculated, throwing off the Mexican president and Lacroix as he blended more into the background.

"Captain, there's nothing like that at all. As you saw from your journey, the city hasn't changed much. We've put our faith into this bond we share. There's nothing else I can say to you-"

"Of course there isn't!" Sebastian slammed his fist onto the table, making the presentable glass set rattle and fall over. Juárez was horrified from his anger and again quickly looked to Lacroix for affirmation, Lacroix simply froze.

"I've been doing the goddess's work and I cannot have anymore bumps in the road! I think you need to be more transparent in your inner workings, Benito. It is the only way I think this can aid our relationship."

"I'm not paying for transparency. Where is this coming from? Whatever your father has done to you has obviously left you in this state. I will not be talked to like this by a child." Those words felt like a knife in Sebastian's chest. Hanging his head down with his hands pressed behind his head, his face turned read as he applied pressure. As Sebastian's fingers writhed through his hair, Juárez got up to pour more tequila into his goblet, this discussion would obviously need more to quail his paranoia. But as he stood left to the captain by the drinks table, he noticed something on Sebastian's neck. A thin blue vein which bulged and ran across the length of his neck. It made him hesitate for a moment before he continued the conversation but he signalled Lacroix to look for himself, but the general was still hesitant to move from the wall. Although, his hand was positioned perfectly to release his sickles from his shin guards, unbeknownst to Juárez

"Look, I apologize for that last comment, captain. But I must reassure you, there is nothing Mexico won't do to help you and our relationship," Juárez repeated. Sebastian brought his head back up straight, the red in his face now covered it entirely. He appeared to be more relaxed, his eyebrows rose and his jaw was loose but his eyes was shut as he took a breath in.

"Then resign," he breathed.

"Sorry?"

"Resign," Sebastian said opening his eyes, "That's how I know your serious." Juárez was beside himself.

"What difference will that make? Mexico will still go strong even without me and believe you me, if this got out that you had a hand in it, my people will not trust you ever again," Juárez barked.

"I won't have a hand in it," Sebastian got up and drew his sword out, pointing it at the president's throat,"I'll have this in it." Lacroix panicked and released his grip on his concealed weapon, finally pulled himself out from the wall to meet at Sebastian's side.

"Captain! Be rational, this will not help us!"

"Are you insane!?" Juárez shouted as he slumped as far back as he could into the couch.

"There's two ways to resign, Benito. By the hand that waves you out, or the blade that pierces you. Either way, I have a good replacement for you," Sebastian explained calmly with a slight smugness.

"Wait? You do? That's why we came here?" Lacroix asked puzzlingly.

"This was certainly an update," Juárez bitterly said.

"It is, isn't it? There's only one good option here, Benito…for you anyway. Progress has to move much quicker than usual, I'm just hear to fix the cogs in the machine," Sebastian said. Lacroix tried hard to think as the sweat from Juárez's brow started to drip.

"Before you make your answer heard, tell me something, general," Sebastian said turning his head to a worried Lacroix who try desperately to piece everything that was going on in his head, "Can you handle the role of President?" The shocking offer of leadership was enough to make Lacroix's lip tremble slightly as Juárez's expression of fear only got worse. This was not what the French general pictured nor was it the situation he'd hoped for upon entering the castle, but he knew he would have to answer and like the Mexican president, there was only one good option.

"Yes," he answered softly.

As the room went quiet, Juárez pushed the sword away from his face and quickly sprung onto Sebastian, dragging him over the opposing couch. The two men tumbled to the ground with a thud and rolled around, battling their way to the decorated blade. Lacroix watched as the two clawed at each others faces, never moving to intervene as both outcomes seemed to be up for grabs. Either way he remained silent as Juárez wrestled his way on top of Sebastian, hitting him a flurry of punches that connected with his nose making him bleed. Sebastian soon fought back, wrapping his hands around the Mexican leaders neck and began to squeeze. This allowed Sebastian to lift his upper half from the floor but Juárez retaliated with a head butt that released the captain's grip. Juárez quickly rolled off of him, thinking that he was dazed to reach for the blade but Sebastian grabbed his ankle and dragged him to the ground again. All the while, Lacroix backed away from the scene, retreating behind the couch that Juárez sat on. He stood there, still with dread as he watched the two duel on the floor. Sebastian now had hold of Juárez's long black hair and pressed his face onto the floor multiple times, it unfortunately only rattled the president as the carpet floor cushioned his blows. Juárez cracked the pirate leader with a quick elbow, the bone connecting straight into Sebastian's prominent cheek as he fell to the ground. Juárez soon was up again, standing to watch the pirate stagger up, using the wall for leverage as Sebastian's bloody hands smeared the walls. Both men eyed each other as their breaths were heavy, Sebastian suddenly ran a full charge to Juárez who sidestepped and the captain flipped over the couch, crashing down onto the coffee table, spilling the glass contents everywhere. It seemed to be the end of it, Juárez grabbed the sword while Sebastian laid there. Lacroix braced himself for an encounter as Juárez turned his attention to him, stalking him around the furniture.

"Wait, Monsieur, I'm on your side! We can negotiate here!"

"If it's on his behalf, I'll have no part in it cabron!" Juárez yelled.

"No, please! I had no idea of this! I wasn't even going to go through with whatever it was!" Lacroix tried to reason as he circled over to the second couch, "Just bring the sword down on him. I have the coach waiting round the back, it'll take him away discreetly."

"Wait, you planned something?" Juárez said shaking his head.

"I've noticed a pattern. The days have seen him change and I don't understand why. What was it you were pointing at-" Sebastian was heard struggling to shake off the impact of the table, slow grunting came with the accompanying sound of glass cracking. Tiny pieces stuck in his skin as he stood. Juárez and Lacroix watched the wounded animal crawl on all fours as he pushed himself up to face down Juárez again, only to then collapse back down face first in glass shards.

"Quick, Monsieur, just do it. It's the only way to save both of us!"

"And how do I not know you'll follow through on orders without him?" Juárez wondered as he lifted the sword slightly.

"Please, I don't want anything to do with this stinking country! All I want is a retirement. Pirates pocket as much as they want except the ones who protect them-"

"Silencio! I've had enough! There is no free thinking with this relationship," As Juárez finally let his fear turn to anger, Sebastian grabbed a broken goblet and struck into Juárez's leg. He shot out a sound of pain and Sebastian now had hold of his arms as the men did battle in a test of strength. Sebastian used his to push Benito away from the lounge and through the door leading to the President's suite. The lavish room filled with plump cushions and a high rose bed perfectly complimented the office room, although there would be no peacefully slumber here. Benito Juárez's wife had been hiding inside keeping her peace but as soon as the door came flying open, a scream left her and Lacroix finally took action. The sickle was drawn, the metal slid up from the shin protector and Lacroix held it to the woman's neck as he tightly held her hands.

"Let's let this play out," he whispered into her ear as her husband and the pirate Captain continued to battle. This would be quick though as Sebastian bit Juárez's hand which had hold of the sword. Sebastian got up and brought his boot down on Juárez's hand making him squeal as the sword was brought up from the ground and swung around to be brought down into the presidents chest. His wife screamed out a loud frightful "No!" as the captain's finishing blow left the sword standing inside a gushing wound. Benito's eyes gazed up into the ceiling with the little time he had left, struggling to lift himself free from the cold steel of the blade. Sebastian loomed large over the Mexican president as he stared into the man's soul which was about to leave his body.

"Your resignation has been accepted, Mr President," Sebastian said. Just then, Juárez gritted his teeth and grabbed hold of the captain's trouser leg, gripping the fabric in a closed fist as he muttered his final words.

"I'll never...resign." As his last act if defiance was heard, Benito Juárez took his final breath and fell limp beneath the might of the sword. His wife was released and she fell to his side as the blade was pulled away from his flesh, leaving a pool of blood to soak into the carpet. Sebastian's rageful stare burned into Lacroix, who still held his sickle, praying that another duel of fates wouldn't happen.

Sebastian walked over to him and faced him head on.

"Thanks for the help."

"Well, you had it under control, captain. I merely kept my peace and watched it play out," Lacroix lied.

"Hmm, good choice. Very good distraction by the way. Who on earth would not own an entire country?" Lacroix hid the true feelings of his increasing work behind a guffaw as he clicked the sickle back into his knee bracing, wiping away any suspicion.

"I'm sure you can handle it general. Mexico is now in our hands, with no trouble in the foreseeable future," Sebastian hoped as he turned to head out, "Oh one thing's on my mind, you bribed the guards didn't you? I take it that's why you took so long when arriving inside?" Sebastian wondered. Lacroix could only play into the captain's thought process to save his skin at this point.

"Ah you caught that did you? Oui, captain. And you'll be glad to know that your driver is around the back of the castle. In case, anything was to arise." Sebastian turned back around and patted Lacroix on his shoulder, accepting the events as he saw it, believing in the Frenchman's bluff.

"Well, President. Enjoy your spoils," Sebastian said, looking over his shoulders to the corpse of his predecessor and his mourning wife. As Sebastian left the room, Lacroix's sleazy eyes crossed over to the grieving widow. As she knelt with her hand in her husband's hand, the woman cast her eyes onto Lacroix, watching him pace slowly towards the door. The general would not be exiting the room, rather he would seal off the bedroom with himself and the widow locked away inside. The doors would close quietly before the wretched screams of female terror encompassed the office space with the blood of a former leader running under the thin gap.

Mayor Longstaff did not sleep at all that night. He resided at the captain's desk after everyone had departed for the night. Stationing himself by the fireplace which he stoked. A sense of isolation wrecked havoc in his thoughts for the past few days, like a leech it didn't let go, much like how he was with a bottle of rum. Even though he had a glass poured, it was only half drank, choosing to favour small sips that he would keep lingering on the tongue as he tried to think of something. It wouldn't be a plan of action but a plan of self-reflection. Had he done the right thing? If not, when would be the opportunity to do it? There was always going to be that wonderment if he should've left. Taken off like Sebastian's father in a moment of turmoil, perhaps it was the faces of his former colleagues that drove him to maddening self thought. People who he communicated with daily, now replaced by colour coded faces that drove every action the captain wanted without any hesitation. In essence, his role of quartermaster would be the one who could challenge his executive power, although Longstaff believed that he now would become obsolete at any given moment and be swept away in the dungeon below. His silence was then shattered as the doors to the captain's quarters flew open, with the young messenger boy returning in a hasty fashion, panting and excited about the news he was about to deliver.

"Quartermaster! I have urgent news that must make it to the captain!" Longstaff got up slowly from the chair, to tired to care to tired to explain.

"The captain isn't here, boy. But I'll take a message for when he returns from Mexico," Longstaff said without enthusiasm.

"Oh, it's going to be a great day when he hears this, sir. The Maelstrom is finished." That sentence forced Longstaff to open his eyes all the way in disbelief.

"It's finished?" Longstaff asked. It only dawned on the quartermaster that he hadn't moved in hours when the Maelstrom was in sight from the office window. He rushed over opening the two panels and beheld a specimen of destruction. The workmen were already drinking themselves to death after a job well done while the slaves were dutifully whipped back to their barracks, away from the camaraderie. Longstaff saw the vessel with worry as he cast doubt into the intentions. A simple defence fix? Or a weapon surely to be captained by the ever degrading mind of his captain. Time would tell if the bells would toll for Sebastian's enemies, but time would tell if Longstaff could cut the cord.

CHAPTER 24

SAIL AWAY

The American bounty hunter inspected the boat that was loaned to him and it ticked all the boxes, Strong, fast and durable. Payday was within his reach, all he had to do now was report back to D.C. For his journey, the sea would provide a misty outlook, flooded with a thick haze that would trouble the best navigator. The lanterns he lit on the bottom of the mast, near the wheel and at the bow all had this dull glow that did well to illuminate the important areas of the boat. It was only a small passenger boat but it was the best passenger boat that ol' Boggs could get a hold of. As the boat creaked along the shoreline, the bounty hunter heard the faint sound of running on sand. A crisp crunch came from the jogging man who wore a blue bandanna got closer and closer until it came to an abrupt stop at the stern of the boat.

"Message from the Bluebeard's, sir," The young man called out as he reclaimed his breath. The bounty hunter took slow steps over, making him wait until his upper frame leaned over the wooden edge.

"What is it? I'll be leaving in a matter of minutes, can't it wait?" He said.

"Sadly not. The Bluebeard's are about to start the reaping, sir. They want to know if there's any strong points you know about," the young man said.

"Tell that grimy son of a bitch that any slave checkpoints are crucial. You get them to revolt and they'll follow just about anything you do. They got nothing to loose, believe me, I know."

"But what about the captain? Is there any places that could be of importance, sir?" The young man chimed in quick as the hunter was about to leave.

"Get right up to the front door. See what happens," The bounty hunter said. He reeled in the anchor and the sails caught a breeze from the east, turning the ship in a thirty degree angle. As the ship pulled away, the young man, brandishing his colours waved to him and shouted a message of excitement.

"Thank you again sir! The revolution is going to be a success! Just you wait and see, we'll be free pirates again!" All the bounty hunter could do was look out to sea, steering the small boat up north to America as the fog made the boat vanish like it was a ghost. Before his body wasn't visible to the young man's eye, the hunter pulled out a pendant from underneath his shirt, gazing deeply at the haunting portrait of a distinguished woman on the left side while a doughy faced child was to the right. He knew what he had done in the last few days was crucial for him and for them, it would be the last time the hunter ever set foot outside of the American south again. Home was where his heart was.

CHAPTER 25

THE MAELSTROM LIVES

For a glorious day for the christening of the Maelstrom, the sky's were dark, the wind howled and the worry behind the Maelstroms ability to set sail was rampant. Soon after the captains return, the Bluebeard's began their sweeping effort to disrupt the occasion. Protests that had been in isolation for so long, had now come to fruition. The groups traditional look and message of a life without a governing body wasn't resonating with many people, but there was always that one person who took a great interest. Sebastian's troubles with the group would be blocked out thanks to the black bow politicians that wiped the floor in the snap elections. A fire was raging, but it was silenced for now. Even though he had a lack of interest in a small, rag tag group of extreme traditionalists, it would be foolish to not have them in the corner of your eye. He had already soothed the sting of his fathers betrayal he would hate to have a familiar scar open up at a time where his control had never looked greater. The familiar group presided by the door as Sebastian walked up to them, brandishing a sleeker look with new garments and trinkets around his neck. The goddess Oki was still the centre piece of the gold chains, hanging over his heart. It was very royal looking, the astonishing amount of gold that had been melted down was a sight to behold, the captain was presenting himself like a king. A far cry from what the original settlers had in mind when it came to their captain. Klaus, Longstaff and Pastor Albert also dressed formally, donning more suitable pirate-esque garments like the worn trench coat and boots. A style traditional buccaneers would have when sailing for adventure, now an attire of formal address. Sebastian wasted no time in protocol, barging past them all to open the doors while the three men hurried behind. The guards too were also scrambling to form the protective formation when the captain exits the castle, the change in behaviour was out in the open now and the looks from the guards was now one of confusion and worry. The wine had now become to hard to resist. Sebastian took a swig from his hidden flask the contents of the rich flavour, swishing them around in his mouth, making sure it stuck to his mouth longer as the slits of his teeth had now turned a burnt red. The occasion now felt like a hindrance rather than a national event to the captain, a dramatic change as the scowl on Sebastian's face aged him, taking away his plucky spirit and hopeful demeanour. Across the docks, the workers and slave force lined up single file, about to face the man who would christen it's completion, christen it's eventual maiden voyage (Wherever it may be.) They saw a formidable sight, the captain and his closest confidants by his side while armoured guards with pikes and swords surrounded them as they walked down the sand coloured stairs with the black cloud of an on going storm followed them. Getting closer, the slaves saw the unbelievable riches that wrapped around the captains neck, some jaws dropping at the sight of this treasure that was told in story form. The confederate, Colonel Saxton presided over his men and held the bottle that would christen the Maelstrom. Sebastian and Saxton didn't speak because of the magnitude of the ship they stood by. What more was there to say? Sebastian held the bottle, wrapping his fingers around the bottle's neck as his eyes scaled the ships size.

"Gentlemen! We are now dominant. We are the rage of the sea. We are the vengeance of the sea. We are the souls of the sea. Make no mistake about it, the Maelstrom will carry us all into the goddess Oki's arms as we seek to do her bidding. No more will we be seen as the scum of the earth. We were once looked at as vermin, now we will be seen as the predator," Sebastian turned the bottle around, raising his arm up, "I, Sebastian Teach, christen you, the Maelstrom, as the islands burning light!" The bottle smashed across the Maelstrom's body and the celebratory claps came from the workers (As they were told to). All Sebastian could do was stare at it, months of planning finally culminating in a specimen of sea dominance while the rain started to fall across his face. Longstaff felt empty, he could no longer see perseverance of the islands, he could see its destruction coming in the form a ship that had not been tested out at sea. A failure in waiting, a sickness of a determined soul that had broken under the weight of a political system that he had been a part of for years. It was as if every glass of rum he had in his life had surfaced back up through his stomach and the feeling of being sick was inescapable. While everyone's attention locked on firmly to the captain and the Maelstrom, Longstaff saw someone approaching to the west. A man in ragged clothes, dyed in blue, stormed up the docks with anger. Longstaff soon saw that the man was carrying a pistol, cocked and ready to take the shot. He ran through as quick as he could to reach the man just before his arm raised to pull the trigger. However, Longstaff didn't push the gun away, he pulled and aimed it squarely into his chest. As the trigger was pulled and the shot rained through the ears of the onlookers, Sebastian watched as Longstaff slowly fell to the floor, his knees buckling as he kept hold of the man's hand that held the gun. The Bluebeard struggled to break the quartermaster's grip as he watched the swarm of guards and the captain rush down. Two guards brought the man down with a fierce tackle while Sebastian rushed to Longstaff's side, holding him as he gently slumped back.

"Sebastian...."

"No, please, stay with me. Stay with me!" The captain cried as his grip tightened and his emotions screamed out.

"A pirates...life...wasn't for me," Sebastian's eyes started to well up as Longstaff's final words left him, "Please...find yourself again..." Longstaff's eyes closed as his head flopped back and his death was embraced. In that moment, the vulnerable side of the captain came out again. The memories flooded Sebastian's mind as he brought his head down on the quartermaster's bloodied chest, mixing his tears with the blood. For a moment, the sounds of commotion all seemed to fade away, Sebastian cold only hear himself cry out in agonising realisation that one of his closest friends was gone. Someone who would always hold him in high regard. The sentiment may been different in the final days of Longstaff's life, but with his dying words, the former mayor of Tortuga gave Sebastian words of change, hoping that it will change him in the coming days. The understanding of those words would resonate in Sebastian for as long as he would live, then they would be closed inside as the anger came out. Sebastian screamed in torture that shook everyone nearby, causing them to freeze in place. Sebastian drew his sword and the guards prepared themselves for the eventual slaughter by yanking the assailants arms behind his back. The captain grabbed the Bluebeard's neck and directed the sword for the jugular, but before the blade was even close enough, Sebastian held the blade steady. Trembling slightly, the emotional toil on the captains face showed him as a vulnerable and terrified man. Those words from Longstaff pierced into his soul, *What would this achieve?* he thought. Another dead man lying on the streets. It felt petty, the death of his quartermaster needed to be more on a larger scope rather than stomping out cockroaches. Sebastian lowered his weapon, composed himself as the guards waited in anticipation of his orders.

"Bring him to the castle, men. See to it that he is rested and fed."

That anticipation now was bewilderment. Both the guards and the man in question looked at each other in dumbfound from what the captain requested, but he didn't raise his voice. It was as if his anger had reached a new high, perhaps this was more dangerous than what the captain previously showcased. Nevertheless, the took to his order and walked the Bluebeard member to the castle with his arms still bound by their grip. Behind Sebastian, where Longstaff laid, Pastor Albert was on his knees, whispering in prayer as Klaus visibly held back a tear. Uncomfortable as it was, Sebastian know what needed to be done.

"Albert, he deserves a proper send off," Sebastian said somberly.

"Certainly, I'll arrange the church-"

"No, here is where he'll lay," Sebastian pointed to the Maelstrom, "It's only fitting that he shall be laid to rest in the confines of the thing he held dear. How he held me dear." A suffering pause of reflection saw the others console the young captain as the remaining guards covered Longstaff's body with crude tarp before carrying him away. The emotions would only be carried until the captain made his way over to the rows of slave workers, who had been standing still throughout the events that just transpired.

"All of you listen! Some of you are delinquents, rule breakers, deserters. People who I actively despise! Yet I will not look on at this vessel and see your fingerprints on this. I see this as the goddess Oki, in a form which carries her very essence across the oceans. We carry her essence. Now you all were promised a reward for your commitment, and by the rulings of our slave masters, I've been informed that there were no hiccups along the way. So for that, keep your head high. You all are no longer slaves, you are the first crew of the Maelstrom. And your first order is to get this mammoth of a machine going, our first voyage is in an hour's time! Move!" The new crew didn't waste time, they scurried like ants onto the giant boarding platform of the Maelstrom. Saxton barked out the order again to keep the formidable stare of the captain away from him as he too was on observation. Klaus came to the captains side quickly in a panic.

"Surely you jest, captain? The Maelstrom hasn't even been tested. You cannot jeopardise your position like this-"

"And do nothing? Something tells me that this place wasn't ran correctly since I was in Mexico. My quartermaster was killed right in front of me, and you think I should hold back? I believe it's you who should hold back sir!" Sebastian shoved the tall Klaus till he buckled against the wooden dock rail. "If you know what's good for you, you'll get back in that castle and remain there until I return. I have a bug to squash." Klaus protested until his voice was distant, it fell of deaf ears as the crew made way for the captain who stormed on board the ship. An endless amount of ropes weaved through the ships floor like snakes in the sand, the men squabbled like chickens as they rushed to get the vessel up and running and Sebastian was now at the helm of the ship, overlooking the one hundred plus man made project. Confidence and pride wiped away his determined scowl of revenge as he took a moment to reflect upon himself. *This was brought about because of me*, he thought. From inside the belly of the wooden beast who's skeletal decor reminded the crew of deaths embrace through depictions of suffering and treachery, coal was poured into the guzzling engine which spurred on the turn wheel hidden beneath at the bottom of the Maelstrom. Two men waited anxiously for the order to release the levers that would lift the breaks. A level above them, slaves turned unprepared crew adjusted the cannons, lines of them all connected by a single rope running all the way around the body. Up above, the sails finally were unravelled from the towering masts, bringing down a black sail which connected to all three masts. Sebastian saw the one lone man scale the middle mast as fast as he could. He almost wanted to shoot him down for the sheer fun of it, the crewman looked insignificant due to the size but eventually made it to the small crows nest. After a quick jostle, the colours of the I.I.C were flying proudly, showing the demonic skeleton captain, driving his dagger into a bloody heart while another prays to him. Sebastian gripped the helm, fastened himself for the initial jolt of life that would be spurred on my his command and relaxed himself by downing the flask from his coat pocket, tossing it aside as the red flowed down his mouth like blood.

"Colonel, release the Maelstrom," Sebastian said calmly. With that, Saxton repeated the order loudly to the crew in front of him which set off a chain, repeating all the way through the ship until the long start up process whirred into action, with the breaks of the of the paddle wheels being yanked down to the floor with a thud. Under the water, they slowly began to push, the start up had begun as the two men rushed above them, signalling for the men to shovel more coal into the engine. With a deep menacing creak, the Maelstrom hummed its way forward with an expel of smoke being pushed from the bow of the ship. The archangel figurehead who's body was alluring but her head a skull like the fallen bodies underneath it, clawing their way to her bosom, roared as the black smoke exhaled from her mouth. The anchor with a weight that would leave a formidable crack in the ground beneath, clicked back into place and the ship rumbled at a speed that was unparalleled to any other at sea. The crew were stunned as the initial jolt threw them to the ground and all they could hear was a roar that echoed the very thing nightmares are made of. Sebastian could only smile disturbingly as he took control of the beast's direction. With a sharp turn, the helm was swung all the way round to the left and the Maelstrom did so, creaking still but surviving the first few moments away from the castle dock yard. The Maelstrom would circle its way around the island of Cuba, heading to the south and then to the south east, where it would be seen by the I.I.C's main islands: Cuba, Jamaica and Haiti. Before it's arrival, the south of Cuba was overrun by protests. The Bluebeard's ensnared the public in it's rough demonstrations that continuously disrupted people going about the day. Swords were drawn, violent altercations, yet no sign of the military guards leaving the ordinary bystanders to fear for their lives. It would only be magnified once the Maelstrom was in sight. Only a select few would channel the message of the Bluebeard's calling with real emotion, the others knew it's true purpose, causing the violence that only brought more eyes to them. Market stalls and homes were ransacked, broken and left to burn in the name of progress until the law showed up in the form of a giant monster out to sea. The town of Fallen Gull fell silent and watched as the vessel glided across the seafront, until it came to stop. Starboard of the ship faced the shoreline, miles away the crew of the Maelstrom gazed out to the island, some seeing a former life or a former home. Sebastian observed more on the smoke and fire from the seaside town. Seeing the devastation from his hourglass, as well as the looks of astonishment from regular people and the disruptive Bluebeard's, there was no way the Maelstrom could fail now. The final test of the ship would begin.

"Mr Saxton. Fire the cannons on that town," Sebastian ordered. Saxton was staggered by this, but having seen his closest personnel fight against him, he simply carried out the order and repeated it. This did not sit well with the crew, some bursting into fits of rage over this.

"Are you insane?! We'll take out more of our own than the Bluebeard's! You can't do-"

"Don't argue with me! The captain has granted you your safety and a paid position aboard this ship. You will do what he says or you'll become a new piece on the wall!" growled Saxton, "Now, load up the cannons!" The crew sucked in their new found pride and continued their duty. The second deck with the cannons were all loaded until the latch was slowly lifted up, a long board that stretched the length of the ship rather than individual hatches. A formidable sight, if the crew wasn't ladened with hesitancy or the nutritional body of a wet rat. In terms of ammunition, there was enough to leave the entire town in craters and wreckage. They waited for the order, hands grasped in the lighters that would make the cannons sizzle before an ear shattering blast. Finally, Saxton saw Sebastian nod his head and the Colonel sounded to fire. One by one, the large cannons erupted with a fiery cloud of smoke, the first wave of five cannons striking the shore line making the sand fly high. The next batch hit the rock foundation at the edge of the town, shattering the earth and smacking the faces of unprotected women who were a moment ago watched the ship stop like they were witnessing a miracle. Some were thrown back from the blasts while others were reeling from their wounds which scared their faces in a deep bloody mess. A women in a white cap crawled on the floor trying to find her teeth which had scattered along the ground while another rushed away with her baby in her arms. Another wave decimated the marketplace, destroying wooden structures with a sickening crack and bursts of splinter sprung everywhere. The Bluebeard's now tasted the sting of retaliation as one member took the full force of one stray cannon ball, caving in his chest as it sent him hurtling towards a wall. Explosions rumbled in the air as the onslaught continued to rain down on the town of Fallen Gull, the screams of many could be heard but were faint to those on board, yet they would soon be gone by the time the cannon fire brought hell down on the town. As the bodies flew and the town crumbled behind him, one lone Bluebeard who discarded his picket sign, bolted forward through Fallen Gull's notoriously tight pathways. It may have been a marketplace but only convenient made for those who lived there. It came as a blessing when a small home or store crashed to the floor, another road block in the feat of escaping the onslaught of fire. A balding crew member who watched the General's hand, hoping for the ceasefire to be signalled watched with tears in his eyes as he stood in the middle of the staircase that lead to the armoury. Still, the crew didn't hold up, they continuously loaded and fired the cannons until finally the hand was brought down. The balding man finally ordered the ceasefire down the hatch as his voice broke and the emotion spilling from his mouth as the saliva spat out. Sebastian hadn't moved or changed his expression as he watched the carnage from afar but he finally came round to walking away from the helm. Colonel Saxton watched every member on the top deck like a hawk and with his hand on his holstered Colt. The look of realisation in the mens faces were everywhere, some unable to understand the ramifications of what they'll be made to deal with once word spreads. The Generals fortune came true as a young man from the armoury pushed past the balding man and came in a near feet of the captain, screaming his frustration with a determined sprint before he was cut down from a quick head shot from Saxton. The shot rattled the ship more than any wave could. The crew up top froze in fear while the rest on the levels below looked up, wondering what had transpired. This didn't even phase the captain, who's look of admiration beamed across to all the crew members, waiting in retreat as the twitching body of the attacker laid in front of them.

"That is how you assert yourself," Sebastian said, pointing over to the charred land, "Not by words, but by force, which is what we've always done. This is what piracy has always been about. These islands are ours and we all swear by a code, as did I. If you disobey, disrupt or defile the land our goddess gave to us to treasure, then I will be the blade that cuts you down. I'm done dancing around ridiculous hurdles that strangle the very thing we swore to be! Now I want you all to look that and know how dominant we are. The Maelstrom was built for this very reason. To make us feel like we've regained control. Every hardship that stands before us will not look so intimidating now, will it?" Sebastian asked. The crewmen shook their heads and mumbled the appropriate response, a far cry from the jubilation that Sebastian expected.

"Cretinous slaving swine!" Sebastian withdrew his flintlock and fired up, once again scaring the crew as they backed away or crouched down holding their ears, "Feel proud of yourselves! This ship made you slaves no more! And if you don't show your love to me, then I can easily throw you back into the camps with nothing to your name! Am I understood?" The once tepid reply was now a hearty war cry, with raised fists and expressions that hid the guilt.

"Now all of ya, back to your stations. I want this ship returned to the castle docks at once!" No hesitation in the orders that fell on their lap, the crew returned to their posts like obedient lap dogs.

"Colonel!" Saxton hurried over.

"Aye, captain?"

"Mr Longstaff's body. Where did they place him on here?" Sebastian asked quietly.

"Third deck, sir. Just before the furnace," The general said.

"Take me there."

The two stepped below deck, it was dark, only occupied by four men who were moving crates of cargo, organising the entirety of the Maelstrom's ammo and food supply. They did not dare lay eyes on the captain and moved closer into the darker spots of the deck as the fallen Mayor Longstaff laid on two long rifle crates with a white tarp covering him from head to toe.

"Get them out of here," Sebastian said as his eyes looked down on the body, "I wish to be alone. His venture into Oki's arms must be between me and him," Sebastian said, keeping his head down in remembrance to his fallen friend. Saxton obliged by the captains request and beckoned the four men sculpting away in the corners of the deck to leave with him. With the ominous glow of one lone lit lantern, Sebastian pulled back the tarp slightly to reveal Longstaff's face. Cold, blood-soaked and at rest. The familiar stench of rum that radiated from the quartermaster's sweat sunk into his clothes as the release of his bodily fluids dripped over the crates. That's when Sebastian let go of the anger, the sense of being a leader determined to bring the islands and anyone who stood in front of him under his control slipped away for a few moments and he started to cry. The emotion dripped onto the tarp, his anguished cries of love for the former mayor of Tortuga echoed in the deck of the Maelstrom. So much so that the crew could hear it from above and below, believing in a sense of toll that the ship would bring onto all of their lives. Sebastian let out a cry that broke him, bringing him down on his knees sobbing as he gripped the tarp, pulling more off of the body. Longstaff's hand was pulled out, his thick hand dropping to Sebastian's level. He wiped away his tears and looked upon the relaxed hand that was stained by his blood, his tears continuing to flow as he held onto it with his. In that moment he was a little boy again, remembering back to a simpler time where his responsibilities were little but his importance was still great. And yet this hand, who was not of his bloodline, gave him so much hope and love more than what his family ever did. His thoughts then turned to his father, comparisons of the two were often exchanged when he was younger and even so till the quartermaster's eventual death. While Longstaff's image brightened, Sebastian's father rotted into a painted image of a monster. A monster that left him finally find himself while Longstaff looked on proudly. *Why did you do this to me? I don't hate you, I hate what you did,* Sebastian thought. He wanted no more of this. If this was going to be the straw that broke the camels back, then let it. Sebastian rose to his feet, wanting to look at his friend one last time before the cover would shield him forever. All of a sudden, a sharp pain radiated through his head making him press against the left side of his skull. The sharpness subsided but his vision was now blurred and his direction became staggered. *Is this the boat?* He thought. Couldn't have been, the Maelstrom was riding along calm coastal waters, it couldn't possibly be the cause. Sebastian slowly backed up against one of the beams, keeping himself straight as his vision became distorted, warping everything around him. Through his eyes the deck became damp, barnacles blossomed everywhere and the ceiling dripped while the wood rotted. "This isn't happening," he said, trembling as he stood firmly by the beam. Sebastian would soon spring to life as something slithered down the beam. The sound coming closer to his head wasn't normal, it sounded like it was coming from something under the sea, the sound of movement thrashing against water. The body of an eel swam around him once until it sharply flicked it's head back and flashed its jaw at Sebastian, throwing himself to the ground in horror, he backed himself away towards the stairs to the upper deck as he watched the eel fly around the deck chamber. It slowed as it reached Longstaff's body, weaving around the curves of his body as Sebastian looked on in fright.

"Keep away from him!" he cried. The eel then twisted himself around and the shock of its tail tapped the body's chest making it jolt. As the eel swam away into the darkest corner, Longstaff sat up quickly making the captain scream for his life as the corpse began heaving in air. Sebastian wanted to curl up into a ball as he watched

Longstaff's body slowly bring his head up, locking eyes with the frightened soul who hung onto the stairs bannister, trying to scamper back up to his feet. As Sebastian got to his feet, Longstaff pointed at him, his bones cracking with every slight movement of his hand. The suspense of what this vision could bring next was was inescapable yet scary as Sebastian's curiosity made him stay frozen in place.

"Longstaff?" Sebastian said quietly.

Longstaff's mouth then excreted an ungodly amount of water and bile. Sounds of wrenching came from the corpse until small krill escaped his jaw along with seaweed and seashells. It did this for a good ten seconds before the flow of water stopped, however it did so as Longstaff started to choke. Sebastian could see something lodged in the quartermaster's mouth, he wanted to help so badly but he knew the man was dead, he couldn't do anything to help yet it still made him step lightly towards his fallen friend. After a moment, Longstaff brought up what looked like a glass, covered in slime and blood as his extended jaw cracked back into place. He brought it up to his face and looked at Sebastian with a sly grin, brandishing his childish smile that Sebastian knew far to well.

"Here's to you...captain," Longstaff gargled, spitting out whatever water was left, "Oki, knows what you did. She's got a message for you, you know what it is?" He asked. Sebastian shook his head in disbelief as the tears ran down his face again.

"You're a failure," Longstaff cackled, "You're a failure!"

"Stop it."

"And not only that, you're a murder! A genocidal prodigy who never learnt how to wipe his own arse!"

"Stop it," Sebastian said again, getting angrier.

"You've let you're family down! You let me down, son. Cause you know something? You would've been better of drinking yourself away into obscurity, like I did. At least that way, you would've been a fucking disappointment that was fucking happy!"

"Shut up!" Sebastian darted for the corpse with his sword drawn and swung at the quartermaster's head. The head rolled away as the body fell back down on the crates. The nightmare was over. Sebastian breathed in heavily as his gaze was fixed on Longstaff's head. As he came to, the walls were not covered anymore, the smell of moist sea urchins was gone and no more water dripped inside the below deck. Sebastian realised that the illusion was gone, but it still felt all too real. The only thing that was real was the fact that Longstaff's head was removed from his body. The captain dropped the sword to the ground after he realised what he had done. Sounds of footsteps hurried down the stairs as Colonel Saxton wondered what was going on.

"Are you alright captain? We heard screaming."

Sebastian's lip shook as he thought of words to describe the incident, but he stopped himself. There was no reason to. *What would that achieve? Disruption*, he thought. He brought his sword back inside the hilt and made his way to the stairs as Saxton stared at the table.

"Make sure the body is burnt. Put it in the engine below for all I care," Sebastian said pushing past.

"Captain! The head?"

"Hang it up somewhere. It's just a decoration now," said Sebastian.

Even though he was miles east from the islands, the bounty hunter could still see the dark cloud of smoke that came from one of the islands. A sight as clear as day and sounds of calamity. His slow journey gave him front row seat to the beast of the sea that blasted it's cannons in rapid succession. He had hoped, and so did his contractors, that whatever this thing was wouldn't have made it out of the port. It was a success, a colossal success. It seemed the grand plan would become a lot more difficult as the walls of the I.I.C had a formidable weapon. This however would not cross the man in the ten gallon hat mind whatsoever the second his boots touched down on the south side of the Texan shore line. Only the heads of D.C would handle this, and he was hoping that nothing unfortunate happens to the post office in that stretch of time.

CHAPTER 26

FATE

The battle map was scrolled out across the presidents desk. As the president studied the coastal areas of Florida and Alabama, his two Generals; Grant and Lee stood across the other side of the desk. In this instance, Lee had re-obtained his role as General but it wouldn't be for long, nor would the partnership with Grant.

Across the line of southern Florida, President Lincoln pushed small circular pieces across it and directed his two Generals.

"Cuba is the main course, the other islands will fall shorty after Cuba is captive. Dead or alive, the signed treaty obtained by my contracted man will stand forever. Captain Teach will have no choice, he's lost either way. You both will man stations in the southern regions of the two states," Lincoln instructed.

"What about Mexico, Mr president? They're an ally and could prove to be either a strategic attack or retreat," Uslyess said.

"As much as those possibilities are in question, one would have to think about Benito. He's a diplomatic man, Grant. He's not the character for intervention. I just hope my letters have got through to him when defeat is staring him in the face."

"And the ship? Storming the castle stronghold is one thing, but unless that ship is sunk, you've got no way of entering the islands," Lee said.

"Our forces will learn if that thing is a complete wreck or an adversary, Mr Lee. The picture will be painted very broadly in the newspapers once it's been broke to the public. Pirates have an image, so let's not get creative," Lincoln said.

"When will we roll out?" Grant asked.

"Immediately. By the time we get there, I would've instructed the press to alert the public along with my presence along the coastline."

"You-you're coming with us?" Grant wondered.

"Of course. Diplomacy has to be our forefront, Mr Grant. Even though we know the outcome, who's to say if the captain has a change of heart and won't put up a fight," Lincoln said.

"That's a very optimistic outlook, Mr president, but surely you don't think he will put up a fight either way?" Lee questioned.

"It won't just be me. His father is accompanying me. I think if there's ever a way to better your chances, it's with him. He was the first to make contact after all." The two generals shared a similar thought of doubt with the presidents actions, nevertheless, sucked in their pride and agreed.

Across from them, a few rooms down the hallway, Edward Teach was in the same place as he was before he left the islands for America, resting in his bed with his thoughts once again on his son. The president's proposition for tomorrow was harrowing. He had hoped it didn't come to this but now that security was in his corner, he felt more at ease. His son was going to be a man with a vendetta, Edwards name was probably on a traitors list of the highest order. Possibly spoken around the islands like a bogeyman or Judas. He couldn't imagine the state of shock the islands were in right this very moment but Edward had an idea as to what his son had transformed it into. He sat up from the lush linen, rubbing his hands along the white sheets as he tried to imagine himself back in the days when the two of them were inseparable. It was the only way to escape the feeling of emptiness that had stuck with him since he arrived in Washington. Edward cast his mind back, a decade ago, when him and Sebastian attended a festival on the island of Haiti. He was amazed by the fire display team of slaves performing for guests along the beaches. They breathed fire in a dazzling display that made the young Sebastian clap frantically at the sight.

"They're like dragons!" He yelled. Edward smiled, he had been smiling all the way through the show as he was away from the stress of work. This was only one of the few days he could actually bond with his son like a human being, sprinkled with trips and activities. That day was one where he could do both and, unfortunately, was the last one. The next few years after that were the hardships of being shaped up to be the next in line.

Even though Edward was adamant about becoming the captain with Norton's health in question, it didn't stop him for an eventual curve ball. As he cast his smiling face onto his son that day, and Sebastian doing the same, the memory vanished and Edward was back inside his rented quarters. Just as he snapped out of it, a knock was heard at the door and Edward answered it. It was the Vice President, Andrew Johnson, Edward had become acquainted with him during his touchdown into the states.

"How are you keeping?" The vice president asked.

"Not well, to be honest. I wonder if this is how executioners feel on their first day on the job," Edward said disparagingly.

"Mr Teach, I am sorry, but emotional support is all I can provide at this time, I'm afraid," Johnson said bringing himself inside the room, "We can only hope that this can be dealt with civilly."

"It won't. I'm sure of it. You have no idea what that ship can do if it is unleashed along the shores. If he wanted to, he could invade the east coast at the snap of his fingers," Edward said.

"That's what drew the president to address this. It's the reason why the war hasn't been declared to be over. There's something immense to gain and the only thing standing in the way is your son. You know how much at risk there is I don't need to brief you anymore on it," Johnson said. Edward wandered around the room with his hands on his hips, contemplating what his inevitable role will be in the exchange.

"I pushed him to be like this. Rebellious. I could've easily let him have his way from time to time and that would've soften the blow to make this less difficult…but…"

"You painted too much of yourself in an already existing picture," Johnson observed. Edward looked at the vice president with understanding, nodding as Johnson went on.

"Ideal as it sounds, it never bods well. It's what many people in Washington have been trying with the president."

"Have you tried it? You are his VP after all."

"If I did that, Mr Teach, then I'd be out of a job. My views are always in question here. But for you, it's a chance to redeem yourself in life. You came here to end piracy, save your son and start a new. It's bold, but you're half way there," Johnson said.

"But what will this new life entail for me? This country is careening into a new direction either way at the end of all this. Can you guarantee it'll be safe?" Edward asked. Johnson had no affirmative answer yet he had his response served at the ready.

"I can say that it'll be a work in progress. One which you can easily express yourself over. Think of that freedom next time you feel afraid here." Johnson bowed his head as he showed himself out the door, knowing that he couldn't contribute anymore to the conversation.

"We leave for tomorrow at dawn, it'll be quite the journey." The doors closed and Edward was alone again. The second he was alone, he reached under the desk and brought his bag of belongings out from underneath. Rummaging inside, he came across an old locket underneath his clothes and pressed it down, opening egg shaped door into a world where Edward was like his son, entranced with hope and excitement for life. He had recollections of what his father said to him when he was Sebastian's age, it was vague yet he remembered the sentiment. He had only wished he could emanate the same energy as him, unfortunately, nothing in the pirate world could be done twice.

As the Maelstrom docked back into the castle dock yard, Sebastian was not his normal self. He stared out from the helm, seeing the workers frantically throw the lines across the Maelstrom's large frame yet he was in a trance where he retreated back into his mind. Inside, his thoughts turned back to when he saw Longstaff speak to him, horror's that would scare any man, woman and child. What he contemplated the most was that he would have to relay it back to his peers and his public. Would they trust him after the disaster at Fallen Gull? It froze him to the point his hat blew off of his head from the wind, tumbling down the stairs until Colonel Saxton stopped it with his boot. He didn't startle him by calling up to him, rather walking closer at a slow pace in case he startled him like a wild animal.

"Captain? Are you departing?" Saxton asked quietly. Sebastian didn't respond for what seemed like the longest three seconds in Saxton's life.

"Tell the men they may get a small break and then they're back on this ship," He finally said. "For what purpose, sir?"

"I wish to remain on the ship until further notice, Colonel. Inform Klaus inside that he is to hold the fort until my safety is certain," Sebastian went on.

"Safety? Captain, you're more than safe when inside the castle-"

"No! I cannot let them see. Do you hear me? They'll be coming for me if I'm inside that cursed place."

"Who? Who will be coming for you?" Saxton said worryingly.

"They all will," Sebastian said in astonishment, "Everyone will. The Bluebeard's, the naysayers and the traitors, they'll all know where I am. Here I'm protected. Just bring me as much of the wine as you can. Just say I'm away from the island." Saxton didn't know what to think. The captain had gone from a bloodthirsty man out for revenge to a paranoid recluse in a matter of hours. *What could've been fuelling this?*, he thought.

"Certainly, captain," Saxton placed the hat on the top step and stepped away off the Maelstrom, wrapping his brain around these spontaneous orders. Having no idea where the favourite wine was kept, Saxton first thought was to see Klaus who remained in the castle via Sebastian's angry demand. Once inside, the young messenger boy brushed past him out the door with a spring in his step. It took him buy surprise but didn't rattle him. It must've been something from Klaus. Reaching the captain's quarters, the door was left wide open and Saxton saw Klaus presided over the captain's desk, hanging his head down as he loomed over.

"Sir?" Saxton said, making Klaus jump.

"For god's sake! Just knock," Klaus said loudly.

"Apologies. The captain has, uh, made a slight request which you could help me with." "Yes, yes, what is it?" Klaus said, trying to hurry along the conversation.

"He wants the wine brought to the Maelstrom. He didn't say why but he may be thinking that-"

"Top floor of the castle and get some of the crew to help you with it. There's at least a crate of it left," Klaus answered.

"But, sir, this request seems to be very odd with the captain's behaviour-"

"What else is new!? Now do what you've been asked to, that's an order!" Saxton hurried back out of the office to find the wine like he was requested. Klaus returned to his relaxed state, breathing deeply as he fixed his gaze back to the table. What sat in front of him was studied multiple times, Klaus made sure there was a broad statement, no misconceptions, no interpretations, nothing that would show a conspiracy. Everything was laid out in black and white like it was requested. It would be a shame to those who read it, but also a chance of escape and contention. Once received, there was no going back.

Rourke stood in wonder as he watched the raging smoke coming from Fallen Gull. It had been burning all day, the smoke seen for miles. The once loved street that produced knick-knacks and the islands greatest fortune tellers was now rubble. He watched out as a small boat docked, it was the messenger boy from the castle. Rourke knew it would be concerning Cuba yet fear was not found on his face, more of contemplation. All in all, he would realise his true potential as the new head of Jamaica if the message was what he expected.

"Governor Renfold! Message from the Captain!" The young messenger boy called out as he sprinted up the docks, brushing past workers as they watched him head to Rourke's side. Rourke opened the letter and read its contents, brief and direct, the message was clear and so was the name written on the bottom left.

"Very good. We have a response plan in the making," Rourke said.

"You want me to get back to the captain, sir?" The boy asked.

"No. You'll stay put. It's safer here than it is over there. You'll resume duties for me now, boy. Make yourself busy at my quarters, now," Rourke ordered. The young messenger did as he was told with no hesitation and made his way to the governor's building, leaving Rourke by the dockside still looking out to Cuba. The directive was formed at the captain's desk and now the practically of the task had to be performed with precision to ensure the best outcome. For Rourke, it meant disregarding everything for the sake of safety. He now understood the bravery Edward had taken to slip away from the growing madness. Perhaps the pirate life was dying, but who was to say it would be a boring. The next few days were to be a cautious time, no one knew exactly what would happen or what would come of the islands in Sebastian's path, but either way, Rourke said a small prayer in his head as he remembered Sebastian. The hope had been crushed and the real life ramifications of preserving such a way of life in the ever changing world was disastrous. Rourke had sensed this with every captain's cabinet he had been apart of, the changes were small but this was now drastic. He could only pray that Sebastian would be the last pirate not to go down in a fight.

In the confines of the third lower deck, bottles piled up and rolled across the wooden deck floor as the Maelstrom swayed. Sebastian sat slumped against the last crate, devouring the addictive wine that had caused him so many turbulent nights and visions. To him, it was like nectar, soothing his overwhelming thoughts of dread with a throat stinging sensation of relief. And with five bottles in, Sebastian was in a sensation he never thought he could top. The wine had made his throat dry, his eyes saw nothing blurred images that spread across his vision like an oil painting and hos speech was non-existent, splitting out nonsense and random noises. He rocked himself to the movement of the boat, giggling as the smallest movement felt like an incredible dive off of a cliff. Sebastian would not have this high for long though as the contents of the wine in large amounts began to take its toll on his body, he sweated profusely, his muscles were tight and if he rocked any more, sick would surface. At one point, the verbal diarrhoea spilled out something coherent as Sebastian struggled to stand. "Whheerre are YOU!" Sebastian bellowed to no avail, it quickly returned to a collection of grunts and noises. With no coordination, Sebastian picked up one of the rolling bottles next to him and threw it across the deck, it colliding with the wall and smashing into pieces. Two seconds went by and Sebastian was once again a blubbering mess. He cried while falling on all fours, crawling away from the bottles and up the stairs as he still chugged back the throat stinging wine. A long and uncomfortable climb, Sebastian dragged himself along the hard staircase till his ribs were sore with his knees clipping the steps. He eventually made it to the top deck, yelling and moaning still, trying to find the apparition that appeared to him while he was sober that morning. To the trained ear, anyone near the Maelstrom would mistake him for the ghost as the misty night clouded over the island. Finally he stood, stumbling back slightly near the hole he had emerged from. His misty eyes looked around, not knowing what to look for, the thoughts in his head shifted round and round as he tried to focus on one thing. It saddened him further as he was he alone, throughout the year of his captaincy Sebastian had been subjected to betrayal, family woes and separation. While Cuba recovered from its wound, the infection brewing from the Bluebeard's idea of revolt was only spreading. Sebastian now felt like a lone wolf in a pack that had separated from him. It dawned on him that his actions have caused the opposite of his vision, piracy would viewed more unfavourably than ever. The people had already seen expulsion, delusions of grandeur and attacks on home soil too devastating to be forgiven with a simple sorry. These thoughts surrounded his whole world view subjecting him to a breakdown which came with a terrified scream that echoed around the castle area. As it faded, Sebastian stood still and waited if someone would come, whether it be a guard or a ghost of his memories. It was neither. He was a lone pirate on a ship christened to bring back prosperity. Not a word more left Sebastian's lips as he just observed the components of the giant creaking vessel. As he stood alone, Klaus was watching from the balcony of the castle, making out the darkened shape of the captain from up above the tallest peak of the castle. It was neither a look of dread or worry, Klaus had done all he needed to do, all he needed was to now escape at the correct time. But he took a moment to reflect on what he was seeing before him; a young drunken leader of a crippled nation of islands. It wasn't as turbulent as when Norton was in charge but the convincing of nations from abroad helped ease troubled waters. If only he knew, Klaus thought. Klaus had seen captain's go down before, but this was a drama most people involved couldn't recover from, more or less an entire nation. He retreated back away from the balcony to get some rest, he would be leaving tomorrow and there was no point in letting anxiety derive him of sleep. Even though the plan was coming into place, who was to assume a bump in the road could happen.

Sebastian watched the balcony from the ship, unbeknownst to Klaus. Sebastian recognised the figure immediately, tall, frail and hooded. What would've been had he not fallen into place like they wanted to. Traitorous blood was what he could smell, it was one thing he excelled in. *It wasn't me, it was them. The snakes in our garden*, he thought. Even in a drunken state, he knew everything should've gone his way, with or without his fathers influence and the only person in his corner was dead. In the cold winds of the night, Sebastian vowed to be the victor and come dawn, the islands would change for the better.

CHAPTER 27

TERROR

As Klaus awoke in the early hours of the morning, his deceptive guise made the guards continue their morning rituals without any concern over the captain's whereabouts. He was dressed formally this day, opting to brandish a long coat with a tucked in shirt and fitted slacks. With these garments, he took to look at himself inside the captains bedroom, using the massive mirror by the window to see himself in full view. The white beard had been trimmed last night, followed by a long and luxurious bath which Klaus helped himself to through "Captain's privileges". For a moment, he saw himself with the fresh set of clothes and pictured himself as the captain, *What a world that would be*, he thought. It made him smile smugly as he buttoned up the collar and patted himself down. Klaus saw that the sword was missing from the holder along the bottom cabinet underneath the mirror but it didn't perplex him, he knew he had it and he didn't care, everything that was of value to these islands were soon to sink. A knock was then heard at the door and the guard showed himself in.

"Sir, the Captain has asked if you could wait here for him. He has business to discuss with you."

"Certainly, how long will he be?" Klaus asked.

"He didn't say sir, only that you remain here. He is worried about the rebel Bluebeard's." That pleased the once shrouded gatekeeper. *The threat of the rebels would certainly keep the captain put like a scared little mutt*, he thought.

"Thank you," Klaus said and the guard returned to his post, closing the door. Klaus was beginning to think the possibility of a quiet surrender while the Cuba burns itself down was probable. After all, it would be up to the Americans to clean up the mess from within. Klaus walked over to the window and embraced the warm sun on his pale skin properly without being blocked by the bulky hood he became accustomed to. There was nothing but the quietness of the room and seagulls from outside. His eyes squinted open to look out towards the dock but something was missing. Something very big was missing. The Maelstrom was not docked at the captains port. Staggering to make sense as to where it disappeared to, Klaus was then sent hurtling towards the ground as the walls behind the massive luxury bed scattered across the room with a mighty bang. As the dust settled and wooden floor cracked, Klaus in a panic looked all around the room to eventually find a cannonball, which had shot through the mirror and wall behind it. He didn't know what to do as another was fired through the conjoint room and soon bricks walls began to crumble beneath him. More and more hit the castle at high speeds, the sound of the roaring cannon fire was frightening to Klaus as he called out for the guards. He rushed to his feet in retreat, bursting out to the main halls where he saw paintings and wood floor being destroyed before his very eyes. There was no one in sight, no advisor, no maids, no guards, they had vanished. Klaus was left to the slaughter as suddenly the walls began to crumble. The floor shook as he ran down towards the stairs trying to reach the entrance when all of a sudden a cannonball struck the main foyer, hurtling Klaus violently onto the stairs. His back bent awkwardly and the back of his head began to bleed. His ears rang and his vision was blurred. Any movement was pain as he grunted out, all he could see through his impaired sight was dust and stone shooting all around him as the muffled booms came from every side. As he looked up and his vision became normal, he could see the sky up above from the tallest floor, the roof had been blasted off while the inside of the tower was visible. He relished this sight as he had done the suns morning rays, staring fondly at the slither of cloud that floated high above. The towers stone frame soon began to crack and buckle, the final stage of collapse was about to happen, but before he did, Klaus recited the small chant that he had learnt whilst undercover and in that moment of recital, wished to see his friend again. Klaus closed his eyes for the last time as the tower finally gave in, stone and wood cascading down below to the ground floor like a waterfall where everything was buried in a dusty tomb. The castle was now a small cloud of dust that rushed around as the air blew. The Maelstrom was far away from the dock but was still in range to perform the attack. The crew were again in a state of disbelief, holding back their emotions for fear that Sebastian or the accompanying Saxton would do. It seemed viable to their survival that they remained on the ship as to what would transpire on the islands would certainly change the balance of everyone's survival. Sebastian just watched with no emotion, staring at the castle like a sunken abyss, a body being put in the ground, it was neither satisfying or fulfilling, it was a step he had to take. In his own head, he saw this as progress without any hesitation, a way to battle the demons both on land and his head. With a wave of his hand was all it took to get the Maelstrom rolling again with Saxton being the usual mouthpiece to sound off the orders. It was almost as if the former Colonel could read the young captains mind as the ship moaned forward. The Maelstrom would power through the gap between Cuba and New Providence, two targets that were in Sebastian's range of fear induced attacks on his own people. The people in question were confused, dazed, scared and vengeful. The castle falling and the destruction caused by the captain himself before the early hours of the morning would send signals throughout saying: The captain has gone AWOL. The Bluebeard's saw this as a triumph, a visual aid towards their message, who was to care for them if the powers that be fall? Only they would have a different answer than the one they were perpetuating. The coastlines of the islands screamed back at the monstrous ship stalked through the water gap it would take to venture east. Sebastian was now the most hated man in the islands history and he was proud of it. The fury was soon to set the islands ablaze again.

Trying to pass through an angry mob, Pastor Albert watched in astonishment as the violent uproar pushed past him, seeing before him the rubble that was the castle. Confused and grief stricken, Albert wondered to the goddess Oki as to what had happened. How could've this happened? he prayed. In the end, seeing this was too much to handle, like a recluse, he hid himself back inside as he watched the guards try to obtain some order before the coasts were to become violent ordeals. Inside the church was peace but not for a sound mind, Albert was lost as he looked around to see empty, turned up seats in a place where worship was necessary. He resided to the top of the stage where he sat down on the edge, burying his chin in his chest. The emotions began to swell but he held back, even when there was no one around he didn't want to look weak in the eyes of his goddess. It was impossible to beseech explanation, it was seemingly the work of forces beyond his control or understanding. Albert however, felt remorse for gas lighting his devotion that had been renewed by Sebastian, feeling like his words of praise were nothing but an opportunity for the seizure of people's attention, away from the captain's real intentions. The message was lost in translation he felt, Oki was the protector of the seas and those who claimed it, not one to destroy itself from within. Just before his hands could cover his eyes to let the tears flow to the floor, the church doors opened and two guards stepped inside with a third surveying the outside should anyone breach.

"Pastor Albert, we would like you to come with us," A beefy guard to the left of him said.

"If you're here to sacrifice me to the wolves then so be it," Albert said in defeat.

"No sir, we're here to escort you off the island. You will be taken to Jamaica, where you will be under Governor Rourke's protection."

"Protection," Albert said with sarcasm, "Me? An arbiter of hope?"

"Indeed sir. Klaus requested the immediate departure of those associated with the captain." Albert soon realised where Klaus was where he last spoke.

"Is Klaus-"

"Unfortunately sir. He's not been found, but he was inside the castle this morning," Albert slumped back again upon hearing this, "This was the last message he delivered," The burly guard handed Albert the letter and he read quietly as the guards stood raring to go. Whatever Albert had been feeling before suddenly vanished, like he was relived of his own self inflicted guilt as the words made sense of the situation. His life would be spared of this awful doing and justice, he felt, could be served and another could be spared. Then, a realization occurred as Albert brought down the letter.

"How soon do we have the vessel to escape?" He asked to the guard.

"One at the waiting, holding a few men of our own, sir."

"What was to become of the men down in the chamber?" Albert continued.

"Few had died sir, few are still down there."

Bluebeard's raged against the machine as the patrol guards fought against their effort to shoot at the captain even though his distance outweighed the shot power of their pistols and rifles. Swords were drawn and steel was clashed, blood was spilt and the land was soon ash. The Maelstrom fired from both sides of its body, hitting the land the sailed past with extreme precision. There was to be an effort to make sure there was no one left standing by the end of the onslaught. The Bluebeard's had thought quick from the previous encounter and with a stream of successful take downs, they managed to bring in heavy duty of their own. Cannons that had been used for decoration were ripped away from their stone walls and we're now targeting the Maelstrom. There was only three in total, yet they were spread out to cover the Maelstrom's long body. That didn't stop the hell fire as they frantically tried to get the weapons loaded, the Maelstrom continued it's onslaught, breaking down walls and barriers, ripping away the floor and killing anyone caught in it's way. As Sebastian watched from the helm, he couldn't help but bring the spy glass up to his eye for a better inspection of the damage, yet his mind was still in a state of erosion that broke down his sense of reality. Instead of injured citizens and rebellious Bluebeard's, the captain saw rows of people standing in a line, all looking back at him. They weren't real however, they were corpses from the days of old. No matter how much cannon fire came down on the land, they all stood there, watching and judging.

Sebastian was momentarily frozen while the earth was scorched in front of him, a face of bravery glared back at the ghostly horrors that he saw through the spy glass, breaking in an instant when Saxton barked: "Captain! Boats to the east!"

The spy glass was closed shut to its tiny form as Sebastian hurried to the starboard side. He could see the boats approaching, rows of them, not battle ready, some where loaded with men blasting their flintlocks with little effect on the ship, the others were smaller and some were row boats. The row boats didn't carry anger, they carried those who were still blindly loyal to the captain, cluttering onto what little they had left to take refuge with him.

"Sir, they look like they're fleeing," Saxton observed.

"A graceful end is what they deserve," Sebastian said bluntly wiping away any compassion that started to blossom from the American.

"Captain-"

"Wipe them out! No one steps foot on here except me! They're probably filthy assassins, now do it!" Sebastian exclaimed. Saxton was now biting his jaw down hard, visually subtle behind his scraggly beard. Reluctantly, he followed through and the toll it took on the crew was weighing them down, how much more could they stomach of this bloodshed? What the men on the boats was about to see was a quick death. As they waved out to their captain, their hope was not lost, they knew he would let them onboard. The men on the row boats rose to their feet as they frantically got closer, one sail passenger boats had the speed to cut through them, it would soon become a sight of grave desperation. The hatches of the Maelstrom slowly rose up and the cannons rocked forward while the crew aimed them down. Much like Saxton, their hopefulness was about to drown beneath the water below, sinking deep into their stomachs was dread that weighed them down like an anchor until finally the first shot rang out. A miss fire at first, a small beacon of hope to the many that held on to their boat for dear life against the impactful splash that landed in front of the small row boat, maybe this was a test of loyalty, but as thought came, it went in an instant. A second shot of another cannon decimated the two men in a row boat, their bodies flying in the air before hitting the sea with a hard slap as the wood flew into the air with the water. Panic ensued as everyone scrambled to turn around and sail back to shore but it was to no avail. The cannons sounded off with loud bangs that rattled the eardrums of the stranded men before silence embraced them. Shots splashed into the ocean as the boats were taken out one by one, crumbling into wrecks that would scare off anyone from the surface. It was now uncomfortable to watch for the colonel, who turned his back on the horror. In doing this, he showed his vulnerability, some of the crew noticed him mouthing a silent prayer. He turned their attention back to their work as he placed his hand on the pistol he had used earlier. Sebastian now was looking out to nothing but wreckage, the cannon fire had ceased as no targets moved from the ships perimeter. Sebastian could see the bodies laying face down in the sea as the blood surrounded them in a crimson circle. All the while the ships sunk, a lone row boat was untouched, yet twitching inside was a body of a man, still alive and clutching onto his son, no more than six years old. They looked up at their captain, the child crying as his father struggled to keep his eyes open, he showed Sebastian his hands, opened and reaching out to what he thought was salvation. In return, Sebastian beamed a stone cold look of pity, pity that they would sacrifice themselves to be under his wing. The day had been filled with a rage that destroyed the I.I.C from the inside, who else could be saved? As he watched them plead, Sebastian saved them from their bond of faith, with a shout of "FIRE!"

Days had now passed since the President left for the shores of Florida, Vice President Johnson remained at the desk, steadying the ship as the balance of the war was still in play. The day was dull, uneventful to where Johnson wondered why he got up that morning. It had been four hours since he awoke at six am, and the paperwork was all that he met, no staffers, no aids, no one to greet him. Not even a simple good morning. While a pleasant exchange would've been nice for a morning, Johnson was greeted to knocking at the presidents office doors.

"Enter," he answered and a man in black arrived with detailed papers.

"Mr vice president, this is urgent and it needs your attention," the staffer said, placing the papers down in front of the vice president.

"What is this?" Johnson asked.

"Telegram from California's governor, an attack is imminent. The Mexican president has just sent a threat that the southern reserves are in their cross hairs." Johnson was puzzled but oddly calm by this new information.

"Watch that the patrols keep an eye at the border, it's hardly a threat," Johnson dismissed.

"Sir, this is urgent. The president could be nearly at the southern end of the country, we have no idea what the I.I.C could be planning here. If Mexico follows through that means-"

"Mexico is not a contender. If the I.I.C has planned this from the very beginning then I would start believing in what my local mystic says," Johnson said brushing off the paranoia, "Mexico are still in a state of rebuild and the main priority, which is that ship, is nowhere near in range of the state. If an attack is building from them, they'll be dismantled after the first shot. It's hardly worth threatening over."

"But sir, the gold reserves?" The man urged.

Johnson never frowned nor showed worry, showing his presence as a cool and calculated man than the worried mind of the president he served. This was a time to show confidence in the people who had doubts over him.

"We'll have more of that soon. I shouldn't worry," Johnson said smiling. The man in the black suit was shocked by this but remained silent, taking back the papers and tucking it under his arm as he exited the presidents office. Johnson reclined back in the presidents chair, feeling a sense of satisfaction after the exchange. Even though he would be unchallenged now, in his mind, Johnson took the time he had at this desk to prepare himself should ever an event be likely where he would take the title of just president. But in also, gain some fortitude towards his peers who had judged his appointment. If this was the only interaction he would get from his busy day, he didn't mind it.

The wind swept between the presidents men as they stood on the edge of the country, gazing out to sea with a dark cloud following behind them. The horses neighed as the weather picked up and they stood parked by the presidential carriage. President Lincoln stood across the far west of them, standing beside Edward Teach who has lost all emotion in his face. While both General Grant and Lee stood away from each other, using the troops available to separate them, they both felt at ease as to what they were about to achieve with this crossing. It was unsure if they were to cross into the territory of the pirates or the pirates come to them, Edward however, knew he would have to stare town the belly of the beast which resided in his son. The plotting of the I.I.C's downfall that had been building for months was about to be achieved, although who knew what lied in store for the men about to colonize the Caribbean islands.

"Edward. How far did it take you by boat to reach this crossing?" Lincoln said, raising his voice to best the howl of the wind.

"A few days. Why?" Edward asked.

"If you had to guess, how long would it take a ship like the Maelstrom to cross?"

Edward was about to answer but he shut himself off. Unable to invest himself in the plot, Lincoln laid his hand across his shoulder, caring for the father's inner struggle. Never breaking his stride, Lincoln removed himself from Teach's side as he walked over to consult General Grant instead. "General, from my understanding, this ship could have speed unlike any boat we've ever seen. How soon will the artillery reach us?" Lincoln asked, whispering the last line.

"They're about half a day behind us sir. We may have the men but there's no telling what that thing could do to us if it arrives before then," Grant said.

Lincoln held his hat tight in both hands as he nodded his head.

"How long do you reckon that smoke has been burning for?" Lincoln wondered as the men watched black smoke rise from the farthest reach of the horizon.

"Difficult to say, sir. But if that's come from one ship, it only highlights my point about the artillery," Grant said.

"Then let us be extra careful. I shall instigate the dialogue whether we journey forth or they come to us," Lincoln said. To the far side of the two, General Lee stared down the barrel of his eye glass, surveying the open waters. Behind them were a squadron of soldiers in their union blue uniforms, opening the cargo of weapons at their disposal. The usual casket of rifles, six shooters and scoped snipers were displayed along the ground, resting on stretched out tarp. The erection of small tents for the president and his accompanying party were being made as the sliders braced for a night of waiting as their comrades behind them would be arriving in the early hours of the morning.

"Mr Lee, Mr Teach. If you would be so kindly to step in the tent with me, we can discuss the arrangements of talks. Men, at your stations," Waved Lincoln and the men all went in their directions while the presidents party went behind the tarp curtain door. Four foldable wooden chairs were propped up near a slim table, all looking like the wind could take them into the air if the tent was not fastened properly. The four sat down with the generals to one side and Lincoln in the middle with Me Teach at a comfortable distance.

"Now that we've established a base near our target and the Generals army in hot pursuit of our location, we can begin briefing. So far, from what our own eyes can see and the intelligence given to us by our inside sources, the captain has engaged with the rebels that we installed," Edward looked at the president with interest, "The likelihood of the captain remaining in place at the island of Cuba is low. The Maelstrom ship was due to be sailed and the spurring of the insurrection effectively will drive him out. Our insider also informed me that the ports will effectively be controlled. No one one will be leaving except the captain, leaving us to go in and secure things, upon which it will be controlled by our implant. Mr Teach..." Edward suddenly feel his heart racing as his name was mentioned. *This couldn't be happening*, he thought. Not now.

"At this moment, we are unaware of your counterparts whereabouts. It remains to be seen if they have survived this ordeal, but from what we know, you know the islands better than anyone-"

"Mr President, I'm going to have to decline. I offered myself to the US for protection of me and my son. That's what I'm here for. There's one thing I will not do and that is go back to that cesspool of ingrates and animals," Edward said sternly even though his expression showed fear. Both Lee and Grant looked at each other for a moment as the president leaned forward with his hands locked together.

"So that fear was not just about your son, I presume? It seems this goes even further." The more Lincoln went in deeper the more it took its toll on Edwards secrecy. His illusion was crumbling fast and needed to be stabilized.

"Mr President, my last name bears more than my actions. I'm part of an ancestry routed in the islands creation. I'm a black spot on the Teach name. With how my son has portrayed me in my absence will surely be taken with anger. I should refrain from ever stepping foot there."

"What if we offered you anonymity?" Grant suggested.

"What's the point? What's the point of someone holding onto an appointment when he has lost any and all care?" Edward said, his voice cracking slightly.

"Fortitude amongst wreckage is how we rebuild, Mr Teach. I see your story as one of character. Confined to a system that doesn't suit your interests. You felt uncomfortable, out of place, wanted it to change for the better. And when you go against the grain, you come out as the villain. I felt that throughout my entire first term. And I assure you, it's never easy," Lincoln explained. Edward was comforted by the presidents humanity, understanding the route cause of his dissatisfaction that had plagued him since childhood. Edward slumped forward as he rubbed his face with his hand.

"Your safety is guaranteed, Mr Teach, but your worth is still to be proven. Surly that drive has been with you given your record?," Lincoln finished.

There it was. The inevitable drive that he once had brought forward to him again. Edward lamented on that dream, a dream that had come close, then carried on by his son. He nodded and Lincoln patted him on the back as a conclusion was met, Edward would in some way control the islands. But what he would inherit was sure to be seen.

"Brave of you Mr Teach, once the handling of the islands has been understood, the United States can be it's provider of aid and support in exchange for its treasure reserves."

"Mr president!," A young soldier burst through the tents gap, "You better see this!" Startled by this, the four men rose from the tent and went back outside as the sun began to set. The soldier handed the president the spy glass to observe the sea, Robert Lee discreetly took his out as well. The Maelstrom was in view, distant yet formidable. The sheer size of the ship captivated three out of the four me, Edward had seen its construction, he knew what to expect.

"My god, that thing is moving faster than any vessel I've ever seen," Lee said, handing his spy glass over to Grant so that he may share his astonishment.

"Hang on, there's smoke coming from the stern," Grant described, "Has it been damaged?" "There's no way, that's…"

"Engine powered," Edward finished for Lee, "Both steam and wind power that monster."

President Lincoln watched the longest as he watched the ships voyage, it didn't seem like it was going to head in their direction, the President had to act fast.

"Son, how much gunpowder do we have at the moment with us?" He asked.

"One crate sir, the rest are arriving with the cannons."

"Right, tell your commander that I want a massive fire to burn here. We need wood and the powder to produce something that can be seen out for miles. I want the flag flying also," Lincoln ordered. The young soldier hurried over to the tents as he gave the president a salute of assurance that his orders would be met.

"That'll be one way of getting his attention. Gentlemen, take it in turns getting some shut eye, we don't know if they'll be hostile, but I hope we and our country can survive this." The four men stood at the edge of the country, looking out and watching over the Maelstrom as it was an ant. They stood like giants for now, but once the ship had come further, they would be the insignificant ones.

Across the miles and miles between them, Sebastian steadied the helm as the crew prepared what artillery fire they had left as the lanterns on the mast and in the lower decks were lit. Colonel Saxton came up the captain's side to report, "We have use two thirds of the cannon fire. If we want to continue this war path of yours then I suggest we dock soon." Sebastian seemingly ignored the colonel, never breaking his cold stare that stretched out to the furthest wave. Annoyed, Saxton continued, "It's brewing, you know it is. You can't keep this up for long."

"When we reach land, you and everyone else on board can leave. I won't stop you but certainly won't go down to mutiny," Sebastian said defiantly.

"For god's sake, what has gotten into you? This is beyond a joke, this charade you put on is a joke! Why would you run yourself down to the grounds of desperation like this?" Sebastian's eyes flickered, his thoughts turned to the colonel now.

"Why? When I took the life of my predecessor, I swore to uphold what I loved. I was prepared for that very moment. Then it slowly became a shell of itself and I would've been the scapegoat. I will die happy knowing that if I go down in the next few days it wont be to a fucking mutiny! I'm a pirate and that's what I'll be to the very end! I won't be kissing the floor to anyone unlike you," Sebastian said gritting his teeth, spitting out the words like a venomous snake.

"The question is colonel; Do you want to jump ship now? Cause that'll happen with the snap of my fingers, not yours." Saxton knew he could draw the pistol, but what would be the response of the crew? Sentiment among the crew was unreadable so there was no way of telling if Saxton would live should he relive the captain from the ship. His eyes soon shifted away from Sebastian as the colonel noticed something in the distance as the sun vanished and the night sky brought the twinkle of the stars out. Another twinkle came from land, one that was growing in size and colour. Sebastian noticed this and turned to face what Saxton saw. He pulled out the spy glass and looked out, a fire, a massive one that sizzled with sparks shooting up into the night. Minuscule now but none the less it pivoted the intoxicated captain to turn the helm slightly in its direction. Drawn to it like a moth, it seemed the Maelstrom would be making land fall in the next few hours. Colonel Saxton walked away from his side, never drawing his gun, never gripping his dagger but cutting into the captain's pride with realistic consequences.

"I don't need to jump. I'll step off calmly, just like everyone else on this ship, "he said to the back of Sebastian, "But you, you have to decide if you want to salvage whatever character you have left. Cause are kind ain't welcome there."

CHAPTER 28

DEALING WITH THE NEIGHBOURS

In the early hours of the morning, two before the sun would rise, the Maelstrom had docked at Florida. The US flag flew with grace as the fire that lured the captain and his crew over still burnt fiercely. President Lincoln, along with generals Grant and Lee, two members of the squadron army brandishing rifles and Edward Teach stood ready to meet with Sebastian, who brought Colonel Saxton and his crew crawling up the steep sands. From below they looked like ants, scurrying up their new found home but pretty soon they'd be either gentle creatures or angry warriors. Behind the president was the army legion that followed along with the artillery, presented in rows that outnumbered the oncoming crew along with its leader. Edward stood ready, emotionless yet his heart was rapidly pounding out of his chest. The second father and son would lock eyes again, it wouldn't be pretty. Sebastian was seen first, his face lit from the orange glow like a vengeful spirit as his legion of crew hands was behind him. The light from the fire did him no favours in making him seem sane, his wrinkles from dehydration and nothing but a wine diet were prevalent, his clothes were worn, crinkled, the only thing that looked presentable was his hat. Colonel Saxton showed up beside him, he was worried, not stoic. Lincoln caught sight of this immediately to use to his advantage in the negotiations. The crew were no better, staggering alongside one another like obedient puppies being pulled by one single string. The party of pirates halted and we're now a few feet apart from each other. Silence sat between the two, never engaging, the crackling of fire was all that was heard and all Sebastian could do was look at his father with a disappointing frown. Lincoln finally ended the tense stare down, clearing his throat to get the captain's attention, which it did.

"I do hope your journey here wasn't too chaotic," he said calmly.

"It wasn't. I could tell it was planned," Sebastian said in a cold manner.

"Mr Teach, it's time to be completely honest. There is no going back there. This has been in the works for a while," The president continued. Sebastian gave a quick glance back at his father, knowing it to be true.

"Whatever you've done will have to be trialled. There are plenty of witnesses and this war will end in your surrender."

"I was the scapegoat, wasn't I father," Sebastian kept his eyes on Lincoln but his words made everyone turn to Edward.

"You were setting me up from the very beginning." Edward looked down to the ground for a moment before admitting the truth.

"We all did, son. Rourke, Klaus...Saxton." Sebastian snapped his head to his left as Saxton stood tall with his hands pressed against his back, giving General Lee a nod of mission accomplished. The colonel then moved away from his party standing straight with the president before extending his hand for a handshake and joined the opposing line. Staggered but not shook, Sebastian awaited the next line of the presidents "dialogue".

"If any of you have confidence in your captain's ability to govern, then stay where you are. If you do not have confidence, then step behind with us," Lincoln called out, reaching the furthest line back of the pirate crew. Sebastian couldn't believe what he was hearing, if this was democracy, he hated it. The worrisome looks of the crew all shared a similar look of tiredness that had plagued them since they put their faith in the young captain. Seeing his mind falter and his actions barbaric as they come, they saw no other way. Finally out stepped one brave worker, his face was cut and he held his beanie cap in his hands, exposing his balding scalp. As he looked at Lincoln and his party members, it would be the first time he smiled since stepping on the Maelstrom which loomed over the sea behind them. Sebastian only saw cowardliness and his anger, driven from the bottles of wine made him snap again.

He drew the sword of his grandfather and pointed it towards his neck. The crew backed away in fear while the two union soldiers standing either side of the president aimed their rifles, ready to fire on his command.

"Sebastian!" Edward cried, finally releasing his distress as his son stared with malicious intent.

"There's no point to this! You have nothing left to prove," Edward pleaded.

"Even now, you want me to do what you say," Sebastian said coldly.

"Mr Teach, you're outnumbered here. Put the sword down and we can discuss things," Lincoln said. Sebastian knew he was right even though his grip on his sword was the tightest he ever held it, he slowly lowered it and the crew behind him started to shuffle forward. They crept past, giving the captain a look to be sure his erratic behaviour wouldn't make him start swinging the sword that cut down others before them. Soon, like the president said, Sebastian was on his own, the last pirate to do battle.

"Now, captain, there will be a swift transition. The islands will eventually be held by the Bluebeard's until the replacement head's living accommodations are met and if you retaliate, you will stand trail for your crimes of harbouring Confederate statesmen during a period of war."

"Is that it?" Sebastian shrugged, "A public display of me when your adversary is standing right next to you? No one will buy your sham-"

"And no one will buy you as a pirate," Edward interrupted, "Now please son, ditch this idiotic persona and just turn yourself in. Don't you think I've sacrificed enough for you? This is the only way you can have a normal life without these dreamlike notions of immortality. There's no winning as a pirate, my father knew it and you will to." The words his father laid out onto him were hurtful, shattering the very little hope of being the best pirate leader in all of the world was hanging on by a thread. Sebastian held that thread however, tighter than he ever held it before, spurred on by the negative rhetoric his father had stuck with all these years. He saw no other option other than spiritual guidance and drive.

"No. Mr President, if I am to go down, at least let me do it my way," Sebastian brought his sword up and pointed at the President, "You and me. Fair deal, fair duel." Lincoln kept his composure, listening to the captain's offer while slow building unrest for the safety of the head of state came from the president's party.

"With the goddess Oki watching down on me and through her channelling the spirit of the sea's, I challenge you to a fight of honour. If you win, I'm yours to do what ever. If I win...well we'll just have to see how that goes."

"Mr President, this young man knows that if he tries anything of the sort we can gun him down before he even thinks about crying parley," Grant said sternly.

"No! For the love of God, this isn't what I wanted!" Cried a frustrated Edward as he came to the President's side, "Don't do this. You're only giving him what he wants and he needs to be taught that I'm right."

"Mr Teach...win or lose, he gains nothing. What he does get is a lesson, a lesson that you never taught him," Lincoln's cold remark with an icy stare made Edward step back, "Respect is earned, not handed to them. I accept your challenge!" Everyone from the generals to the newly acquired deck hands.

Lincoln tinted around and the sea of soldiers made way for him as he stepped over to the burning fire by ol' glory. He watched the fire continuing to burn, marvelling at its natural beauty and terror, it was a final moment where the president could tend to his thoughts, memories eventually delivering a small prayer onto the fire and flag like an altar. An altar that embodied the spirit of his country as he prepared to do battle.

"Gentlemen, let this war be over with," Lincoln placed his hat down where he stood and ripped out the axe nearby that rested near the chopping block. His hands glid across the handle and he felt the sharpness of its blade.

"Form a circle!" The president ordered and the soldiers formed around Sebastian as the generals and Edward stood to watch behind them. Calm and collected, Lincoln turned and marched inside as the irate pirate stared him down with the sword by his side. The human arena all watched with dread as the two stalked each other like tigers, treading lightly on the soil as they went either way. This was no gladiator fight where applause would be heard whoever the victor was. Sebastian had been waiting for a moment like this, a shining showcase of his hungry blood thirst against Lincoln's cool and calculated fight style. This was young lion against old lion. With a push of his left foot, Sebastian made the first move, swiftly bringing his sword towards the president of the United States with an overhead swing that missed by a mile as Lincoln stepped away easily, not once bringing the axe up in defence. However, he gripped it tight with both hands as the pirate leader brought himself back up, still stepping forward, closing off the available space. Another swipe of the sword, this time diagonally left which Lincoln counted, the wooden handle pushing it away. Sebastian was now gritting his teeth like the animal he had become, his father studying him like a keeper in the zoo. Sebastian then lunged again, pushing the sword from his great grandfather forward which Lincoln again counted, this time following up with a swing of his own, an upward slice from the axe nearly grazed the young captain's forearm as he retracted his arms back. This time Lincoln came forward, the axes smaller frame made it easy for the president to make successful chain combination of downward swings from the left and then the right hand. Sebastian managed to dodge them and as Lincoln went for a third strike, a half circle swing at the mid section was brushed aside by the opposing sword. Sebastian could see the power in the presidents attacks, his face only wincing slightly as the speed increased with every swing. That axe was second nature to the president as he came again with a quick chop down near Sebastian's feet, to the captain's advantage, the axe was slightly wedged in the dirt. Sebastian gripped the sword with both hands, looking to drive the sword cleanly through the presidents back but he escaped the clutches of death in a split second, backing away till Sebastian had slotted his sword down further than the axe could. In an unconventional twist, Lincoln delivered an uppercut that rattled the pirate so much that Sebastian lost his grip and fell to the floor. The crowd of soldiers along with Lincoln's entourage were shocked by the presidents foul play yet pondered the pirates ability to fight, was this the hell raising cut-throat the rumours had been saying? Staggering back up to his feet and retrieving the sword up from the ground, Lincoln once again spoke directly to his opponent: "Don't be shocked. You're a pirate, I didn't expect you to follow the rules so I broke them first." Sebastian in a rage came at Lincoln with hard strikes, slashing furiously as Lincoln countered with the wooden handle. The two traded shot after shot of their instruments of death, furiously trying to tire the other one out. In the crowd, General Grant grew intensely more concerned for the president, as he slid his hand on the handle of his flintlock pistol, trying hard not to seem like he would be the first to draw fire. His emotions were heightened as the crowd saw in a sharp turn of the duel that Sebastian sliced Lincoln's left arm. His blazer sleeve was torn open, the blood from his upper arm coloured the white shirt in damp and darkened mess. Lincoln was not phased yet he could feel the impact on his arm slowly coming over him, he dared not look at it. A quick dart forward and Sebastian was again on the defensive, the president came again with chops that rattled the foundational steel that Sebastian's sword was made from, the hardened grind of the axe blade scratching and marking it with every hit. In a desperate attempt to get the other hand (and a receipt from the uppercut) Sebastian thrust his shoulders into Lincoln's stomach, pushing him down with an awkward tackle where the two men now wrestled each other with their bare hands. Sebastian pressed his left hand onto Lincoln's right arm, keeping the axe away from his face while his other unloaded on the president's face. Three blows to the head came down harder each time until Lincoln's lip was cut and his eye was slightly bruised. Sebastian smiled with glee as he was in control but it wasn't for long, Lincoln wrapped his legs around the young man's body, grasping them hard until he could maneuver Sebastian to the ground, the president's amateur wrestling background coming into play. Surprisingly dropping the axe, Lincoln used both hands to wrench Sebastian's dominant hand which had hold of the sword, twisting the muscles until the sword was dropped to the side. Everyone saw the duel was no longer about formality as the two were now in a battle of physical dominance. Sebastian tried his hardest to break the hold but the president kept applying the pressure, he looked to keep on top by switching the hold. Sebastian managed to wiggle free which meant he could crawl on his stomach towards his sword but the arm rake was switched over to a neck hold as Lincoln knelt on the young man's healthy spine. Sebastian's head felt like it was going to be ripped fro his shoulders as the pain was gradually increasing. Not one for torturing an opponent, President Lincoln asked Sebastian: "Submit?"

Defiantly, Sebastian answered with a gritted, "No!" Upon hearing this, Lincoln released his grip and got back to his feet, picking up his axe as he watched the pirate crawl to his sword, resting his hand on the back of his neck as he too rose. With a click of his neck, Sebastian didn't run, but paced up to the president, bringing his arm around for a backwards slice, but Lincoln brought the axe sideways on to Sebastian's left shin. The axe blade drove into the bone and the young pirate let out a scream of agony as his legs buckled. As the tears streamed down Sebastian's eyes, he saw the president trying to bring his weapon back out from the bone. Edward turned away as he couldn't bare to see this kind of action any longer. As the president pulled away the axe, it flew across the arena and the opportunity arose. In a flash, Sebastian struck Lincoln's foot, driving the sword through flesh and bone until the sword stood on its own. Lincoln cried out which made everyone uneasy, Grant was counting down the moments till he wanted to fire, ending the madness. Sebastian hobbled up, putting most of his weight on the opposite leg so he could punch the president viciously. The two traded blows, even though Lincoln couldn't move, he was unafraid to fight bare-knuckled. One after the other they came, landing on either the head or the abdomen, the blood poured from both men by this point and they were struggling to stay afloat. They gasped for breath until Lincoln had enough, he tugged and pulled the blade out from his foot, a gush of blood spat from the top of his exposed boot. Sebastian came in, the two now struggled to pull the silver sword away from one another, seeing it as the only way to end the fight. Sebastian yanked back to bring the blade pointing at the president's stomach who pushed back, the blade etching ever so close till the tip was just making contact with skin. Lincoln countered this by side stepping before giving the young Sebastian a knee to the gut, winding him as was shoved to the ground. Lincoln now had the sword of Blackbeard in his hands, only acquiring a split second to admire its craftsmanship before turning and pointing the sword at General Grant who had pulled the gun from his holster, looking to end shoot the pirate leader as he crawled away again.

"Honour the agreement," Lincoln said directly to the General's face as the sword pointed to his neck. By the time Grant let out a sharp intake of breath, Lincoln was literally stabbed in the back. The axe was driven into the president's back by a skilful throw from afar, the crowd fell silent as they watched the horror unfold of the commander in chief, slowly fading. Everyone was still as a statue, jaws dropped and hung loose as they stared in horror, the president of the United States was now slowly dropping to his knees, hands still clasped onto Grant, looking at him to respect the authority he had still. Finally Sebastian made it to him, he took the sword from his hand, grabbed the back of Lincoln's head and drew a long slit across the Lincoln's neck. Grant backed away as the blood spilt perfectly down his neck like a waterfall, flowing through the creases in his skin like a rock formation. Abraham Lincoln drew his last breath and fell to the floor as the pool of blood stained the soul of his homeland. Grant in a fit of rage clicked the safety back of his pistol and aimed squarely at Sebastian's head, it was denied however, Edward rushed over to lift the Generals arm in the air, the shot rang as the bullet went off into the sky.

"No! This isn't the way!," Edward shouted, "If this is what my son wants...so be it." He looked over to Sebastian who proudly stood over the fallen commander in chief. Edward watched as his son triumphantly stuck the sword into the ground and took up his hat that had fallen off during the skirmish. Placing it back on his head, dignified in what he had done, with the eyes of many looking at him from all directions, Sebastian proclaimed: "The last pirate, I shall be."

CHAPTER 29

THE WAR RAGES ON

Sebastian sat with little hope. He would be deemed in the eyes of a nation as the catalyst for the war continuing, a scapegoat for the likes of General Lee and the confederacy who had now surrendered fully with the Generals grand scheme coming to a conclusion. Only it didn't end in triumph, it ended with a death. A death whose position had now been thrust onto the hands of one Andrew Johnson who sat the opposite side of the desk. Surrounding him were his affiliates, strangers Sebastian had never seen before other than two Generals. The hat of the former president sat in the middle of them, presiding a dark shadow over the oval office while the new President Johnson twiddled his thumbs while Sebastian remained in a trance of numbness, never moving or bringing his gaze up from the floor. Was he painting a picture of regret? Johnson thought, either way, the trial of a foreign entity in the midst of a home-grown war could provide some easy leeway for the new commander in chief.

"Sebastian Teach. Now former Captain of the I.I.C, great grandson to the notorious pirate Blackbeard, and overall raving lunatic. You will soon be put into public spectacle the likes of which you've never seen before. This isn't like home, Mr Teach, this is the United States, and we won't take to kindly to your involvement in this. You'll be given a full trial, don't you worry about that. Just remember that anything you can give to us now will be much easier for you," Johnson explained in the clearest sense. Sebastian did not move, he remained fixated to a particular patter from the office desk and his face was a relaxed neutral expression. Johnson looked to the others around him, all of them seemingly nodding for the next procedure, like they were guiding Johnson through the routine.

"Very well, if silence is what drives you to the cell quicker that's fine by me. But eventually you will cough up everything you know for a smooth transition. Uslyess, have the guards take him." Grant walked around the group to help Sebastian up from his chair, still staring at the ground as he turned around to be escorted out. As the assistant opened the door, a familiar face was seen, Edward Teach had been waiting outside, listening in as much as he could. The exchange between father and son was brief, no concern, no animosity, just brief observation.

"Edward, I will see you now," Johnson said, calling him in. Edward came inside cordially, observing the walls and design of the oval office as he chose to stand before the new president.

"The paperwork of deed ownership to land that you have requested has been forwarded. As in token of gratitude for your compliance in this matter, Mr Renfold and others will also join you in the living arrangements," Edward was relieved to hear a few names had survived the chaos of the islands, "As it retains though, you'll still need to attend the trial of your son in a month's time."

"Why? I know what the verdict will be. And if anything it'll cast doubt into your people's minds about me and anyone associated with him."

"Very true, yet don't forget it is also General Lee here who will also be compensated for his public surrender. We don't wish to burn bridges in this administration. That's what Mr Lincoln would have wanted. Right now we need to piece ourselves together as a society-"

"By making my boy a spectacle," Edward interrupted.

"Sometimes one distraction can make people forget hard times, Mr Teach. I don't want squabbling, we have a death to think about right now and if I don't deliver a smooth ending to this operation, there will be hell," Johnson went on. Edward neither complained or complimented the work being done, this was what he wanted after all, although, he thought very little about the complications. Imperfections dragged his thoughts through the mud until they covered the success in a thick brown mess, all he could do was what he was told.

"One thing that you can be useful for is seeing if your son holds any information about the islands the United States could use in its aid mission for the islands. We need anything that can give us the edge to aid the people there," Johnson continued.

"I'll see what I can get out of him," Edward said, turning around to make his way out of the office. Before the doors closed, the group began to matter again with the thoughts turning again to Mexico. The door closed and Edwards mind began to clear, if this was what he'd have to deal with in Jamaica then he'd close every door he could.

As the darkness of the night began to settle in, the view from Sebastian's so called "window" wasn't within his reach. It was too high above for him to see but his bedside was at an angle where he could see out to the stars. Unfortunately though, Sebastian didn't feel like star gazing tonight, he slumped forward as he sat on the edge of the bed, the come down of the wine were beginning to set in, Sebastian was in continuous cycle of depressive thoughts, going hand in hand with his body's slow collapse. He felt weak, tired, at any moment he would want to slump onto the bed to drift off into a deep sleep that his body craved. Sebastian felt like he was in a state of relapse, grasping back the knowledge that he knew was him before a slow descending madness fell on him, for which he had no explanation for. It never occurred to him it was the wine but perhaps it would be a topic of conversation as his father arrived into the room of his cell block. A guard stood outside, as he unlocked the door for him to proceed inside. For some reason, Edward walked with tepid footsteps as he made his way to the cell door, fearing that his son may lash out, even though Sebastian heard the door squeaking open and the rustling of keys. As Edward faced Sebastian, who was giving him the cold shoulder, Edward began to fidget with his hands before speaking.

"So... You wanna tell me what happened back at home?", Silence was met to which Edward had to try harder.

"OK, I'll lay it down for you if it makes it easier," Edward pulled over a small stool from the corner and brought it up to his son's cell to sit on, "The second we knew our lives were at risk, we had to reach out. People were dying on the streets day after day, it was only inevitable that soon the bodies would start piling up we questioned Norton. I had frequent contact with all members of the plan, I'm sorry to say son, but you got in the way," Sebastian still didn't move, that type of comment would've been a death sentence earlier on but Sebastian didn't have the stomach for it anymore.

"I know things weren't how you remembered it, but that type of thing cannot be replicated. We have to move forward, son. This whole thing of being the pirate of the ages is fruitless. Now, when this trial is over, you and I can be somebody. You'll have to serve your time but you can battle this, you're young and to think when I'm gone you'll live a live of luxury and security in Jamaica!"

Still nothing Edward said made Sebastian move.

"Do you know, I never actually understood why being a pirate meant so much to you? Hell, I didn't even ask you."

Sebastian suddenly turned to face his father, showing his weakened and dishevelled face with sunken eyes that stared into his soul.

"It meant the world to me, and that world thought you were a part of it." Edward left his head hang as he sunk in his lips.

"I wanted to prove so much to you, and you used me for something that I wasn't comfortable with," Sebastian's voice started to tremble, "You've destroyed everything are family fought so hard to create for everyday people wanting an escape. And you've handed them back into the jaws of a similar beast."

"A beast in recovery, Sebastian. These Americans are no different from where my grandfather came from. But unless you want those jaws to bite down you have to give me information."

"Information?" Sebastian questioned.

"It's the only way to make your term more sensible. The president will make it look the worst in the papers, the public will be happy and then you can slip into peace. Now, how does that sound?" Sebastian pondered the consequences for a moment, aptly suited to his notoriety from within the recovering states of the union and also to the confederacy. It did not suit him. Even in his hangover of derangement, the idea of fame through fear still glistened to him like a distant star, a distant god even, like he was so close to achieving its treasures. In an instant, Sebastian had the thoughts of piracy in general, reaping the benefits of man, pillaging and plundering and above all else, obtaining a status like no other. Part and parcel of the job but who was to say it wasn't difficult, nor challenging? He knew the right was how to handle this and he was damn sure it wasn't the way his father wanted.

"That sounds...boring," he said, lingering on the word to make it sting more, "There's nothing to hide anymore. I'm all you have left and I know you know that. But what is the president going to think about that? Is he going to take silence or lies? What's the point in truth if that's all you've been fed?"

"Don't do this-"

"No! You don't get to decide anymore for me! No more! You want answers!?" Sebastian screamed, his vocal cords scratching as his words broke. It almost seemed like the wine in his system came back for one last bout with anger management, Sebastian leaned back in his chair, stretched his arms up before spreading his legs and relaxing himself.

"Look to your allies. Cause I had mine. And I think they're more capable than me at some things. Do you think this country will say the same? I for one, look to Oki for the answers, and some of them, are marked with a black spot." With those defiant words, Sebastian looked to the small window again, feeling pleased with his shrouded mystery. All his father could do was hang his head, feeling a lose for words as the cryptic messaging was something he couldn't go on. Edward knew what was to be expected and it seems like that wouldn't be delivered. The two sat in different ends of a spectrum, only one was behind bars and the other had true freedom.

CHAPTER 30

THE FIRE THAT NEVER STOPS

"All rise!" The court judge called out. The precession began like it was any other day but the court was packed. Filled to the brim with politicians from both Democrat and Republican, advisor's, Generals and of course, it's defendant. Sebastian stood but he never sat back down when everyone else had, as the procedural introduction to the plaintiff's case was being read and the crimes expressed by his firm, President Johnson's case captured everyone to the matter. Most had been recovering or still processing the war, now they had to contend with President Lincoln's death and a new government being made. Words thrown against Sebastian Teach were the likes of: "Warmongering", "Genocide" and "Retaliation". None were at the scene yet the picture had been painted by the artist who was never going to see his art recognised. Sebastian knew this now, yet at the time, he was deeply involved in the events. This gave him time to reflect on what was real and what wasn't. What was deception and what was true loyalty to a cause which his father had never seen eye to eye with him. In the end, he came to one conclusion; he had done what any pirate had set out to do. Disruption was the name of the game and he was now on a national scale the likes of which his great grandfather never would've accomplished. Even if he was groomed into the position, they knew not of what his actions could be and they were now deadly destructive in the eyes of many Americans. The islands may have been lost, but his influence certainly will gain attraction.

"...Sebastian Teach. How do you plead before the court?" The judge asked, finishing his opening speech before the court.

"Not guilty."

No fear, only confidence shown in his response. Edward Teach sunk his head in his hands, rubbing his fingers through his hair as small nattering began to build in the courthouse.

"Order! Mr Teach it is with this ruling that in finding yourself not guilty, you will reside in the highest state prison facility until a new date for the courtroom to present evidence and statements has been finalized. You may also do the same in that time should a lawyer be present by your side. In the mean time, you will be escorted out from the courtroom and into your new quarters." The guards surrounded and dragged Sebastian by his cuffed arms as they made their way out of the court. All eyes watched, all eyes beamed their emotions onto him and Sebastian just smiled as he gave a look of smugness. He thought this attitude subsided with his state of intoxication from the wine, but some things, like wine, linger. As he searched the court, finally locking eyes with his father as Edward sat in disappointment, Sebastian took the life he knew to hell and back. A pirates life. It can spread to anyone in any way and any place.

BY TELEGRAPH.

EXCLUSIVELY TO THE STATE JOURNAL

OUR NIGHT DISPATCHES.

IMPEACHMENT.

Meeting of the Senate as Court.

House of Representatives Present.

Johnson's Counsel Appear.

ASKS POSTPONEMENT FOR FORTY DAYS.

The Senate Grants Ten Days.

The Trial Set for the 23d of March.

CONGRESS—THE IMPEACHMENT.
WASHINGTON, March 13.
At an early hour this morning Washington assumed the active, excited appearance for